www.trollriverpub.com
Forever More
The Evermore Series
Book 2
Copyright © 2016 Rachel De Lune
ISBN: 978-1-939564-78-8
Cover Design: Rachel De Lune

are responsible for yourself and the consequences caused thereof.

Dear Reader,

Rachel has worked very hard on this particular piece of entertainment. This book was brought to you by hard labor and love. Please respect an artist's work for the enrichment we try to bring you. I humbly ask that you don't outright steal this child born on paper and brought to you by love. If you come by this book by nefarious means, and you are simply unable to give the change in your pocket for the purchase price, then take it with my blessing. But if you can purchase it and would like Rachel to continue to bring you great books, please purchase a copy to support her.

Thank you,

Troll River Publications

Join the fun with Author Rachel De Lune for giveaways, updates and new release opportunities at: http://eepurl.com/bckw0r

To U.S. Readers

I'd like to take this moment to let you know that Rachel is a writer living in the UK and while most terminology is the same, you may find some words or phrases odd. Knickers are underwear, "realise" is actually the correct spelling for "realize" in the UK and "flaking" is not ditching someone at a party.

Suffice it to say, if you find a word that blares out at you as "misspelled" blame the Atlantic Ocean for this diversity, not Rachel. This book has been properly edited and remains true to UK spelling and grammar. Thank you for your time!

Acknowledgements

This has been an enormous year for me. This realm of authorship is filled with wonderful, supportive people who have given me the encouragement and confidence to write what I want to. There are a few that I couldn't do this without and need to offer my deepest thanks.

As always, to my fabulous critique partners, Elizabeth, M and Kris. Once again you have helped my word jumble make sense and given me support and determination.

To my American Mum, T. You continue to make me write better. I promise that I won't water down the coffee.

To Stephy, who is always at the end of the phone for my brain dump of questions. You settle my nerves and bring my scribbles to life. I hope I continue to write stories you want to publish.

Wendy and Claire (Bare Naked Words), you do an awesome job and I know I'm in safe hands. Thank you. To all of the blogs who have supported me to date, as a reader I love you and as an author I thank you.

Heather, yes, Seb is yours. Sorry folks, she claimed him first.

Rebecca, thank you for the hot guys. Man candy can be such a good writing motivation.

Leanne, keep believing in yourself. I do.

To the wonderful authors I've met on-line. Keep tapping those words out.

To Roxane and Sarah, I love you girls!

My hubs will probably never read this, but he lets me sit in my office and write my stories with very little complaint. I love you, boo. And to Vicki, who is probably more excited about all of this than I am. Thank you for your unwavering support.

Lastly, to the fabulous readers who have read my words and supported me. Your reviews, likes, shares, messages and tweets have filled my heart with joy. I still have to pinch myself. Thank you.

"The only way to get rid of a temptation is to yield to it."
Oscar Wilde

I sit on the bed I ought to share with my husband, in my room, in my house, but this isn't my home. Even after ten years. A home is made up of more than a place to reside and a few belongings. A home is full of love, warmth and memories that bring a smile to your face, even when you feel lost or scared.

It's dark outside but it must be close to dawn. I've sat for hours, motionless, purposely blanking my mind. I can cope with sitting. I'm the first to overanalyse everything, to over-think and replay everything in a loop in my mind, but I can't bear to replay the memories of what happened last night. It's as if my mind begins to shut off when I edge closer, thinking about Seb's words. *"Izzy, I can't deal with you still being with your husband. I don't want you if you keep going back to him. I deserve better. I deserve more."*

My body is on autopilot as I walk downstairs. I survey all of the rooms and belongings: the DVDs, the mismatch of tea cups lining a shelf in the kitchen. I look at it all, and I'm struck that these aren't our things. They are *my* things—my random mix of bowls and plates, my pictures on the walls, my table in the living room, my cushions. I hadn't seen it before, but this house in Bath isn't *our* home. It's my house that I've worked at turning into a home, but it's neglected by Phil.

I continue through the entire house. I can count Phil's possessions on one hand. Only a pair of trainers in the hall and a few dirty shirts in the laundry show he's still living here. It would be so easy to take everything of Phil's and pack it up. *How can I stay here, though?* I don't want to be here. This isn't where my heart is. I want to be with Seb. I take a deep breath and fill my chest. My scream echoes around the empty rooms, filling the air with grief and sadness.

My lungs drain of air and give voice to everything I'm afraid to admit to. *My marriage to Phil is over. I've ruined my relationship with Seb. I'm scared.* Three pivotal facts that are at the root of the emotions that have worn me down and made it hard to think straight. My world has changed over the last few months. My perspective has tilted—changed for the better— thanks to Seb. Finally speaking up for myself in my empty marriage was the starting point. Asking Phil for more than unsatisfactory vanilla sex only drove more distance between us. Having an innocent drink just to escape my empty house also led me to Seb. I never intended to meet a man who could give me everything I dreamt of—the love and attention I'd been starved of for years, the freedom to surrender and explore my sexuality and my darker fantasies, previously locked away in my online world. But I did meet him and he opened my eyes to just how miserable my life was before. I was a coward for not confronting Phil sooner. Now, I might have lost Seb because I wasn't brave enough to face Phil, to demand that he listen to me instead of letting him walk all over me. I should have grabbed my chance at happiness with both hands.

My husband doesn't love me. I don't love my husband. I love Seb. I want out of my marriage. Those four statements are my truth. They feel right. "My husband doesn't love me. I don't love my husband. I love Seb." I say them aloud, claiming them, and it feels liberating. Something shifts within my soul and I'm not bound by my fear of what admitting that love will mean. I shouldn't feel ashamed that my marriage is over. It's not all my fault.

I look around the hallway. A surge of adrenaline floods my system as my body catches up with my mind, and I head for my bedroom and look for a bag. My eyes land on the overnight carry-on, which wouldn't even hold what I need for a weekend, let alone my entire wardrobe. I need a suitcase, or two. The spare room wardrobe is my next destination and I pull both cases down and drag them back to my room. I line up both suitcases and everything gets rammed in, underwear, jeans, jackets. I dump armfuls of clothes into the cases. I wedge it all in, unconcerned about neatness or creases. A few manic minutes later, I have emptied my drawers and wardrobe and have two cases bursting at the seams.

I strip out of my dress, pull on the comfy pair of jeans and jumper I left out, and stuff my feet unto Uggs. I drag each case down the stairs and only pause to gather my essentials, bag, phone, computer bag and keys. Wasting no time, I squeeze the cases into my little Fiat and head to the only address I can imagine going to. Well, the only one that I'll be welcome at.

* * *

My hand is numb from banging so hard on her door. It's 6:00 in the morning on a Saturday, so I know she'll be in. *I just left my husband.* I lose a little of my composure but keep knocking. Jess isn't a morning person, so I lift my hand to pound on the door again. Finally it swings open.

"Who the hell...? What do you...? Izzy?" She looks shocked, stilling with the door half open. "Um, Izzy, what...?"

"I need to stay here for a few-ish days. Will you have me?"

3

"Wow, Isabel, you have *suitcases*. As in plural." She smiles and opens the door for me. I dump my bags in the front room before turning around and going back out to pull my suitcases in from the porch.

"Yes." I brush past her, determined to get everything inside before having to explain myself. Admitting why I'm here to myself is one thing. Saying it aloud will bring it to life. She stands and watches me struggle with my first case. I pull it into the house and drop it at her feet. Seeing my best friend dumbfounded for once, I go back for the other. I stack it next to her, pinning her in the tiny hall, and then head to the kitchen to put the kettle on for a cup of tea. I know Jess will need it, and so do I.

I put the kettle on and make two cups before Jess ventures in to see what I'm up to. She still hasn't said a lot, but I know Jess—it's only a matter of time. She takes the proffered cup and sits opposite me at her kitchen table. I look at her, waiting for her to make the first move. She's gearing up for it. It's clear all over her face.

"So, are you going to say anything?" I press.

"Izzy, what time is it anyway?" She shakes her head. "Doesn't matter. You're here? To stay?" She's shocked. Her voice has gone all squeaky, but she pauses for a sip of tea. Her hair is tied in a messy knot on top of her head, but she can't contain the mass of blondeness working loose. "Well?" she says, as if it's my cue.

"Yes."

"Don't leave me in the dark."

"Well, I've not really worked anything out beyond getting here…" I trail off. "I left him. Phil. I just… I can't stay with him. I can't stay at the house. It's not our home and hasn't been for a long time. I finally saw it earlier tonight, um, last night, but I can't throw him out."

She scowls at me. I hope Jess will understand, and that she doesn't bring up the other man in my life. Or rather, the man who *was* in my life until I managed to mess everything up by being too weak to deal with my failed marriage.

"Okay." She sits forward in the chair. "What did Phil say? I can't imagine he was especially happy."

"Well, he sort of doesn't know. Not yet, anyway."

"What do you mean?" Her face scrunches up in a confused frown.

"He dragged me out last night and forced me to attend his stupid Christmas party. He promised we would talk everything out if I did. He scares me, Jess. Recently, his anger escalates in a way that makes me nervous. I went to the party, but I realised early on Phil only wanted me there to make Sophie, his 'fling', jealous. I ran into Seb there."

"No!" she gasps. "What happened?"

"Things got messy. I'm not ready to go into all of the details just yet, but I ended up back at home. Phil didn't come with me, and he hasn't checked in since I left him. He still hadn't come home when I left to come here."

"Okay. And…"

"And nothing. I just need… I just need to make Phil see that we're over. This part of my life, my marriage, I need to make a clean break before I think about anything else, okay?" My voice is near to breaking, and I don't think I can go into any more detail without my tight hold on the emotional ball of relief, fear and pain slipping, crashing down on me and paralysing me with my reality. I take a long drink of my now tepid tea and wait.

I don't look at Jess. She's sorting through this in her head, and it is only 6:30 a.m. I finish my tea and put the cup in the sink.

"Do you want a hand with your bags?" she finally asks.

"Just up to the spare room, please. If I can have it?" I smile at her.

5

"Oh, Izzy." Jess steps towards me and wraps me in a gentle hug. I let out a sigh of relief. I know she never would have turned me away, but having her confirm it is a relief. She squeezes me again and a single tear falls. I know more will come when I finally admit what the numbness around my chest signifies, that I've let the person I love go, before I really had him. That's when the tears will flow. I hope I don't drown in them. I hope that luck will be on my side and help me to fight my way back to Seb.

* * *

It's nearly midday before I venture downstairs to make some more tea. There's no sign of Jess, and I'm almost hoping that it will stay that way. I can go on in my muddled haze without having to explain my next move to her. Leaving Phil was the goal, but what next? Everything was so clear last night. I was determined to make Phil see I was serious about wanting a divorce. My decision to leave was one I needed to make. I owed it to myself. I've finally got the courage to stand up for myself. I won't question that I'm deserving of happiness anymore, no matter how hard it is.

I go back upstairs to check my phone for calls or messages from Phil in response to the empty wardrobe. If he's called, I'll be shocked, but I'm not holding my breath. I can't be a coward anymore. I need to end things with Phil, and I need to do it soon.

I pull out my phone and dial Phil. It rings and rings. My stomach churns and my heart pounds after each ring tone. I feel sick, and my hands are clammy as I clutch the phone. Finally, the answer phone clicks in and I hear my own voice asking me to leave a message.

Phil won't be without his phone, so I call it over and over—I can't let this go. Phil finally picks up. "What is it, Izzy?" His voice is gravelly and full of sleep.

"I need to talk to you and it can't wait." I project as much authority into my voice as possible.

"Really, Izzy, after your disappearing act on me last night? I'm sure I don't want to talk to you." He sounds angry now, but that helps.

"Where are you, anyway? It's two in the afternoon, and I really do need to see you."

"Well, I'm not at home, am I? Just wait until I am, Izzy. I'm sure you can keep yourself busy with your computer until I get home."

"No, I have something I need to speak with you about, and I'm not home either."

"Why? Did you say you weren't feeling well, or was that just an excuse to leave the party?"

"I didn't stay at home. I'm not there. Please, just listen to me. I'd like us to talk."

"After the way you acted, you've got to be kidding me. And where are you if you're not home?" His tone is now past angry.

"It's none of your business. Please, I'd just like to have a conversation with you without you shouting at me."

"It is my fucking business where you are, Izzy. Don't mess with me."

"Why? You seem to think I only deserve to know where you are when it suits you. I'm fed up with the way you treat me, Phil."

"What, just because I've stayed out and want to know where you are? That's my business to know."

"I agreed to go to your Christmas party. You promised me we could talk without fighting. Why don't we meet somewhere?" I count to ten in my head, trying to calm myself so I don't say anything I will regret later. I've never challenged him before, and he doesn't like the idea that I'm not firmly under his thumb. It's sent his well-organised world spinning.

"Sorry if I can't fit into your plans, but after you ran out from the party last night, you sure as hell didn't fit into mine, so you're just going to have to get used to it. Now, I want to know where you are." No amount of counting in my head can stop me rising to that.

"You're unbelievable. You seem to think I'm oblivious to where you really are when you're out. I'm not. Tell me, Phil, how'd you get Sophie away from that other gentleman she was nuzzling up to?"

"Where the fuck are you, Izzy?"

"I'm not telling you."

"Izzy, stop playing…"

"I'm not playing. It's over, Phil. I don't want to be married to you. I want a divorce." Silence greets me. He's pushed me to this. He's goaded me time and time again, helping me to find the words that I've wanted to say amongst his ugly tirade.

He's still quiet. I've shocked him.

"What do you mean, you don't want to be married to me anymore? It's not something *you* get to choose, Isabel." His words ooze with venom. Gone is the Phil that I once loved more than the world. He's become someone I don't recognise.

"Yes, it is. I want a divorce."

"You tell me this over the phone?"

"You never made the time for me when I asked to talk to you. I'm sorry it came out this way. This is for the best. For both of us."

"Is that it, then? I don't get a say?" The venom has been masked. He's softer in his words, but it's not hurt, not the emotional kind, anyway; it's his pride that's damaged.

"I'm not happy, Phil, and I haven't been for a long time. You're cheating and won't even admit it to me. We've been fighting, arguing. I've been telling you that things aren't right between us but you've continued to ignore me. Not anymore. You knew this was coming. You are as absent from this marriage as I am."

"Where is this coming from, Izzy? You've never complained before. We've been like this for years and you've never complained. What's different about this time?"

I don't know why this should bother me now, but it does. His wording 'this time' implies his behaviour has been like this before. I consider something I hadn't imagined before now. Sophie is not the first time. He's cheated before. He's had affairs in the past, and I've not noticed. I feel sick—physically sick at the prospect that my marriage was always a sham, that I was so blinkered to it. God, did I ever know him at all? This is

9

the man with whom I wanted to spend the rest of my life, have children and grow old and grey with.

"You really have some nerve to expect me to stay with you after this, even though you won't admit to your affairs. It's over. I'm divorcing you. I'll be in touch regarding how we proceed from here."

"Eleven years, Izzy, and that's it? You finish us over the fucking phone. You really are a cold-hearted bitch." The line goes dead.

* * *

"Seb...?"

"I'm sorry, Izzy, but I can't do this."

"No..." My mind panics. *"I love you, Sebastian,"* I blurt. He turns to face me.

"I know you do, sweetheart. Thank you for telling me, but that doesn't help. You still return to Phil. I think you should take some time and think about what you want, Izzy. Really think." He looks at me, my dress half on, half off from his impatience to fuck me, to claim me. *"I think you need to leave."*

"No!" I scream, but it has little effect. The aquamarine of his gaze is tinged with pain and darkness rather than the bright blues and greens that normally shine back.

He doesn't say anything further, just leaves me and closes the door behind him.

"No!" I scream and bolt upright in my bed, pulling myself from my dream. I'm breathing hard and I'm sticky with sweat, although it feels like I have an ice block in my chest, chilling me from the inside out. My dream is still a vivid image in my mind, Seb walking out on me all over again, the cold look in his eyes, telling me that we can't be together. It turns my

10

stomach, and I feel a roll of nausea that I fight off. I take a few moments to familiarise myself with the surroundings. I'm at Jess's place, in what will be my bedroom and home for the next, well, I don't know how long. Rolling to the side, I reach for my phone. It's 3:10 a.m. I slump back down. I'm cold and scared. More than scared—terrified. With my dream so fresh, I can't keep the hurt and pain and feeling of utter loss at bay. All my tears let loose at once, and they overwhelm me.

I cry. I cry so hard I can't get in a breath to fill my lungs. A tight pain bands my lungs, squeezing them tighter, and I start to panic.

"Izzy, what's wrong?" Jess's concerned voice fills the room. She's standing at the bottom of the bed. Light spills from the hallway, throwing her into shadow. "Oh, hun, what's wrong?"

"I... I... I can't. He said... I don't... I don't..." I know I'm not making sense, but I can't speak the words. My tears consume me.

"Shh." Jess sits down next to me and gathers me to her like a small child, letting me cry it out. Her embrace is like a lifeline and I cling to her, desperate to find my way back to safety.

* * *

I wake again. Jess and I must have fallen asleep. She's lying next to me, and I try not to wake her as I extricate myself from the bed. Checking my phone again, I see that it's nearly 6:00 a.m.

"Can you speak now?" Even her soft voice makes me start.

"Sorry, I didn't mean to wake you—either time. I'm sorry, Jess."

"Hey, don't worry. I'm here for you, but it would help if I knew exactly what we're dealing with. Is it Seb?" She sits up, leans back against the headboard and pulls the covers around her to keep warm. I turn and climb back in beside her, tucking the covers in. At this point I have nothing to fear. I've said my piece to Phil, even if it didn't go the way I wanted it to. Jess isn't his biggest fan, so I'll have her support on that front.

"I told Phil I want a divorce. My words finally seemed to get through to him."

"Asking for a divorce was a huge decision. You've been together for a long time. But I agree it's the right thing for you to do. It's been a long time coming and I can't say I'm sorry." She smiles and reaches out to grasp my hand.

"Thank you. I just, I think it took meeting Seb to make me see everything, or at least to help me see what I want. Jess, how did I let things get to this point? How could I not see? Phil said something on the phone that suggested he'd cheated on me before." Jess and I are cuddled under the covers, like we used to do years ago when a good evening ended in a sleepover.

"What did he say?"

I bite my lower lip. "He asked what had changed *this* time, implying that he's cheated before. I never noticed." Saying it aloud makes me feel like a fool all over again. *I've been blind.*

"I'm sorry, Izzy. I am." She doesn't sound surprised. "You really are best without him. I know divorcing will be hard. You loved him for so long. What about Seb? Where does he fit in?"

"Well, isn't that the big question? I don't know myself." I shrug. "It wasn't supposed to be serious with Seb. Honestly, it wasn't, but it grew into something I never thought could happen. He made me feel more than I could have ever imagined." Giving words to the feelings inside of me helps me to think of the positive. Jess remains quiet, happy to let me finally talk this out. "It's been… You know when you work something up in your head? A problem or something you hope will happen."

"Like overthink it?"

"Yes, you think about it for hours and hours until you're obsessing over how to achieve your goal? And then you finally reach it. Jess, being with Seb is like that. It was such a relief. Seb desired, wanted and valued me. After having none of those affections for so long, I was intoxicated. The warmth and love I felt was everything that I'd forgotten about, and was missing with Phil. I love him. I love him more than I ever thought I could love someone, even though we've only been together for a short while."

"That's great, hun."

"I really hope that he's in my future. We've not had a usual start to our relationship. We don't really know each other. I want us to be together, but…"

"But what? What's stopping you now?"

"Well, I'm scared. Scared of a lot of things, actually. How do I know these feelings can be true? That everything between us is real? I spent twelve years with Phil and our relationship amounted to nothing. Seb fulfils a fantasy of mine. What if things with him seem real because of the situation we're in? Seb and I are new and fresh. What if my feelings are simply reflecting that? How can I trust what I'm feeling?"

"Hey, calm down, Izzy. Seb certainly didn't seem unsure when he took you off me at the bar. Have some faith and believe in how you feel."

"Perhaps. We had a fight. Seb said he wanted more than what was happening between us. I just… I don't want to rush a relationship, yet I'm desperate to see him and work things out." My eyes burn as the tears fall again, but I don't worry about them now. I can cry because I love this man and I want to feel everything, including the hurt.

"Well, have you spoken to him since the other night?" I think back to the last moments with Seb, telling him how I felt after all the hurt and confusion of the evening.

13

"No, I haven't. I told him that I love him, but he wanted more. He said he won't keep seeing me if I continue to go back to Phil."

"Well, why don't you talk to him?"

"Do you think? I don't want to seem like I've only finished with Phil because of what he said. I want him to know that I want him for him, and for what we are together. I need to try and separate the two."

"Then you need to tell him. He should understand if he knows you at all." She delivers this with a small smile and another squeeze of my hand. I let her words sink into my foggy brain. Maybe she's right.

"Okay, can we talk more later? I'm still so tired and my face hurts." We both giggle. I'm suddenly so weary. I've been through the week from hell.

"Fine by me, but I'm not leaving. My bed's cold and I'm nice and comfy here." Jess snuggles down just to make her point. "Besides, I'm not sure I'm ready to leave you alone just yet." With that, she turns over and goes back to sleep.

Three

On Monday I contact a solicitor recommended by the firm we use at work. If I'm serious about leaving Phil, I need to show it. The solicitor, one Mr. Osbourn, goes through the process of the divorce, which seems fairly straightforward. I give him the outline to our relationship and that he's cheating on me with Sophie. He asks me if I've discussed the divorce with Phil and if he might cause any problems. I tell him that I want to end things amicably, which he is pleased about. I fill out the details he's asked for as well as a cheque to cover his fees and the cost of the divorce. The only thing I need to forward on is our marriage certificate. For the first time in almost a week, I feel lighter. I stop to grab a bottle of wine on the way home from work and text Jess to say that we're staying in tonight.

* * *

"Cheers!"

We clink glasses, cuddling up to each other on the sofa.

"So what grounds did you state on the divorce? Did you put Seb's name on the paperwork?"

I'm momentarily stunned. "No! It doesn't work that way. I outlined everything to the solicitor. About Phil, that he's been cheating on me. Phil's adultery will be the grounds for the divorce. Him finding out about Seb would complicate things. I've put up with his behaviour for so long, but the solicitor said that this is the best way to go. I've got to get my marriage certificate and try and find Sophie's details somehow, still. Then the solicitor can send off the petition."

"Why do you need Sophie's details—she's Phil's bit on the side, right?"

"Yes, I want to name her as the co-respondent."

"Really? I thought you wanted amicable?"

"I do, but at the same time, I want Phil to hurt for what he's put me through. I'm pleased I've done it, Jess, but can we not go into the details right now?"

"Okay, okay, I'm sorry. Please, you know I was trying to be nosey. Change of subject. What are you doing next week?"

"You mean Christmas? Nothing. I'm working right up to it. You?"

"I'm around but will be at my folks' on the day. You'll be more than welcome."

"Thanks, can I think about it? I want to contact Seb. I need to make the first move, and I'm... hopeful." I smile to myself, thinking how good it would be to spend Christmas with Seb. As my wine goes down, my mood goes up.

"I'm proud of you. I know this hasn't been easy on you. I might remind you that if you'd not bottled up your feelings, it might have been easier." She smiles at me and quirks her head to one side, teasing me again.

"Thank you. Are you still okay with me staying here? I'm not sure how long it will be before I'm ready to move out. I need to start paying you rent."

"We can deal with all of that after Christmas." She looks at the empty bottle on the table in front of us. "Do you want more wine?" Her mischievous grin has spread across her face and I can tell she's hoping I agree.

16

"Sorry, I really shouldn't. Half a bottle is my limit. Any more and I'll have a hangover for work."

"Fine. I suppose it is a school night. See you tomorrow."

"Good night."

It's the first night that I want to hear Seb's voice more than I don't want to pick up the phone.

He always had the ability to calm and soothe me as well as command and control me with his words.

Making my way to my room, I sit on the bed and scroll to Seb's number. My pulse kicks up a beat and my stomach knots with anticipation. I press call. It rings. And rings and rings. As the voicemail kicks in, I'm rewarded with a few brief words: "Sebastian York, leave a message." At the beep, I shock myself and actually speak. *No more easy Izzy.*

"Hi. It's me... I've wanted to call before today. Every day, in fact, but I've had some important things to get in order first. Can we talk? I miss you." It's all I can say. I pause before hanging up.

I hope he'll talk to me, so that I can explain how sorry I am. Then, hopefully, we can look forward. I want to offer Seb the 'more' that he asked for, to be able to reciprocate what he's done for me. I cling to that hope as I try to find the sleep I'm always in need of.

I get up early the next morning and stop by my house before going to work. Phil hasn't contacted me and hasn't returned any of my texts attempting to start talking our separation through properly. *Why should he change that habit now?* We need to talk about the divorce settlement and what we do with the house.

At least the locks haven't been changed. I let myself in and take a tentative look around.

"Phil?" I call. His car isn't in the drive, but I don't want to get a surprise and find him here. I go to the spare room and pull open the draw with all our important paperwork. I take my passport and marriage certificate out. I go into the kitchen and take off my wedding bands. My eyes tear. They were a symbol of everlasting love and marriage. Now they only hold the memory of what went wrong.

I leave the rings on the kitchen sideboard. I don't leave a note.

Four

I arrive at work and grab a cup of coffee before settling down at my desk. It's my little ritual. I phone Phil and leave a short, polite message, informing him that I'll be filling for divorce.

"You're getting divorced?" Mark's question makes me jump out of my skin and I die a little on the inside. I'm absolutely clear that divorce is the right thing for me, but I'm not sure I want to share it with the world just yet.

"God, Mark, you scared me."

"Sorry. I didn't mean to eavesdrop. It's quiet in here and I was getting a drink." He sounds a little embarrassed.

I relax and try to talk about it. I'm going to have to at some point. "It's alright. I should've been more private. I didn't think anyone was in. And yes, I'm getting a divorce."

"Is that why you were off for those weeks? I know you said it was an emergency." I give Mark a rather frosty glare. I'm not comfortable talking about this or explaining myself in any further detail to my boss.

"Yes. I'm sorry, but I'd rather not talk about it any further." I raise my eyebrows and nod to my desk, indicating that the subject is closed and I want to get back to work.

"Of course. I'm sorry you are going through such difficult times, Izzy."

I post my marriage certificate to Mr. Osbourn over lunch. I don't hear from Phil for the rest of the day, which is his usual MO. However, I don't hear from Seb either. I text him before I leave the office. The whole journey home and the rest of the evening I wait for that little bing. Each email, every social media notification raises my hopes, but no contact from him comes.

While I'm waiting, I do a little investigating. Pulling up Facebook, I do a little stalking until I find what I'm looking for. Sophie Trent's profile. The only person I know who might know where she lives is Jackson, Phil's friend. I scroll through my numbers and hit call.

"Hello?"

"Oh, hi, Laura. It's Izzy."

"I don't think Phil's here, I'm sorry."

"No, I was actually after Jackson if he's home." My voice has a squeak that betrays my nerves. If I can't get an address then I won't be putting Sophie's name on the paperwork.

"He's not home either. Can I help?"

"Well, actually, do you know Sophie? Sophie Trent? She was at the Christmas party."

"Sure, she's been friends with Jackson for ages."

"I'm trying to get in touch with her. Do you have her address?"

"Why do you need her address?" Maybe the truth would help here. It does sound a stupid request, and if any of my friends gave out my address as easily as this I'd be livid.

"Look, I know she's been seeing Phil. I'm leaving him. I just need to clear the air with her. You know, face-to-face." I grit my teeth, not wanting to give away the real reason behind the call.

"That bad, huh? She lives on Upper Camden Place, although I'm not sure of the number. I'm sorry it didn't work out." Laura doesn't sound at all surprised.

"That's fine. Thanks for your help, Laura." I end the call and Google a search for the postcode. With my newfound knowledge, I fire off an email to Mr. Osbourn.

A loud bang and the sound of movement wakes me. It's 2:30 a.m., and I think I hear Jess giggling downstairs. She's not alone. The giggling dies but is replaced with low moaning.

I squeeze my eyes shut and bury myself under the covers. I cannot deal with hearing Jess get frisky with a guy. *Way too much information.* I hear more banging and footsteps.

"Which door, Jess? Mmmm… which door?"

"Right, right, this one." Another bang and then silence. I pull my head out of the duvet and wait. Nothing. I relax and thank Jess for having thick walls. At least she's having fun.

I check my phone, but there are no new messages.

Please, Seb. Just tell me you're OK, that we
can talk soon. I miss you. So much. Love Izzy

Christmas is fast approaching. It's usually a lovely, homey time of year. I love giving presents and seeing friends, but I have been dishing out excuses to many about my plans over Christmas. A few mutual friends have sent text messages of 'sorry to hear' and 'is there anything I can do?' about the news of me and Phil. It seems either he's happy to discuss our breakup or Laura has been talking.

I've left him a handful of messages since I dropped off my rings but I've heard nothing yet. My sadness and guilt have been replaced by anger and frustration.

On the plus side, Mr. Osbourn and I have gone over all the details for the divorce petition which has been filed with the court. He advised that I should be seeking Phil to pay all the costs of the divorce, plus half of his pension, the savings and all of the proceeds of the sale of the house. That's not what I wanted. Half of the house and the savings plus paying for my costs was what I deemed fair, although whether Phil would agree was another matter. Mr. Osbourn also advised against naming Sophie as a co-respondent. I was disappointed that she wouldn't be dragged into this. She deserves this, and it would serve Phil right. But he said that it would likely complicate matters further. I want this divorce over with as soon as possible. Reluctantly, I agreed.

Christmas Eve is a short work day, and I'm thrown out at noon by security.

"Hey, merry Christmas Eve!" All giggly and excited, Jess greets me as I walk in the door, and I can't help but smile back at her as she grabs me into a huge hug.

"You have a surprise in your room. I think it's an early Christmas present."

"Oh, thanks, Jess. I've not really planned Christmas this year."

"No, silly, it's not from me. Go up and see. I'll be right behind you." In my overactive imagination, I picture Seb sitting on my bed, ready to welcome me back into his life. Of course, he's not in my room. On the desk, though, is a beautiful arrangement of flowers—white hyacinths, purple irises and alstroemeria in an elaborate display. They are stunning and fill the room with a sweet perfume. I know they are from him. They are too similar to the last flowers he sent—striking and original. It couldn't possibly be anyone else.

I look for a note and hope for a letter. I find a small card.

Dearest Isabel,
Wishing you a Merry Christmas
Sebastian

I stare at it.

"Oh, Izzy, they are gorgeous. Are they from Seb?"

"Yes." I can't keep the amazement and worry from bubbling up and choking me. He's reached out. That's a good sign, a very good sign.

"They are so unusual. What do they mean?"

"What do you mean? They're flowers."

"The Victorians loved their books on flower meanings. They say they represent specific emotions or feelings." She pauses. "Red roses are the obvious—love. But I'm not sure about these flowers."

"Do you think Seb would really send me a message with flowers?"

"They seem pretty unusual, like the ones he sent you last time. You know him, is this something he would do?" I think back past the last few months to when I first met Seb. He was always different. He listened to me, took the time to see me for who I really am. My heart flutters with possibility.

I hadn't thought about the flowers having a unique meaning before now, and suddenly all I want to do is fire up Google. I buzz past Jess and reach for my iPad. Jess jumps on the bed next to me, giggling again. *Come on, come on!*

I will the screen to work and quickly type 'flower meaning' into the search bar, then wait for a long list of possible sites.

"White hyacinths mean beauty and irises stand for a message." I slump back down, thinking about what Seb is trying to say.

"What about the last flowers?"

"The alstroemeria? This reference says they mean devotion."

My eyes water and I can't quite stop my heart from hoping. Is he trying to tell me he still has feelings for me? I desperately want him to love me the way I love him. When we were together, I thought he did. I could feel it.

"Izzy, did you hear what I said?"

"Um, what?"

"I said, what are you going to do?"

"I want to fight for him."

"Oh, thank god! Right, phone him… Now!"

"Okay, but not with you here."

"Ohh, I promise I won't say a word." She's grinning from ear to ear and it's infectious.

I nudge her out of my room as I clutch my phone against my ear, waiting for Seb to pick up. He doesn't, so I fire off a message.

> Thank you for the flowers. I'm ready. I want us to work. I love you. Izzy

How did he know where to send the flowers? He must know I'm not at home, and that gives me hope.

> I meant what I said. I won't go back to what we were doing before. S

He responded! I'm caught between relief and nerves. *Had he been ignoring me previously?* I shake off my doubts and tap his name on my phone again, hoping he'll pick up this time.

"Hello." He answers on the third ring, all chocolate and velvet, sending shivers down my spine. The short build-up of anxiety evaporates on his first word. I've missed him, and right now, that's what I want to focus on. That, and getting back to him.

"Hi."

"So, you've decided?"

"My decision was never between you and Phil. I just needed to find my courage."

"And...?"

"Seb, I miss you," I choke out. "I feel lost and I want to be with you. Please believe me. It's always been you." I can't hold back and cry.

"Oh, Izzy, please don't cry. Shh..."

"No. I've been awful to you. I never considered how my actions would hurt you. I was too wrapped up in my own world, but I love you and hope with all my heart that I can make things right." I pause to gather myself before carrying on. *Get it all out, Izzy.* "I'm sorry, Seb. I should have had more courage and told Phil that I wanted a divorce a long time ago. I have now. I've filed for divorce. I've done it." I hear him let out a small gasp, but I can't let it distract me from what I need to say. This is my confession and I'm finally talking, albeit through tears and snot. "I love you. I just, this is all so crazy. Is there any way we can work at recovering what we had?"

I take a few shuddering breaths and hold on to a sliver of faith that Seb feels the same way, that he did want more, after all. I wait… and wait a few more moments until I don't think I can stand the suspense. I've crumbled and laid myself emotionally bare to Seb. Our fate is in his hands. My fate.

"You tell me this now when I'm miles away and can't see you."

"You want to see me?"

"Of course I do. Didn't you understand when I said I wanted more? What we had at the start quickly changed from a temporary affair to a relationship that promised much more. I hoped that you believed enough in us to take that final step and leave Phil, but you didn't. I won't continue to be second in your life."

"I want to see you. I want us to be together."

"Are you ready to see me, Izzy?"

"Yes. Please…" I beg and I'm not ashamed about it.

"I'll warn you, right now I'm caught between wanting to spank you senseless and worshipping you. It's been a long week."

"I'll love both from you. Please, Seb." He sighs audibly. I press. "I can come over. I still have your key."

"I'm in Manchester at the moment. When will you need to be home? How long is your Christmas break?"

"Boxing Day evening. Are you staying at the same hotel as before?"

"Yes, I'll meet you in the bar. Drive safely, Isabel. That's an order."

* * *

Nearly four hours later, I'm parked, and walk, bag in hand, through the entrance. A magical green spruce decked in white and silver twinkles at me in the lobby. Beautiful glass and crystal ornaments hang from the branches, each placed with care. The elegant tree brings a sense of hope to me. I have been rather distracted from the regular goings on of Christmas, and this sight makes me smile.

Now, standing looking at the tree, meeting the man I love for a rendezvous of passion, I finally feel Christmassy. The misery of the last week has evaporated. The conversations ahead of us won't be easy, but I'm not afraid. Not anymore.

I'm nervous, and the butterflies are back in residence. Seb told me to meet him in the bar—the bar where we first met at the hotel—and it seems fitting. The bar is nearly deserted, a combination of Christmas Eve and the late hour. I sit awkwardly at one of the bar stools and start twiddling my fingers. My stomach is churning in knots and I just want to be wrapped in his arms. *Please, please, please!*

I texted him as soon as I parked the car, but so far, I've had nothing back. Waiting is torture. There isn't even a barman I can order a drink from, so I'm stuck with only my thoughts for company. Why did he have to be all the way in Manchester?

I feel him before I see him. All the hairs on the back of my neck stand up and I start tingling in anticipation. "Merry Christmas, Isabel," he purrs at my ear, sending my pulse dancing through my body. He doesn't touch me, just hovers his mouth by my cheek so I tilt my head back and up towards him. "Let's go upstairs. Come on." He steps back and offers his hand to help me. I gratefully accept.

His handsome frame holds a tension I wish I could erase. In jeans and a white shirt, he makes my mouth water. His stubble has grown out a little, and I itch to feel it scrape across my cheek—or against my thigh. He collects my bag and leads me to wait for the lift. He doesn't look at me or say a word as we wait, and I can't help but fidget. I'm eager to be with Seb, for him to lay my worries about us and our future to rest. If we have a future. The memory of our strained conversation and the separation I've felt still linger.

The 'ding' of the lift makes me jump. *Why do I feel like this?* Seb steps us into the lift car and drops my bag. As the doors close, he pulls me into his arms and engulfs me in a huge cuddle. He crushes me to his chest and just squeezes harder. I melt at his sign of affection. It's just what I need. He shuffles me a few feet without breaking his hold and presses the emergency stop button.

"For the next day, our time here is just for us, Izzy. I want us to enjoy being together without thinking about anything else. Can you give me that?" My eyes close and the tears run freely at his words. My tears are happy ones, and I struggle out of his hold to wrap my arms around him and kiss him. I kiss him and it's wonderful. His tongue pushes and penetrates me as his lips crush mine, revealing how much more he wants. We expose our base need for each other through this kiss. He takes control, holding my jaw, and slows my overzealous attack on him. He turns the kiss into a slow, sensuous act, which has me desperate to be under him. "Yes... Please," I mumble, agreeing to his conditions. I would agree to anything after that kiss.

He pulls back but cradles my head in his hands. His beautiful aqua eyes bore into mine, past even my teary sheen. His gaze carries an unspoken promise that the next few days will be spent revelling in one another. The message heats my blood.

He releases the stop button and the doors open shortly after. We walk to his door and he pauses to look at me, fishing the key card out of his pocket as he does. He grins and looks at the door.

"What is it?" I ask, grinning back at his infectious smile.

"Don't you remember?"

Now I understand. "The same room?"

"The same room. Coming in?" He holds the door open for me with his free hand, and it's the easiest decision I've made in a long time. I cross the threshold and don't look back. No hesitation. No doubt.

I walk in and look around. I know it's the same room, but I feel different about being here this time. I gaze out of the window, and the twinkling lights of the city remind me of the lights of the lobby Christmas tree. *Fitting, really.*

I sense Seb behind me. Just being near him sends a low pulse of current over my skin, making me hot with desire. His hand gently sweeps my hair to one side as he plants soft kisses on my neck. "I'll turn the heat up. You've got far too many clothes on for my liking, Izzy."

He moves away from me but I remain still. We've never been together as just us, without the pretence of exploring my sexuality. *Will it be the same?*

"Why are you still standing there, sweetheart?" He turns me to face him and his eyes are dark, filled with blues and greens.

"I... I wasn't sure."

"Oh, sweet girl. I want you naked beneath me, and if you don't hurry up and start taking clothes off..." he pauses to run his finger down the centre of my chest to the top of my jeans, "... I'm going to strip you myself." My breath catches at his words, and the familiar ache at the bottom of my stomach makes me want to squirm. I run my palms up his chest and rest them on his shoulders.

"As you wish." I smile with my eyes, and it sparks the reaction I want. Seb pulls off my jumper and unbuttons my shirt.

He peels it from my shoulders to my wrists, restraining my arms behind me. His hands move quickly, fulfilling his threat to strip me. He picks me up, carries me to the bed and pushes me back so he can pull my jeans and knickers off. I start to struggle to free my arms but he's not undone the buttons at my shirt cuffs and I can't free my hands.

"I wanted you naked, but seeing you like this, Izzy… Keep the shirt on."

Bound by my shirt, my arms are trapped on either side of me. Seb strips himself, then crawls over me, heading straight for my mouth. The passion that spiked in the lift surges back with a vengeance, but I can't touch him. He starts to kiss my mouth, my throat, down my chest. He pulls my bra cup down and sucks hard on my nipple.

"Mmm…" I bow off the bed. My clit throbs at his touch and heat sweeps over my skin. He continues to play with my breast, licking around my nipple before flicking it with the tip of his tongue and sucking softly. "Seb, please." I'm begging him already.

"Shh. I want to get lost in you, Izzy. Just let me." His words hold the desperation I feel. I want to give him what he needs.

He moves his attention to my other breast and pulls my leg out wider to cradle him. He trails his fingers up my leg as he gently kisses around my nipple. His touch is a faint tickle across my skin and draws a deep response from me. I'm wet and my sex is aching—aching and wanting. I feel needy for him to fill me—make me come. His fingers only skim the apex of my thighs and up to my breast. I moan, and I can feel his smile. He begins tweaking my nipple with his fingers, just enough to make me pant, while he flicks and licks at the other breast. He immerses me in sensation. I lose myself to him.

"Mmm… Ahhh!" My mewls and pleading fill the air as I vocalise my desire.

"I want to hear you, Izzy. I love how you sound."

I groan and my hips begin to thrust. I can feel his thick erection pressing into my leg and I want him. I want him to fuck me. *Please, Seb, take me, fuck me.* He pinches harder, sucks harder, and it's painful in the most delicious way. Everything he does, I feel in my core. My clit throbs. All my muscles begin to tighten, and I can feel the build of my climax in the pit of my stomach.

"That's it."

"Oh pleeease!" As I plead, he pinches hard while ravishing my nipple with his tongue. It sends me over and my orgasm pulses through me without him even touching me.

"Fuck, you're so sensitive, so full of need. I'm going to bury myself in you now." I'm still coming down from my climax as Seb shifts off of me. A moment later he presses back on top of me, and his eager cock is coated in my wetness as he slides through my slick folds. "God, so wet." He thrusts into me. We groan together at the exquisite feeling and he pauses to rest his forehead on mine.

This. This feeling is what I want—what I crave and what I've missed. His hips begin to rock against mine and we're both lost to the feeling. I'm climbing already. Each thrust is faster, more urgent, and I can see the tension in Seb's jaw as he pulls out and surges back into me. His gaze captures mine and I want to surrender to him—surrender all of me to him. So I do. He thrusts one more time and hits against my clit. My orgasm crashes over me. "Thank fuck." His curse tells me he's held back. He slams back into me, his frantic need to fuck me overtaking him. His own cries of pleasure ring loud in my ears as he comes hard, and then collapses on me.

In my blissful cocoon, I'm aware of Seb shifting beside me, but my eyes have already closed.

I open my eyes, and Seb watches me from where his head is buried in the pillows. "Can you take my shirt off now, please?" I smile into his now warm eyes.

"Yes. Merry Christmas, Izzy."

"Merry Christmas, Seb."

"Right, now we need to sleep. It's already morning and you've had a long drive." I let him manoeuvre me to reach my cuffs. He pulls the covers back, my invitation to snuggle under. "Thank you for coming to me, Izzy." His thanks shocks me for a second. I thought he wasn't particularly keen on the idea of me driving up to see him.

"Thank you for letting me. I'm glad I did. I missed you." My voice breaks a little at the relief that we've connected again.

"Shh. Sleep now. We can talk tomorrow, alright?" I nod into his skin. He turns the light out and wraps me in his arms. I give a huge sigh and try to stifle my yawn. When I hear his breathing slow, I whisper very softly, "I love you." Sleep claims me.

I'm warm and still sleepy, my head is groggy, but I sense something on my back. I stir. The sensations drag me from my slumber. Feather-light kisses rain down on my back. I must have ended up on my stomach during the night, and Seb's soft lips are making a trail over my back.

"Umm, good morning. That feels amazing."

"You have a beautiful body, Izzy. I've been watching you sleep but couldn't help myself. Good morning." He kisses down my back all the way to the base of my spine. I start to move, shifting my hips and arching into his touch. As Seb registers my approval, he skims his hand down the side of my body to rest on my hip. His fingers grip my flesh and pull me closer to him, closer to his mouth. He replaces his lips with his tongue and slowly draws it up the centre of my spine.

I groan, heady with desire. He continues the trail with his tongue and it's erotic, so personal, and I melt, my stomach now sick with need.

"You like me stroking you like this." It's not a question.

"Yes," I purr.

"Good." He moves down to the base of my spine again, but instead of repeating his tongue torture as I thought he would, he pulls back the duvet.

"I'm naked." I squeak my protest and turn to look at him over my shoulder. The burning look in his eyes stops any further fight from me. He moves down the bed and takes my left ankle, pulling it to the corner of the bed so my legs are spread wide. My breathing and excitement level kick up a notch. Wanton desire runs through my veins.

His tongue runs around the inside of my ankle. He grasps my foot and stops me from wiggling it free. "Stay very still, Izzy," he commands. He's taking control, and I love it. It's what my body craves and clearly responds to. I'm relieved. I worried when he said these days would be for "us," not as "Isabel and Sebastian," the formal names he'd insisted we use during our previous games of D/s. I wondered if that meant he wouldn't dominate me, but the look he just gave me, together with his commands, has vanquished those doubts.

Soft, slow licks travel tantalisingly up the inside of my leg, getting closer and closer to my sex. I instinctively tense and begin to draw my legs together. *Relax, you know it's going to be amazing.* Seb notices. He grabs my thighs and pushes my legs even wider.

"Don't deny me, Izzy." I try to relax and he presses my legs a fraction wider again. "You look delicious and wet." The anticipation he's building is painful and I want to press my legs together to relieve the growing ache. "I think you're a needy girl. Now, do you want my tongue on your pussy, licking and sucking on you until you come on my mouth?" *Oh my god.* My brain is scrambled. His words ignite a toxic mix of desire and need in my blood. My clit swells, eager to feel Seb's touch.

The sensitive flesh of my thigh quivers as his tongue dances a sexy trail upwards. I'm both mortified and desperate all in one. Just as I think he's going to reach my slick lips, his tongue tickles the inside of my other leg and I moan in frustration. "You're impatient, I see." He's laughing at me. *Yes, I am. Please!*

He repeats the trail with his tongue, starting at my ankles, and I zone out to the hypnotic sweep of his tongue on me. I feel how wet I am. Every lick of his tongue registers on my clit. When he reaches the apex of my thighs this time, I'm panting hard.

"Please, Seb... Please touch me." I've become accustomed to begging. I'm still not ashamed.

"My pleasure, Izzy." He pushes a finger inside of me with exquisite slowness, and I nearly come apart. Inch by inch, it slips inside of me while his other hand keeps my leg outspread.

"I can see your juices coating my finger. It's running off you, you're so wet." My muscles clench at his dirty talk, my orgasm coiling. "I'm enjoying the show, Izzy, but I want more. On your knees for me, head and chest down, arse in the air, legs wide."

Huh? I'm thrown off a bit, but I do as he says, all with his finger buried inside me. When I'm in position, he draws his finger out just as slowly as he pushed it in and repeats. Over and over. He doesn't speed up and it's enough to drive me crazy. He keeps my orgasm at bay while sending my body into overdrive.

"Please. Please, Seb, please. I need to come," I plead with him, but he doesn't change his tactics. "Seb, more. I want it harder, faster." I'm grinding my hips back and down onto his finger now, wild with the need to come. He slips another finger into me, which only serves to inflame my desire, but he allows me to fuck his fingers. My inhibitions at being on display to him are long forgotten. "Yes... Oh god, yes."

"Fuck, don't come!" He withdraws his fingers from me.

"No! No, why?" He pulls me back and thrusts his cock into me before I can say anything else. He pulls me back so I'm almost sitting on him, my legs still wide. He reaches around to pinch my clit and he growls in my ear.

"I wanted to watch your beautiful pussy weep with desire for me, but you are too impatient." He thrusts up, hard. "And you fucked my fingers so wantonly." *Thrust.* "I want to fuck you into next week." *Thrust.* His words are sexy as sin and I'm ready to explode. My orgasm tightens everything inside me. "Come for me, Izzy." He squeezes my clit between the soft pads of his thumb and forefinger.

I come apart on his lap as he grinds through his own climax. "I think you may have forgotten your control again. We'll have to work on that." I smile at his words, remembering when he first spoke them to me before spanking me over his breakfast bar.

"I look forward to it." I sag against him, completely spent. I collapse forwards and crawl off him back up to the pillow. Seb pulls the duvet over me and I want to go back to sleep. Again.

"I'll let you sleep for a little bit, but I'd really like to spend some of Christmas with you. And not just in bed."

"Okay," I whisper sleepily as I doze back off to a happy place.

* * *

It must be the middle of the day when I wake. I turn over in bed and stretch out for Seb, only to find the bed empty. I wrap the duvet around my body and venture out into the living space. Across the room, Seb is arranging a small table with plates and cutlery. A trolley is behind him with a number of dishes and plates and two silver cloches. I'm arrested by the view out of the floor-to-ceiling windows of the city far below—the same city that bore witness to my punishment when we were last here.

"You can't stand there all day, Izzy. Go put some clothes on so we can have lunch. Hurry up before it gets cold." Seb's already dressed in jeans and a dark grey t-shirt, stretched across his torso as an invitation for me to stare. He looks up and gives me his sexy smile. I smile back before wrestling the duvet back the way I came.

I'm in a dream world: Christmas with Seb, the man I'm head over heels in love with, at a hotel where he is showering me with attention. I can't shake my own grin as I hastily throw my jeans and a jumper on. I re-emerge to find Seb sprawled in a chair at the little table, sipping on something pink and bubbly from a champagne flute. I join him. A full Christmas spread is before us and it's perfect. He stands and helps me into my chair.

"How on earth did you get this all arranged?"

"It's a hotel, Izzy. I ordered it up."

"Yes, but it's Christmas."

"I know. Hence the Christmas dinner." I'm warmed by the sentiment that we are relaxed enough with each other to have these playful moments.

"Thank you. It looks wonderful. I didn't really have any plans for today."

"Oh, why not?" He starts on his food, spearing a slice of turkey and a roasted parsnip, topped with cranberry sauce.

"Well, I hoped that we would spend Christmas together. Jess invited me to spend it with her if not."

"What about Phil?" The air holds a silence after his question. *Didn't he believe me when I told him I'd left him?*

"What about him? I'm not living with him anymore. I've sent off the papers to petition him for a divorce. Spending Christmas with him was hardly appropriate." The sass in the answer earns me a disapproving look and I cower a little inside.

"Will you tell me about it?" I owe it to Seb to be completely honest. Seb has a right to know why I'm getting a

37

divorce, but I can't help the shame and embarrassment that I'm feeling.

"Well, after I got home from your flat, I was a mess. I couldn't sleep and ended up wandering around the rooms of my house... just looking at where I was. This was my house. But it wasn't a true home anymore. I didn't want to be there or part of a life that was unhappy. I know leaving was something I should have done a long time ago, before I'd even met you, but I wasn't strong enough for that. I packed up and left for Jess's. I hired a solicitor who has filed petition papers, the first step, and told Phil. He accused me of changing—said that I'd never reacted this way before to his little flings, that his behaviour wasn't a problem before. I realised then how blind I've been." Seb hasn't looked at me during my little speech, just continued to eat his turkey, which makes it easier for me to continue. "I wanted to tell you how I felt about you, but I also knew that I needed to do this for me. I had to sever things with Phil for my benefit, not just because of what you told me. I think I would have either way. It was long overdue, and certainly something right for me. Jess has been great." I pick at my food, taking a few mouthfuls.

We continue eating in relative silence, stealing glances at each other, smiling and giggling a little across the small table. It's like the first date we never had—charming and sweet.

"You know, you were an adorable bundle of nerves the first time I saw you, but you can't deny that the attraction was instant. If it wasn't for that training course, it's likely we never would have met again." His smile is mournful and I feel it, too. There are so many 'what ifs'. There still are, and we need to get to those. Just not today.

"Thank you," I say, suddenly grateful beyond measure for everything Seb has done. "For helping me find my courage. I'm sorry we didn't start like a normal couple should."

38

"That wasn't meant to happen for us. We have our own story, okay?" Seb whispers. Tears start to form in my eyes and his hand engulfs mine, drawing my eyes to his.

"Sweetheart, it's okay. You're here now."

I stare into his eyes. The blue has turned dark, and I know that after both our confessions, he's feeling like I am—emotional and grateful for reaching this point and in need of cementing our feelings in the best possible way.

"We need to get out of this hotel room."

"Why?" I thought he was going to drag me back to the bed, not suggest we leave. My brows furrow and I give him a look that can't be mistaken for anything other than disappointment.

"Because," he says with a grin, "if we don't, I'm going to fuck you again, and as good as that is, I want to take you out."

"But it's Christmas."

"I don't care. This is our first Christmas together and I can actually take you out for a change. I intend to do just that. Even if it's just to walk around for a bit." He kisses the end of my nose in a very un-Seb-like gesture. "Come."

After he wraps me up in his scarf, we head out of the hotel. The weather is pretty un-Christmassy, grey and overcast with a cold bite in the air, and I appreciate the extra layers I dressed in. We don't talk, just meander about through the streets of Manchester. Seb has a death grip on my hand, something I've never felt before, and it does wondrous things to me. I feel bright and happy—contented.

There are few other people out. All the shops are closed but it doesn't deter Seb. He guides us slowly about and I relax next to him, silently enjoying his lead. We travel up one long road from the hotel before veering off and walking a little further. I hope Seb knows where he's going, as I have no idea and my sense of direction is poor, even if we have been going in a relatively straight line.

39

We enter a small garden area with Christmas lights twinkling in the gloom. A mix of old and new buildings surround it. The red brick buildings and modern glass and concrete play against the lush green of the grass. I spy another couple walking through holding hands and wonder about them. Are they in love? Do they have a secret that only they know about? It makes me smile, and I look up at Seb.

"What is it, Izzy?"

"Oh, nothing. I'm happy, that's all." He leans down to kiss me, sure lips guiding me and coaxing me into the kiss. Goose bumps travel up my neck and I run my hands through his hair to pull him closer.

"Hmmm. You're going to have to get better at that—telling me what you're thinking. Come on. Let's head back. I don't want you to get cold."

"Okay, lead the way."

We wander out of the park and take a different path back to the hotel. We pass more shops, closed for Christmas. The windows look sad with the lights off, nothing sparkling or moving in the displays. After a few twists and turns, we arrive in a small square dominated by a brick church. Its strong lines and brickwork are beautifully set against arched windows. It's beautiful—old and new at once.

"Did you get married in a church, Izzy?" Seb's question interrupts my appreciation of the building.

"No, why?" He doesn't respond, but pulls me gently forward, clearly wanting to move us along.

"Well, it's a lovely church," he murmurs as we leave the area, following a few small streets this way and that. His question has me thinking, though. Perhaps it's just trying to know me more. Having talked about divorce earlier and ending up in front of a church makes for a logical explanation, surely.

I'm sure we must be close to the hotel. My hands are now small blocks of ice, despite being thrust into my pocket or wrapped in Seb's hand. I think we're about to turn the corner to it, but instead, we appear in front of another impressive building. It's not a church this time, but a gothic building dominating all of the others with its majesty. The complete mix in architecture on our short walk has surprised me—the old and the new, modern with traditional. Will Seb have to be here for long? I push the thought away and focus on what I want. Warm and comfy. "Are we nearly back yet?" I sound like a whiney child and I don't care. "Nearly, Izzy, nearly. Come on." He's laughing at me again.

* * *

"When will you be back in Bath? How long is your job going to keep you in Manchester?" Seb and I are back in his room, spread out on the sofa, curled up and drinking wine. You could call it a perfect end to a wonderful Christmas Day, but I can't keep the dark from creeping into my mind.

"I'm due to be here until the end of January, so a few weeks." My heart sinks at the daunting stretch of time. We were only apart a few days and I went mad with loneliness.

"Oh."

"Don't worry. I'll work something out. I don't want to be away from you for the next four weeks." He smiles down at me and squeezes my hand.

"Can you do that? I mean, you have a job."

"Yes, and I'll work something out. Don't worry. It's not going to be tomorrow, but I won't be away for long."

"Thank you."

"Don't think you're getting off that easy, though. There are definitely some benefits to being away from you as well." He's casually wrapped his legs around each of mine, securing me to him on the sofa. "Yes, I'm going to give you some instructions that I'd very much like you to follow. I know how good you can be at doing what you're told." My heartbeat spikes and I'm definitely interested in what he wants me to do. He nips

41

at my ear, licking the outer shell while pushing his now hard cock into my lower back. "Have you finished your wine, Izzy?" *Wine? Oh!*

"Um, yes…" I place my nearly empty glass on the sofa table.

"Good. I want you in my bed. Now. Go." He sits me up and smacks my bum, encouraging me. "One more evening together, sweetheart. I intend to make it count and ensure you can still feel me in you for the next week. I want you naked on the bed when I come in. Do you understand?" I'm frozen at the door to the bedroom, listening to his rich voice enticing me.

"Yes." His mention of only having one night left sours my mood, but I shove it aside. I won't let that ruin what time we have left. He's already got me desperate for him. His words alone are the best aphrodisiac.

"Good girl."

* * *

I wake up and stretch. My deep slumber hasn't repaired my achy muscles, but stretching them out certainly makes me feel better. Seb promised that I'd be feeling him for a week, and I'm sure I will. Right now, though, I want to cuddle up to him, and as I have the opportunity, that's exactly what I do. I curl up to him and weave my leg over his hip and between his, securing me as close to him as I can get.

"If you keep moving like that next to me, I won't be responsible for my actions." His usually rich voice is tainted with gravel this morning.

"Good morning."

"Good morning, sweetheart. Are you going to behave?" *Am I going to behave?* Something inside of me doesn't want to. Perhaps it's the contented feeling that Seb's brought out in me, the feeling of being safe and happy in his arms, but suddenly I don't want to be quite so innocent and submissive. I want to be naughty.

"Well, it depends on your definition of behaving." I trail my fingers across his chest and down his stomach, stopping perilously close to his cock.

"Izzy…"

"Shh, let me please you. I want this." I climb onto him and start kissing and licking his chest. I've got one goal in mind. Until he can come home, I want him to remember the feeling of my mouth wrapped around his cock. I pump his thickening cock in my hand before gently kissing the tip. I open my lips around the head and slowly tease him, dipping him inside my mouth and pulling out only a fraction of the way. He's hot and hard, and as I taste him a surge of determination spurs me to make him feel me the way I want him to. I'm desperate to ingrain the feeling of my mouth on him. I tongue the underside and lick around and around.

His hips flex. He wants more. *Give him more, Izzy. Show him how badly you missed him.*

I settle back on my heels and open my mouth wide for him. I take him as far to the back of my throat as I can, and then pull up, slurping as I do. I ignore my inhibitions and suck harder, longer. I adjust to the encroaching feel of him in my mouth, taking him a little deeper each time. His groans are the encouragement I need to continue with added vigour. I release the base of his cock and see if I can suck him to the back of my throat. I inch him down but feel my muscles tightening at the intrusion and swallow to try to relax past my urge to gag.

"Fucking… Jesus Christ, Izzy. Again." He grips my head in his hands, clearly signalling for me to stay in position. I pull in air through my nose and calm my rising panic and aching jaw. I descend on him once again. This time, I anticipate the feeling. I want to cough but I swallow frantically to stop it.

"Izzy, I can't. Fuck, I'm going to come." His warning is quickly followed by his hips surging forward, and his hands grip hold of my head, effectively fucking my mouth. The restriction is uncomfortable, but knowing that I've driven Seb to come this passionately allows me to push past my discomfort.

Warm liquid hits the back of my throat and I swallow it quickly before drawing my lips up to release him. I'm pleased with myself, or rather, with Seb's apparent pleasure. His inability to hold back has done a marvellous job making me feel good about myself. He pulls me against him and releases a big sigh.

"We're going to have to work on a few things." His tone kills my happy feeling instantly. *Perhaps I didn't do it right?* *"O*ne, you need to learn self-control and patience. We'll start like we did before, and being away will help with that. And two, I'm going to have to stop myself from shoving my dick in your mouth every time I see you. Fuck me, Izzy, that was intense. Thank you. This is the only time I'm going to thank you for doing something I told you not to do." His admonishment is hidden within his praise, but I'm only interested in the praise.

"Okay."

"Okay."

We finally drag ourselves out of bed, happy to lounge in our little bubble. After the heat from my show of affection earlier, we're now relishing the warmth of one another.

"Why aren't you spending Christmas with your family? Why are you working?" Now that I'm on surer footing with Seb, my curiosity leaks out.

"My mother and father live in the US. New York City. They moved there about fifteen years ago. We don't see each other much, maybe once, twice a year. I don't have any brothers or sisters, and the friends I do have, I see when I choose. Christmas isn't a big deal for me. You said yesterday that you weren't seeing your parents. Do you normally?"

"My parents live in Canterbury. Phil and I moved down to Bath for our jobs years ago. We wanted to be on our own so I don't see my parents too often, although I normally would go home at some point over the holidays. They're okay with 'no plans for this year but I'll see them soon'."

"You aren't close to them?"

"I wouldn't say I wasn't close to them, but I've lived my own life for so long it's just the way we are. We talk on the phone occasionally as well. I'm probably closer to my dad than my mum."

"And you see Jess's family?"

"Yes, Jess and I have been best friends since we met in Bath. Her family live just round the corner from her, so I see them often, usually over a Sunday lunch. It's nice."

"Hmm." Seb pauses and I wait for another question. "Right, we need to get up. It's past one already and you'll have to head back soon." The little glimpses of Seb's life and of mine we're sharing are novel. I've been with the same person for so long now that getting to know the somewhat mundane things about Seb is shiny and new, and because it's Seb, I'm happy to provide the information in return. I'm desperate to ask more about his parents and find out more information about the man I love. And about New York, but I know I'll just get all excited. *Another day, Izzy.*

I shower and change while Seb orders some lunch. Time seems to be against us, and before I know it, I'm packing up my bag. The time in our bubble hasn't been nearly long enough, but it has certainly mended my heart.

"So, when will I see you next?"

"Not until after the New Year. I have some commitments that will be hard to get out of. Come January, it will be easier."

"Oh, okay, um… that's fine." I purposefully check my bag again to distract from the tears glistening on my lashes.

"Sweetheart, I'm sorry. You have New Year's to celebrate and then we'll get the details firmed up. It will be something to look forward to, I promise." He pulls my face up

45

and wipes away the lone tear with the pad of this thumb. "Don't cry. This time apart will only be a few days. Come on now. This hotel will forever be special to me. For the first time, you and I have been able to spend time together freely. I got to take you out and hold your hand with no guilt and no time limit. This hotel is where you and I began. That will always be precious to me." His eyes radiate warmth, and the tears fall as happy tears after his words. He cradles me against his chest and gives me a minute. "Now, have you got everything?" He pulls me through the hotel suite before pausing at the door. "We'll have a lot to talk through when I'm back, I promise, and thank you for not giving in to your curiosity. I know you have a hundred questions, and I do as well. We'll get to them soon." He slides his hands around my neck and pulls me in before taking my lips. His kiss is slow and deep and tells me everything I need to hear. "This isn't a goodbye. It's a see you soon." I smile up at him a little more confidently now.

* * *

"Hello?" When I arrive back at Jess's, a dark and still hallway greets me as I swing the door open. All the lights are off, so I don't expect an answer. It's just after 7:00 p.m. Although I've only been gone two days, it feels like a lifetime. I put the kettle on to heat and take my bag up to my bedroom before returning to make the tea.

I slump on the sofa, weary from the drive. I snuggle in and clasp the hot mug between my hands, the heat radiating through my skin, and marvel at the comfort that a good cup of tea can conjure. I text Seb to let him know I've returned safely. Amazingly, my mood hasn't taken a nosedive.

I'm taking control of my life. I'm making decisions and following them through. That is a huge accomplishment for me. Plus, Seb is in my life.

Work is a welcome distraction from thinking about Seb, and the office is quiet with the lull between Christmas and New Year. Normally, I wouldn't be working, but I can't complain given the amount of time I was MIA before Christmas.

I lock my phone away so I don't spend every five minutes texting Seb. It doesn't help that he checks in with me every couple of hours. Sometimes it's just a quick hi; other times it's more… explicit.

> I'm thinking about how good you taste when you come on my tongue. S

> I don't think I've heard you beg enough, Isabel. Be prepared to beg. S

> Are you still frustrated? Can you still feel my fingers in you? S

It's only been a day and I already ache. I squirm in my chair and try to rid my mind of the sinfully erotic images dancing across it. They're completely unsuitable for work, but there isn't anyone here to notice my blush.

> I love the texts, but can we save them for
> after work? You're very distracting. Izzy

I am determined to get through these couple of days before New Year. I know that Seb and I are going to be together. Just a few more days until I see him again.

At home, I retreat to my past fantasies, browsing my Tumblr blog feed and some of the other BDSM sites. Since Seb, the pull of these has lessened. Now I know how the bite of the crop feels against my flesh. Now I know about the heat and pain that flash before the dull, lustful ache takes over.

The visual stimulation is a poor substitute for the real thing, but it keeps my mind occupied.

My phone wakes me from my deep slumber and I reach over to silence the alarm before realising that it isn't my alarm, it's my phone. "Hello?"

"Good morning, Izzy."

"Good morning, Seb. It's early. Is everything alright?"

"Yes, I just wanted to check in on you, and I wanted to hear your voice."

The sentiment warms my heart. The little things he says are slowly rebuilding my faith in love. "It's nice to hear yours as well. What are you doing today?"

"I have meetings all day, which leads me to the other reason I called. What are you wearing?"

"Um, a camisole and knickers. Why?"

"I want to imagine you lounging in silk and lace while I sit around all day at a board table going over contracts." I can hear the annoyance in his tone and I'm happy about it. He doesn't want to be away from me anymore than I want to be

48

away from him. "I have a plan for later tonight. It will require you to do as I say." His tone has dropped to that sinfully deep timbre that sends excitement pulsing in my veins.

"Okay," I breathe.

"I want you to be naked in your bed when I call you at 9:00 tonight." He pauses. "Isabel?" he growls, and it warms every part of my body.

"Yes, yes, I will."

"Good girl. Now, you need to get to work. I'll call you later, sweetheart."

Phone sex. Seb's conversation from earlier can only mean phone sex. That thought has made me hot and fidgety all day. The hands on the clock don't take pity on me and creep around at a painfully slow pace. Luckily, Jess is out when I get home, so I don't have to worry about making an excuse for an early bed.

I snuggle under the covers just before nine. Anticipation thrums through my limbs, but it isn't enough to keep me warm, so I wrap the duvet around me. I've been thinking about all the different things Seb might say to me or tell me to do, and I know if I dip my finger between my thighs, I'll be damp. The dirty texts seem to have stopped after I asked Seb to tone them down, but that doesn't mean I don't re-read them before I go to sleep without him.

The phone buzzes and Seb's voice brings my body to attention.

"Good evening, Isabel. I trust you're suitably prepared. Are you naked for me?" *God, his voice!*

"Yes, Sebastian."

"Good girl. Now, I want you to follow my instructions, just as if I was with you in the room. I want you to listen to my voice. Put the phone on speaker so you have both hands free. You're going to be touching yourself, and I don't want you to

49

worry about the phone." I tap the button and slide the phone onto the bedside cabinet.

"Ready."

"Good. Start slowly and imagine that I'm standing at the bottom of the bed watching you—watching you make yourself come at my will. Don't talk unless I ask you a direct question, but I expect you to acknowledge and tell me you're following. Understand?"

"Yes, Sebastian." My pulse quickens and I push the duvet off and slip down into the bed. I lie on my back, and my eyes focus on my imaginary Seb. He stands over me at the foot of the bed.

"Slowly start to caress your beautiful skin, Isabel. Run your hands over your stomach, your hips, and up to your breasts. Feel your skin, the warmth from it."

"Yes." My skin pebbles with goose bumps as my fingers follow his orders. My touch replaces my memory of Seb's and my stomach tightens in anticipation.

"Open your legs wide. I want to watch your pussy get wet for me. Spread your legs and keep them there. Keep touching your skin. Run your hands down your thighs, but don't get greedy. Have you done that, Isabel? Have you spread your legs for me?"

"Yes," I pant. Frustration floods me, turning my slow burn of longing into a blaze. My pussy aches for his attention, weeping in protest. "Good girl. Start playing with your nipples. Pinch and roll them between your finger and thumb. Start slowly. Play. Find what feels good. I want you to pinch harder, then release. Pinch and release. I know how you love me playing with your beautiful pink nipples. Imagine I'm teasing you. I'm squeezing them hard and making you squirm under my control."

Small moans break free of my lips at his words.

"I can hear that you like what you're doing. Keep doing it, Isabel. I want you to be glistening and wet for me. I want to see your desire running out of your pretty pussy for me. Are your legs still open for me to watch you?"

"Yes, yes, Sebastian," I pant. My body writhes from the pent-up desire he pulls from me. I've never had phone sex before, and rather than the lukewarm pleasure I feel when I masturbate alone, my body reacts wantonly to Seb's orders. I feel sexy, alone in my own bed, yet I'm not on my own. Sebastian commands my actions, and that's what makes this experience so heady.

"Run your hands back over your body. Skim your labia for me. Don't touch yourself—only tease. Show me what you want me to touch, to lick. Tempt me to stop watching you and feast on you. Do that for me, Isabel." His voice is getting deeper and I think about what this is doing to him. I desperately want to ask how he's feeling, if he's hard at the thought of me touching and pinching my nipples, if he wants me to suck his cock as much as I want him to lick me. His voice is an aphrodisiac that I can't control. My thoughts and my actions drive me closer to climax. I want to touch my clit and make myself come, but I don't. I wait for Sebastian. My small whimpers and mewls confirm that I'm following his commands. My will has become his voice dictating my actions.

"Very nice, Isabel. My cock is rock hard at the sounds of you working yourself up. Picture me standing over you with my cock in my hand, as I slowly rub up and down and get off on the sight of you sprawled on your bed. Push your finger inside your wet pussy for me. I can see how wet it is for me. Push inside and imagine it's my finger thrusting inside you."

"Oh, yes," I cry when my finger slips inside my silky core, but it doesn't quench the needy feeling rolling in my stomach. I want to be filled. "More. Please, Sebastian."

"You want more than your delicate little finger in your pretty pussy, Isabel? Do you want to be filled?" I gush with

51

liquid heat at his words. My excitement coats my finger, sliding slowly back and forth.

"Yes. God, Sebastian, yes."

"Put another finger in, Isabel. That's right, but I know you want more. Put three fingers inside you and finger fuck yourself. Fuck yourself and I'm going to watch as I pump my cock." I grind down on my hand, my fingers not going as deep as I want, but I do as Seb commands and thrust them quickly in and out. I pant in time with my movements and I picture Seb watching over me, his cock in hand.

"Yes, oh, just… Yes."

"Don't come until I tell you to, Isabel. I'm going to come with you." I immediately slow my movements to keep my climax at bay. "Don't stop, though. I want you fucking yourself, filling yourself with your fingers. It will be my cock soon. My tongue and my cock and my fingers. Imagine that now—my tongue lapping up your juices as you writhe on my face, bringing you up but not letting you climax until you're begging me. Beg me to push you over."

"Please, Sebastian, please… Let me come." His words have me right on the edge, but I'm waiting for him. I need him to give me permission.

"Come, Isabel. God, come. Yes!"

My muffled cries fill the room as I ride my climax, finally stopping when my pussy stops contracting. We're silent for a few moments and I can hear his heavy breathing through the phone. My climax was intense, beyond what I ever thought phone sex could be like.

"Are you still there, Isabel?"

"Yes." I sigh, contentedly.

"God, that was good. I miss you."

"I miss you, too. I want you to hold me and wrap me up in your arms."

"I'd love to be there to do just that. You'll have to settle for me whispering in your ear as you fall to sleep."

"Alright." I pull up the duvet, snuggling back down.

"Good night, Isabel. Sweet dreams, sweetheart."

"Good night, Sebastian."

***

Tomorrow is New Year's Eve, so Jess and I agree to have an early night. I know we'll be going out tomorrow. There's no point in even trying to stay in. Jess begins to turn off the lights in the living room. I pick up my empty wine glass from earlier in the evening and walk to the hall light switch. Just as I turn the hall light out, a knock at the front door stops us in our tracks. We stare at each other, frozen in place.

"Who would that be?" My exaggerated whisper is much louder than I'd hoped.

"I don't know. You're usually the only crazy to knock on my door at random times." She continues the stage whisper, adding to the tension.

"Are you going to answer it?"

"Do you think I should?" Our back and forth is interrupted by another knock, louder this time.

"Well, I don't think whoever it is believes we're not here." We're still standing in the hall with the lights out. The landing light from the second floor casts a wedge of yellow down the stairs so we're not in pitch black.

"I'm not going to answer it. There's nobody who should be knocking at this hour." We head to the kitchen, but as I turn, Phil's voice booms from outside.

"Jessica, open up!" The glass slips through my fingers and shatters across the floor, cracking the silence in the house.

"What's he doing here?" Jess struggles to keep her voice to the whisper of earlier.

"I don't know. I was hoping he didn't know where I'd gone."

She looks at me, and even through the dark, I can see her scowl. "Well, Izzy... think about it. Where else would you go?"

"Jessica, answer the fucking door!"

"Oh, he did not just start swearing at me." She marches past me, slams the safety chain across and jerks the door open the two inches the chain allows. "What the hell do you think you're doing? Do you have any idea what time it is?" I stay back in the shadows, my heart thumping in my chest.

"I don't care. She's here. Isn't she. I know she is. She wouldn't go anywhere else."

"Who and what are you talking about?"

Phil tries to shove past Jess, but she blocks the doorway and doesn't budge an inch. "Izzy, I know you're hiding here. I got your message." He jeers. "Giving back your rings doesn't mean anything. When you come out, I'll be waiting for you. Trust me." He growls out his threat, spiking my already pounding heart rate.

"Shut up and get lost, Phil. She isn't here. Don't come back. I'll call the police next time." He bashes his weight into the door, rattling it and shocking Jess. The safety holds. Jess slams the door shut and turns the lock.

"Thank you. God, what is he doing? Does he really believe that this will help?"

"That man is nuts. The sooner you're shot of him, the better."

"I'm working on it, Jess." The light buzz from the earlier wine has turned into a full, throbbing headache.

"Are you going to be alright tonight?"

"Yes, I just... I want to hit something. Preferably Phil." My hands clench at my sides as I imagine trying to explain things to him. "I'll get the glass cleared up and then go to bed. My head's pounding."

"Okay. Look, we'll get this worked out. Just stay strong."

"Thanks, Jess." She gives me a hug goodnight and vanishes upstairs, leaving me to calm my frayed nerves and clean up the shattered glass.

* * *

"Finally! Come on, come on, we need to get going and you need to make yourself look glam." Jess accosts me in the hall as I walk through the door from work.

"Hold on a minute. It's going to take me some time to get ready. What's your hurry? It's only 5:30 p.m."

"Yes, and you haven't been in the mood to celebrate in an age. Tonight, you are making up for it. Now, shower and change. I'll come and get your hair and make-up done in a few. Drink?"

I smile at her enthusiasm and know that tonight I'll have to indulge her.

Half an hour later, my hair is dry and I've chosen my dress but have no idea what shoes to wear. "Jess, can you help me? I don't know which ones."

"It's no wonder you can't decide. You have more shoes than anyone I know."

"They are my thing, and you can never have too many shoes. Even when you think that you do, you still don't. Now, shall I go for the glitz or these?" I hold up one shoe covered in sparkles and the other, a black stiletto with an intricate filigree cut-out design in suede.

"The black. You have sparkles on the dress. Those are more sexy, anyway."

"Done. Now what about the rest of me?" I gesture to my bare face and raise my brows in a silent question.

"Sexy, smoky eyes?"

"Yes, please," I respond. Jess has always had a knack with make-up. We settle for a minimal, natural look that shows off my eyes and lets the shoes do most of the talking.

An hour and two gin and tonics later, we're in the taxi, heading into town. Jess has arranged 'the main event', and tonight, I'm happy for her to make all the plans.

When we arrive, Jess gives the bouncer our names. Magically, he opens the door and we head right in. The bar is huge, split across three suspended levels. Aerial acrobats hang from silks adorning the corners of the building and can be seen from each level. We move towards the bar but are handed champagne by the black-suited waiters servicing the lobby area.

"Where did you hear about this place?" I shout at Jess above the music.

"A friend told me to come. He put our names down on the list."

"He?" I beam at her, already jumping to conclusions.

"Yes. He should be here somewhere."

Jess turns away and starts to traverse the floor, moving around the bar. She stops abruptly and I stumble into her. She's looking up at a guy leaning over the stairs and looking right at her. *This must be the mystery friend.* Jess turns us and we make a beeline for the stairs. Mystery guy is already heading in our direction. As they look each other over, I stand, feeling like an intruder, and my mind skips to Seb. Thankfully, Jess saves my thoughts and makes a speedy introduction.

"Izzy, this is Greg. Greg, Izzy."

"Pleased to meet you, Izzy." Greg reaches to shake my hand and leans in to give me a friendly kiss on the cheek. "Nice to meet you too, Greg. Thank you for inviting us."

"A pleasure. Now, let me get you ladies a drink and we can go dance." He gives Jess a more than friendly kiss before heading towards the bar.

"He seems really nice," I venture, seeing Jess smile after Greg.

"Yes, he is. We'll see."

"Hey, don't be like that."

"I'm not. He's really nice, but don't get carried away and start planning the wedding, okay?"

"Fine. Where did you meet him?"

"At another bar. This is our first date, so to speak." She grins a devilish smile at me and I'm reminded of her late night rendezvous that woke me up the other night.

"Ladies." Greg returns with three flutes of champagne and hands them to us. I tap down the disappointment of not being able to celebrate with Seb. I want Seb to be handing me my drink. I shake it off and put a brave face on. With glasses in hand, we weave our way towards one of the dance floors. I watch as Greg does his best not to smother Jess with his body, clearly wanting to get as close as decently possible in a public place. I'll be leaving without those two later tonight.

"Three, two, one... Happy New Year!" We all shout and cheer. I'm hot and still a little buzzed from all the alcohol, even though I stopped drinking a while ago. I turn to hug Jess but she's wrapped around Greg. They look like they could devour each other, so I choose this moment for my exit. I send a quick text to let her know and head for home.

Once home, I stagger upstairs to bed but want to call Seb before I fall asleep. I haven't heard his voice all day. It rings a few times before he answers.

"Happy New Year, Izzy," his deep, rich voice purrs through the phone, and I instantly feel awake.

"Happy New Year to you."

"Are you at home? I thought you would be out with Jess."

"I was. She met a guy so I called it a night. I wish I could have spent tonight with you. Or at least come home to you."

"And I miss you. Soon, I promise. Just let me get everything wrapped up with work here. Hold on a minute." Seb pauses and I can hear muffled voices in the background. My stomach drops. *He's with someone else?* I strain to hear what he's saying and the response, but I can't. *It's past midnight. Who would be with him?* My head starts to put together a hundred different possibilities. They're all irrational, but my head isn't logical. "Izzy? You still there?"

"Um hmm," is all I trust myself with right now. *Can I ask him? Should I ask him?* I should trust him. Hell, I trust him with a lot more, why can't I deal with this?

"Izzy, are you alright?

"Yes, I'm fine. I'm tired." There is a long pause before he responds.

"Isabel, you seem to forget that I know when you're lying. I've talked to you about honesty before. Now, will you tell me what is wrong?"

"Are you with someone else?" I rush the words, stringing them together in my haste.

"Isabel." His voice isn't the warm, rich, sensual tone he used at the beginning of our conversation. It's now laced with a stern edge that makes me nervous. "Do you really believe that I would be with another woman? Do you have that little faith or trust in me?" Tears pool in my eyes, and I can't stand that I've done this already. "I'm at the work New Year's party with some of the colleagues I've been supporting."

"Oh," I answer weakly. I know, if I think clearly, that Seb isn't like Phil, that he wouldn't do that after everything we've been through. But there is that nagging part of my mind that always goes to the dark place, that place where my self-doubt, guilt and failures conspire against me.

"We didn't talk about how things will work in the future between us, Isabel. You will have to learn to trust me. Not just with your body, but with your heart as well. I want nothing more than to be with you. Now, this isn't the conversation I wanted to start the New Year with. Perhaps we can talk more tomorrow?"

"Yes, I'm sorry, Seb. I just, I suppose my past experience is going to leave a few bad memories. I love you. I do."

"Shh, I know, sweetheart. And I'll be home as soon as I can. You're not alone. Please, just don't let the dark in."

"I'll try."

"Good girl. I'll speak to you tomorrow. Sleep well."

"Good night."

I wake up and remember that it's New Year's Day. I can stay in bed, thank heavens. The conversation I had with Seb last night stayed with me until sleep finally claimed my tired mind, and this morning, the residual effects of the champagne have me feeling like I've been out drinking all night.

I wonder what Seb's doing… God, this is infuriating. I grudgingly pull myself out of bed and trudge downstairs to put coffee on. The house is quiet, as expected. I doubt Jess is awake, or even here for that matter. I need to start thinking about what to do in the next few weeks, and if Jess will be alright if I stay here while I find somewhere else to live. *Not before coffee!*

Seb calls late morning and we talk. It's slightly awkward, especially after my late night accusation. *Why did my mind go there?* He reassures me, again. He also says that he'll be checking in on me, that he wants to know that I am safe. I suddenly feel every one of the two hundred miles between us.

Jess doesn't surface on New Year's Day, and the following day, after my short respite, it's back to the real world of work. The office buzzes with most of my colleagues returning after a couple of weeks of holiday. Mark wishes me a happy New Year before getting right to business and asking for the client files I've been working on. The client projects are much more in-depth than what I've worked on before. They demanded much more of my concentration. Something that I'm struggling to balance with Seb taking up too much of my headspace. *If only I could switch it off.*

While I'm reviewing the optimisation stats I've prepared for Mark, my phone vibrates.

Call me. Phil

Unbelievable! I shake my head in disgust and ignore his text. Calling Phil at work isn't an option. I'd rather my co-workers not overhear my conversation with him. He can wait until I get home.

After negotiating the short drive back to Jess's, I put the kettle on and slump into the kitchen chair. Summoning up the courage to phone Phil back, I hit call and hold my breath.

"Izzy." His cool tone immediately puts me on edge.

"Phil. You sent me a text." I don't want to be on the phone for any longer than necessary.

"Yes, we need to talk. I've received your divorce petition. I can't believe you've done this. How dare you! Well, you know what, I can contest this. And I'm going to."

"What? Why? We're over, Phil."

"No we're not. You don't get to dictate to me."

"There's nothing left between us. We need to move on." I astound myself with how calm I sound. Inside, I'm seething.

"You will not make me the fool in our relationship. 'Happily married' is what my job requires and I'm not risking losing my position because of this stunt, and there is no fucking way I'm paying your costs. You want a divorce you pay for it on your own. As for the house and savings, we both know I have more right over them than you."

"You should have thought about that before sleeping with Sophie and the countless others. We've been over for years. You've been cheating on me for years."

"I'm one step away from being the area manager. You don't get to walk out on our marriage now."

"Yes, I do! You can't stop me. It's not up to you."

"I'm warning you, Izzy, if you mess this up for me, you'll regret it. Divorcing me won't get me out of your life!"

"Fuck you, Phil!"

I hang up before we shout any further. I'm not sure I can take fighting Phil for this, or rather *how* I can fight him. *What can I do?*

"Izzy? Are you alright? I heard shouting." Jess comes into the kitchen. "Oh, hun, what's the matter?" Silent tears have started to run down my cheeks.

61

"Phil's going to contest the divorce." The sorrow and turmoil that Phil has caused are obvious in my voice.

"He can't do that, can he?"

"He can, and the details of the settlement. He'll drag it out. The solicitor told me that there are sufficient grounds for the divorce, so he's doing it just to spite me. I hate him. After everything, he's doing this."

"He's a prick, that's why. Have you told your solicitor?"

"I will. God, I just want all of this to be over and be able to get on with my life. I want to be free of Phil and move forward." My self-confidence is holding on by a thread. Each conversation with Phil reminds me of how stupid I've been. *Why did I put up with this?*

"I know you do, and you will. Just be patient, Izzy."

"Can we change the subject? It makes me so angry, and you know I get emotional when I'm angry."

Jess can't disguise her giggles. "Sorry, you're just so cute when you're angry." She knows full well that I don't do well at getting angry. "When's Seb back?"

"I don't know. He said after New Year's, but I don't want to start pressuring him already. I need to look for a flat. I know you'll let me stay here, but I need to try and get some independence back in my life." I busy my hands and pretend that I've not thought of moving in with Seb as a solution to my housing issue. It's a stupid fantasy, and one that would go against everything I need to do right with this relationship. I want to take my time with Seb and not jeopardise our future by rushing into anything on a romantic whim, even if it's now a fantasy I can see myself becoming absorbed in.

"I get it, Iz. I do. I'll help as well, alright?"

"Thanks. Now, what have you been up to? And how's Greg?" I move the conversation to safer territory.

"Greg and I are good. It's only been a few dates, though. We'll see."

"It looked like you were into him at New Year—or was he 'into' you?" Raising an eyebrow at her, I grin. We both burst into giggles, the perfect antidote to my dour mood.

Seb calls at 9:00 p.m. It's become our usual time to talk. I try to sound positive, but the combined weight of Phil's conversation, flat hunting and missing Seb is just too great not to feel glum.

"I can tell you're not happy, Izzy. Talk to me."

"Phil phoned today. It appears I'm going to have to fight with him over the settlement. I just want it to be over, and he's not going to let that happen. He threatened me and it actually worked. He frightens me."

There's a long pause while I wait to see what Seb will say.

"I want to know whenever Phil calls you or contacts you in any way. Do you understand, Isabel?" His voice sounds harsher, more commanding, and it grasps my full attention. "And keep up with your texts to me. I might be away, but I still need to know you're safe." His commanding voice tells me he won't waver on this.

"Okay, I will text you during the day and I'll let you know if Phil contacts me."

"Good. I'll be back soon. I promise."

"It feels like it's been months since I've seen you. I know that it's only been days, but the thought those days might turn to weeks hurts."

"Sweetheart, I will be with you as soon as I can. I'll see you this weekend."

"You promise?"

"I promise. Now, what have you got planned for the week?"

"I need to start flat hunting, but aside from that, only work."

"Flat hunting?"

"Yes, I can't stay with Jess for much longer. I need to start looking for a place to live." Seb's quiet for a moment. "Seb?"

"I don't want you flat hunting."

"Why not? Jess's isn't a permanent solution. Right now, I need something for me, to show that I can be my own person." There's another pregnant pause.

"After you finalise the divorce, what do you plan on doing?"

"I'm not sure. I haven't really thought that far ahead," I lie. I've thought about being with Seb. Properly. No baggage of a divorce or marriage hanging around my neck.

"You don't need to flat hunt because you can move in with me."

Now I pause. *What?* My heart contracts with love and fear. His offer is everything that I want. In the future. The timing is all wrong now. Surely he doesn't want me to run from my marriage straight into his arms? It's too fast, not right. I need to get the divorce first. We didn't start our relationship the way we should have. I want to make up for that.

"Izzy, are you going to say something?"

"I'm… I'm not sure. Don't you think it's a bit fast? We've not had any real time to explore our relationship."

"No." He doesn't elaborate. The tension is clear even over the phone.

"Will you call me tomorrow?"

"Of course I will."

"Aren't you going to ask me anything else? Try and talk me round?" I hear the huff of his sigh on the other end.

"No, I'm not. If you need some time to adjust to the idea, fine, but this will happen. It's time you understood how much I want to take care of you, properly look after you. I couldn't before, and now that I can, I have no intention of being subtle about it. Remember to keep me posted by text." I'm stunned. How can I argue with him when everything he says sounds so wonderful?

"I will."

"Okay then. Think about us, Izzy. Think about all of the good that we've only been able to grasp at. I want it all the time with you. Good night."

Flat hunting is utterly depressing. Jess and I have gone from one small, dreary room to the next. Nondescript, cramped, one-bed flats are all I can afford while still paying bills on the joint account with Phil.

I don't want my life to take this turn, going backward just to get by, but my options are limited. Plus, the thought of my own independence, taking control of my life, keeps the flame of hope alive. My reality is setting in, and it might not be everything I dreamed, but it's been of my making. My own space is something I can do for me, and only for me.

"They were all horrid, Izzy. You can't possibly consider moving into one of them." Jess isn't shy about expressing her disgust.

"I know, but what else can I do? I can't stay here forever." We both drop down on the sofa, relieved to be back inside and warm.

"It's barely been a few weeks, and I like having you around."

"Thanks, Jess. I appreciate it." I fidget and pull my feet up underneath me, gathering my courage to tell her about my conversation with Seb. "Seb asked me to move in with him."

"What? When? And why am I only finding out about this now?" She's suddenly on full alert.

"I said it was too soon."

65

"Jeez, it is fast. I know you love him, but do you really know enough about him to be thinking of moving in?"

"Look, I already said it was too soon. He's not even back from Manchester yet. I'm worried that if I move in I'll be dependent on him. We've only known each other a few weeks, I'm still married and have been taken for a complete idiot by my husband for the last god-only-knows-how-many years. I don't want to make another mistake with Seb. I'm sure waiting is the better option." I say the words but can't help wondering if I'm being stubborn for the sake of it.

"Just think about the house situation. I bet Seb won't want you moving into one of those grotty places we've just seen. Remember you don't have to go anywhere." She stands up and heads towards the kitchen. "Cuppa?" she shouts back to me.

"Yes, please," I call back.

I have a few more places to view later on in the week, but my initial enthusiasm at starting my new-found independence with a flat has crumbled. As has my hope of finding a hidden gem of a new place. I text Seb to let him know I'm home and try to determine what I want to do, in amongst everyone else's opinions for me.

* * *

Bleary and cold, January is showing its icy teeth and I hate it. Everything is cold. The dingy flats I drag myself to see, my conversations with Seb, even his texts. The week has been horrid. It seems I have hurt his feelings by refusing to move in with him straight away, which is ridiculous when you look at the facts.

I arrive back at Jess's and I'm greeted by a dark and empty house. I shouldn't be surprised, but I'll miss Jess's company tonight. Waiting for Seb to come home this weekend is going to kill me. If he doesn't make it then I will be making a surprise visit to Manchester.

I haven't heard from him this afternoon, but I text him to let him know I'm home and will be waiting for him. I try to keep it light. The last thing I want is to be the insecure girlfriend. *Still working on the trust.* He promised to be home this weekend and that should be good enough for me.

I retreat to my room and glance at the clock on my phone. No sooner do I slump onto the bed than the doorbell rings. I groan at having to drag myself back downstairs, but I do. I open the door to see Phil standing on the step. My hackles rise and I'm instantly filled with dread.

"What do you want, Phil?" I pull the door close to me, blocking his path into the house.

"You don't seem to understand me when I tell you that we won't be getting a divorce. I thought a more direct approach would help." He smiles, a nasty smile that makes my skin crawl. Adrenaline spikes my system. Being home alone with Phil on my doorstep sends an icy chill through my veins.

"No, Phil, I'm not playing. We're getting a divorce. You can't stop it, only cost yourself more money."

"Oh no. After my money paid for the house, you won't be seeing any of it." He takes a step towards the door and I shove my weight behind it to close it on him. He shoves back, stopping me from locking him out.

"Stop it. Go away!" Panic grips my voice and makes me push harder.

"Why couldn't you just keep your mouth shut? Everything was going fine. Now Sophie's pissed at me and people at work are talking, thanks to Laura's big mouth."

Phil is bigger and stronger, but my fear sends adrenaline pumping into my muscles. I force my body against the door. My feet scramble for purchase on the floor. The air burns in my lungs as I hold my breath and force all of my weight into the wood, trying to shove it closed. The door wavers and I get pushed back. Fear clutches at me. My heartbeat pounds and my teeth clench. *I can't let him in. I can't let him in.*

I slip on the floor and fall, allowing the door to swing open. I scuttle backward in the hall as Phil prowls over the entrance.

"You don't get to do this to me, Izzy. You are my wife and I call the shots here. You're a fool for thinking you can try and dictate to me." Phil's enraged voice echoes inside the house.

My legs scramble beneath me as I stand up to him.

"I might be a fool, but not for wanting a divorce."

"Why you stupid…" His face contorts as he pulls back his arm, ready to hit me.

"What the fuck are you doing in my house, Phil! Get out. Get out now. I'm calling the police." Jess's voice rescues my shredded nerves. Phil drops his arm and backs off from me as Jess storms past, coming to my side.

"Well? Out." She faces off against him and he retreats.

"This isn't over, Izzy."

She slams the door shut after him and I slide down the wall and pull my legs up to my chest as adrenaline flees my body. My blood races through my veins and I take a few calming breaths. I sit. Anger and fear stew inside me as I think over Phil's threats. It makes me feel sick. I can still hear him outside and so I close my eyes and block my mind, hoping he'll go away.

"Are you alright? Izzy? Izzy, look at me." Jess kneels beside me, a soft smile on her face. "Why don't you come into the front room. I'll put the kettle on." Fear wins over my anger and roots me in place. I don't want to move. *I'm safe, Jess is home. I'm safe.*

Gentle knocking startles me from the place I've mentally retreated to, but I don't react. It continues.

"Go away, Phil. I'm not opening the door. If you don't stop this, I'll call the police!" Jess shouts.

"It's me. Open up." The deep tones of Seb's voice break through my fear and my body kick-starts. I jump to greet him. I fumble with the lock. Seb flings the door open as soon as the lock opens and knocks me back trying to get to me. I'm engulfed in his strong arms as he pulls me into his embrace. *Safe.*

"Was Phil here? Did he hurt you? Look at me, Izzy." His hands tilt my reluctant face to his. My eyes find his filled with concern. I can only hope I can hide the sadness in mine.

"He was, but he's left. She's just shaken, I think," Jess offers.

"Thank you, Jess." She disappears into the kitchen.

"I wasn't sure when you'd make it back." I look up at him feeling utterly relieved that he is here.

"I was on my way back to Bath when you texted me. You're an amazing motivation, Isabel. Tell me what happened."

"Phil turned up. He doesn't want me to proceed with the divorce. He... threatened me when I couldn't keep him out." I see the steely look transform Seb's face as he processes my words.

"I want you at my house. Now. Come on." I happily comply as he releases me.

"Jess, I'm going with Seb, okay?" I shout through to her.

"Alright, hun. I'll see you soon." I grab my bag on the way out and let Seb take me away to safety.

The tension drains from my body the closer we get to Seb's. Phil has left me rattled, but I don't want him to cloud my time with Seb.

Seb parks the car and proceeds to pull his luggage from the boot.

"You didn't come home first?" I'd have thought he would have dropped his things off before coming to see me.

"No. I wanted to get to you as soon as I could." With every word he says, my heart swells and I forget the nagging doubts of the past week. "Make yourself at home. I'm just going to put this in the bedroom. Have you eaten?"

"Not yet." Seb disappears into his room and leaves me in the kitchen. I survey his home and try to picture myself here. Yes, it's beautiful, but can I see myself living here? With Seb? The house shouldn't matter. The person I love will help make the home. It's just so sudden. So fast.

I've gone from making all of the decisions in my life—what to cook in the evening, where to go, what Phil and I did when we used to be a couple—to being in control of nothing. Phil cheated and I'm likely going to end up in court because he's contesting the divorce. I don't have a house or home of my own. Everything is sliding through my fingers and it's unsettled me more than I thought it would.

Yet, with Seb there is always a glimmer of hope.

"Penny for your thoughts?" Seb's seductive whisper tickles my neck and I forget my introspection.

"I was just thinking about your home."

"Oh, what about it?" Seb comes round to join me on the bar stool.

"Well, I was just thinking about what I'd consider in a home."

"And?"

"And, you interrupted me." I grin up at him, feeling playful for the first time in days.

"You'll pay for that comment later. I want you to think seriously about moving in with me, especially after this evening."

My attempt to lighten the mood has fallen on deaf ears. "It's not that I don't want to move in with you…"

"Good. That's settled."

"No. I don't think now is the right time. Please, Seb. There is so much happening in my life right now. I don't want to rush this and be reliant on you. I want to do this right, when we're ready."

"I'm not happy about you staying at Jess's anymore. Phil knows you're there, and you were terrified when I got to you earlier. What would have happened if I hadn't shown up?"

"Jess was there. And I would have called the police."

"You can't always depend on Jess, or the police, to be there when you need them. I want to protect you and look after you. I want you in my home, Izzy." In his eyes, I see the genuine desire to protect me. Again, I question why I'm fighting this. It's what I want in the long run. But I can't escape the voice in my head that's shouting for me to do something that gives me some independence. Moving straight in with Seb doesn't do that.

"This isn't the evening back I had planned. Do you want to eat? I'll order some take-away."

"That sounds great." I take a needed breath from the tension that surrounds this topic. This isn't the reunion that I had planned either.

We eat in an awkward silence, neither one of us really sure what we want to say. Seb's in constant contact with my thigh, his hand resting casually just below my hip. I know it's there for a reason. I want his hand to caress and console me, to take me back to when he teased me to distraction and I struggled to eat my food. But a flash of disappointment runs through me when his hands stays put for the remainder of dinner.

I sneak a few sly glimpses at Seb from under my lashes. His handsome face has maintained a concentrated frown all through dinner. I want to lighten his mood, but I'm nervous. I don't want to start a conversation about moving in again. My hand moves to slide up his jean-clad thigh. *He's kept his hand on me. Why shouldn't I return his touch?*

I watch his face to see if my movement has an effect on him. I slowly rub my palm in a soothing circle, moving higher

71

and higher with each swipe. My fingers itch to explore and grow adventurous. They span out and reach for the crease of his hip. Seb rewards me with a small re-positioning in his seat. He still hasn't said anything or moved his own hand away. My courage grows and I move my fingers to the inside of his leg and run them up towards his crotch.

"Izzy, don't start something you don't want to finish." His warning lifts my spirits.

"Who says I don't want to finish this?" I look up at him and he finally meets my gaze. Hungry eyes shine back at me and my pulse takes note.

"If you mean that, you're missing something from your room." *My anklet.* I'm off the stool immediately and headed to my room at a pace only just shy of running.

The bed is still un-made from when I left it on that disastrous night, less than a month ago. I take the jewellery box from the dresser and sit down on the bed. I didn't change from work before seeing Seb. Luckily, I'm in trousers, otherwise I'd certainly be wearing tights. I fasten the anklet and let the light catch in the stones, shining their own happy chorus back up at me. I walk back to the kitchen at a more refined pace and wait for Seb's instruction. He's not in the kitchen anymore. I glance around and see he's waiting in his chair in the sitting room. He's brought a dining chair in as well, positioned in front of his chair. I move over towards him but wait for him to take the lead.

"Are you wearing your anklet?"

"Yes."

"You remember what that signifies, what it means when you wear it?"

"I do, yes."

"Tell me. I want to be clear that you understand."

"It means that I will submit to you completely, do as you say without hesitation and trust you." As I speak the words, I feel their meaning throughout my body. They reaffirm everything between us—the underlying current that brought us together, the desire I have to submit to this man and put my trust in his hands, to give up my control freely and willingly. Emotions surge to the surface and I need to concentrate to hold back my tears.

"Very good, sweetheart." Seb stands and prowls toward me. Anticipating his next action has me panting on the spot. Strong hands wrap around the back of my neck, tilting my head up to meet his lips. The kiss that I have been missing all week hits me with crushing force. Lips lock with mine and demand my complete submission. I give him everything, my will, my soul, my love, and he takes. This is what I want. This is what we need—to reconnect with each other.

He releases my mouth and steps back, assessing my body from my feet up. The hurried passion from a moment ago is replaced by the calm and controlled Sebastian that has my body quaking.

I relax and force myself not to fidget. Seb has proven that he won't be rushed and likes to challenge my comfort zone. Finally, he moves towards me and pulls my shirt free from my trousers. His fingers pop the buttons free until my shirt is gaping open.

"Your turn," he commands. I repeat his actions on him, eager to feel his hard muscles under my hands. I want nothing more than to run my palms up his naked chest, but I know not to do anything he hasn't already done to me. He didn't ask me to do that. Once his shirt is in the same state as mine, I drop my hands to my side. His smile tells me I've understood his game.

He slides the shirt from my shoulders, peeling it from my skin and skimming my arms with his touch. When the shirt hits the floor, he looks to me. I smile and run my hands under his shirt and down his arms, feeling all the tension in his muscles. My hands take his shirt, and it joins mine on the floor.

73

We move on to our trousers. As Seb's fingers skim my tummy, my muscles shake, anticipating more of his touch. He pulls the zip down and then slides both hands down and around my bum, rewarding me with a squeeze before the material pools at my feet. I step out of the legs and wait for my cue.

We repeat the game, taking our time with each little reveal until we're both naked. Our restraint is a palpable pulse between us. Liquid desire seeps from my pussy. I anticipate the crush of our bodies, but it doesn't come. Seb turns to take a seat on the dining chair. He crooks his finger, beckoning me over to him.

"Now, I want you to straddle my lap. I'll guide you." He pulls gently on my hips, urging me forward. As gracefully as I can manage, I step around his thighs and slide onto his lap. He's higher than I thought and I struggle, feeling off balance. His hands squeeze my hips, seating me directly against his rock-hard cock.

I can only just touch the floor with my toes, balancing on his hips. When I try to move, it's unbalancing.

"No grinding, Isabel. I want you to stay still and just feel. Understand?"

"Yes, Sebastian," I whisper. My clit presses up against the base of his cock, enough to tease and ignite all of the nerves around my clit.

He keeps one hand on my hip, securing me, while the other hand is playing with my nipple, gently caressing the tight bud. The touch resonates deep in my belly, and I recognise the building pressure of my orgasm. All of the anticipation from this evening makes me ready to explode in a matter of moments.

Seb replaces his fingers around my nipple with his mouth, sucking and nipping with his teeth. I want to move and satisfy my clit, now begging for attention. My pussy wants to be filled. I try to gain purchase on the floor with my toes to rock into Seb, but I only manage a small movement. Frustration

74

claws at me. A moan escapes my lips. "Not yet." He bites my nipple hard as my punishment, but it just causes my pussy to weep further. "So responsive. Can you feel how much your body likes my touch, Isabel? How much you enjoy being helpless?"

"Yes. I want to feel you."

"I know, but you need to learn control and patience." I struggle against the spike of desire that has overcome me. I'm lost to Seb's touch. I lean forward, forcing my breasts into his mouth, and I'm rewarded with his own moan of pleasure, deep in the back of his throat. I grind as much as I can, using the very tips of my toes as leverage. My clit throbs and I feel tiny pulses of static spark through my body.

"Enough!" He reaches for the table and grabs a condom. I wiggle down his thighs so he can cover himself before he wraps his arm around me to lift. He pushes the head of his cock through my folds, then pauses, barely breaching my opening before he pulls me back down onto him.

We both moan in pleasure. I immediately want to ride him but I can't. He's holding my hips down so I can't move. All I can do is take him and feel the pulse of him inside me. I shudder and surrender my body. All of the control is in Seb's hands. Not being able to act allows me to concentrate on just how good his body feels in me. The connection is so rich, so vivid that it fills my soul, consuming me. All of the love and passion I feel for Seb fills my heart and I open myself up to this man, even further than I thought possible.

Everything is heightened—Seb's touch is electric, his eyes hooded with lust and desire. Being at his mercy is where I find my freedom.

Seb hasn't moved. His self-control is firmly in place, but my orgasm is building deliciously, albeit too slowly for my liking. "Sebastian, please, I need…"

"Shhh… Just feel me." He punctuates with a slow, lazy grind of his hips, giving me just enough friction to make me pant. He stills and then repeats, each time moving slowly, controlled. No thrusts, no pumping, just methodically winding me up and opening me to everything he wants.

"Please!" I sob.

"Mine. You're submitting to me, Isabel."

"Yes."

"I give you your pleasure, push you to realise your beauty."

"Mmm."

"Does it feel good? Being helpless under my control?"

"Yes. God, yes."

"Yes, it fucking does!" He finally lets go, pulling me down hard onto his cock while he flexes his hips. My head falls back, completely lost.

"Ahhh!" My stomach starts to quiver.

"Yes," he growls at me, thrusting harder, driving me up and down in a punishing rhythm which only has one ending.

"Yes. Yes…" I cry as he rips my climax from my body, the sheer ecstasy causing me to lose control. My back arches and my weight shifts wildly in his lap.

"Fuck!" His curse and painful grip signal his own release.

Seb pants in my ear, his breath warm against my flushed, damp skin. I feel open to him in a way I haven't before. "Did you feel that, Isabel?"

"Yes," I purr. He lifts us both and I cling to him as he walks us to the bedroom and we collapse into bed. I snuggle into him, wanting to get closer.

"What time do you need to leave?" His question surprises me.

"Leave? I don't have to, do I?"

"Well, you don't want to move in. This is what it could be like." He kisses down my neck and across my collarbone as he murmurs to me. "Do you want this?" His question pulls at my heart. Of course I want this. Tonight has been wonderful— everything I've wanted, plus the veil of guilt that used to surround me has finally lifted.

Can I simply jump into moving in with Seb? I'm not divorced. I'm barely separated. *I can't. It's not right. I need to do this right.*

"Tell me what you're thinking? I can almost hear your brain whirring."

"It's not that I don't want to, Seb, but…"

"But what? I want you in my bed, Izzy. Not just as a date."

"I don't want to mess things up between us, to spoil us. I've only just got you back. Are we ready to go from hardly seeing each other and catching slivers of time to living together?"

"Yes, and we won't. I don't care that you're still married. You're mine. Our story, remember? I want you in my house with me. I've waited too long for you already. I couldn't stay away even when you were still with your husband. Why do you think I'd worry about it now?" I don't have an answer for him. I'm being stupid. I had an affair with this man and fell in love with him. I should be jumping at this chance. I need somewhere to live, and if I'm honest with myself, the thought of having a happy ending with Seb makes me giddy.

He lifts my arms above my head and stretches me out before him, kissing me softly, reverently.

"You know how I could solve this for you. I could simply order you to move in. You'd obey… Look at me. You'd obey, because you want to please me and make me proud."

"That's not fair, Seb. You know… You know that's what I want." His peppering of kisses makes it hard to concentrate.

"Isabel, you will move in with me."

"Please, Seb…"

"That's not what I want to hear, baby."

I look up at him, at his beautiful aqua-coloured eyes, and I'm flooded with all of the good we've shared so far in our relationship. I should have done things differently from the start, and I don't want to make a foolish decision that is based on my lust-fuelled emotions rather than what is best for me. Yet a bigger part of me, the part of my heart that belongs to Seb, wants nothing more than to succumb and agree to what we both want.

I light up from within at his praise and pleasure. I've been lost without him these past few weeks. By saying yes, I can ease both our woes.

The tension radiating from Seb's body tells me how anxious he is to hear my next words. I smile up at him and his eyes give way to a slither of doubt at what words may fall from my mouth. My smile spreads and he finally catches my meaning. I give a tiny nod of my head before he crashes my lips to his in a punishing kiss.

Nine

The next day, hope protects me from any negative thoughts. After I agreed to move in with Seb, I stayed the night. His presence was the soothing comfort I needed. The decision had been made, the weight lifted from my shoulders. I could move in with Seb, make both of us happy, and silence my doubts.

I convince Seb to drop me back at Jess's house and he finally relents.

"Are you going to tell her you're moving in with me?"

"Yes, of course. I agreed, didn't I?" It hurts to think that Seb doesn't trust me to see this through.

"Okay then. I'll see you later. I'll be happy to pick you up." I can see his enthusiasm, and his eagerness is heart-warming.

"Thanks, but it's not necessary. I have a car. I don't have a lot of my things, just a few possessions from the house. No furniture or anything like that."

"You don't need anything else, and I want to help you move your things over."

"Really, Seb, I can manage on my own. Also, I want to pay towards the bills. I don't want to feel like I'm taking advantage."

"Don't be ridiculous. You're moving in with me at my invitation. How is that taking advantage?"

"You know what I mean. I'll pay for food, something. I won't be kept. I've always paid my way."

From the scowl on his face, he's far from happy with my response. I get out of the car and offer a tentative wave. I hadn't considered that being with Seb will mean he'll want to control areas of life outside of the bedroom. My wish was to submit sexually. *What about Seb?*

I leave him stewing in the car and head on into the house. "Hi, Jess. I'm home."

"I'm in the kitchen." I walk through to find her and Greg sitting at the table with cups in hand. "Morning. How did everything go last night? I didn't hear from you after you left."

"Fine, thanks. Sorry I didn't text you again."

"Don't be daft. I'm not your mother. I just wanted to check you're alright, and I'm guessing you are as Seb's back." My face breaks out in a flush in answer to her question. *Seb is back.* I hear a dull thud and see an innocent-looking Jess staring up at me.

"I'm just going to go and put the TV on." Greg makes a sharp exit from the kitchen. He's rubbing his shin. I'm not convinced turning on the TV was his idea.

"And...?" She's waiting on me to say something more. She drums her fingers on the table in a rhythmical pattern. I busy myself with my own cup before sitting down and joining her.

"And I agreed to move in with him." I hide behind my cup, the tea too hot to gulp down.

"When? Why? Are you sure? You were looking for flats. You wanted to have something good for you?" Her hands are flying around, animatedly.

"I know, I know. But that's changed. I do want to move in with him. This is just a little sooner than I had originally planned."

"Izzy, think about this. Are you ready to jump straight into living with this man? You said you wanted to find your own place, your own independence?"

"I love him and I want us to be together." I knew that Jess would start with the reasons why this isn't a good idea, but hearing them makes me want to fight for my happiness with Seb. Starting with moving in with him.

"You've sprung this on me. The last I knew you were looking for your own flat. If Seb hadn't asked you, you would have been perfectly happy to move out on your own. This isn't about you. It's about Seb." She has a point. This is more about Seb wanting me to move in with him. I had wanted to wait.

"Please, Jess. This is what I want. It might not be the ideal timing, but I want to be with him." She gives me that same look as when I chose Seb's side over hers in the coffee shop. I'm taking his side over hers again.

"You've really made up your mind? You won't reconsider, or at least give it a few weeks?"

"No, I want us to be together."

"I do, too. I'm thrilled you're with him, but I don't understand why you need to move in with him straight away."

"Please don't be mad at me. I've loved staying with you and I don't want to leave in this way."

"I'm sorry, Izzy. I'm just looking out for you. You had an affair with him, then you broke up and I had to try and drag you out of the house." She stands up as if she's indignant about my choice. "He broke you, and it's been hot and cold since then. You shouldn't be moving this fast." She storms out of the room.

Her elephant feet thud loudly through the house, followed by her bedroom door slamming shut.

I know that Jess has her own qualms over commitment, and I understand why she's sceptical. But I love Seb and I want us to be together. I don't want to negotiate seeing him. I want to wake up with him next to me.

> I've told her. Izzy

> Good. When do you want to move your stuff over? Today or tomorrow? S

> Perhaps tomorrow would be best. Can I let you know? Izzy

His home. I play around with the words in my head. Can I make it our home? Will he let me? We haven't talked about anything like that, but I am happy to move in. Will Jess accept me back if it goes horribly wrong again? *Stop thinking like that.*

> I'm sorry Jess. I love you x

I hope she has her phone with her.

I am getting restless at home. Izzy has been texting me through the day, which helps, but I want her here with me. She didn't respond to my offer to move in as I hoped she would. I won't take any more chances with her. Hearing her scared and knowing that Phil can get to her makes me see red. She belongs with me and that's final. No way I'm letting that arsehole anywhere near her again.

> You owe me an explanation. Face to face.
> Text me your address. Jess

Shit! I should have known that exchanging numbers with Jess has left me open to a best friend attack. But I needed to get those flowers to Izzy for Christmas. Jess is fiercely protective over Izzy. That was evident at our first meeting at the bar when Izzy, thankfully, agreed to work things out between us.

I type out my response and wait for the inevitable. It seems that Jess will be playing the best friend card on me again. I should be thankful that Izzy has such a good friend looking out for her.

I think back to the Christmas party and to taking the job in Manchester. It was my job to be in control of our relationship, to set the pace and guide Izzy through her sexual awakening. She turned that on its head when I realised I'd fallen for her. Finally, I had found a woman who matched my desires, not just a sub, but a woman who I could foster a relationship with, who I could finally be myself with and have her care for me in return.

That is what I want more than anything else in the world. Izzy is what I want more than anything else in the world.

I pace to the kitchen and pour myself a drink. I'm sure Jess isn't going to make this easy on me. I need her on my side. I certainly don't want to be the new boyfriend who steals Izzy away from her friends.

The intercom buzzes sooner than I anticipate and I go to buzz her in. I leave the door open for her and go back to the sitting room. If she thinks she can come here and change my mind about Izzy, she's sorely mistaken.

"Hello?"

"Come on in," I call out to her.

She approaches with no hesitation or apprehension. She is serious. Her body is tense and she doesn't look happy.

"What the hell do you think you're doing asking Izzy to move in with you?"

"Excuse me?"

"You heard. You vanish and leave her in an emotional mess. Again. Then swan back and whisk her off. Again. I'm sick of picking up the pieces of your mess."

"Hold on a minute. I did not leave her. She left after I asked her for a relationship. I didn't leave. I went to Manchester to work. I'd suggest you get your facts straight before you throw around any more accusations."

"You're splitting hairs, you did leave. What I want to know is why are you rushing this? She's only just getting things together and you just change the game again."

"I can assure you, Jess, nothing is a game when it comes to Isabel."

She pauses, seeming to assess my statement. I stare her down and prepare for her next barrage.

"Well, if you feel that way, why are you rushing things?"

"I'm not rushing anything. She needs a place to live, a home, and I want her with me. Plus Phil knows that she will be with you. She was terrified. I won't have it. Especially when I can help. She's just being stubborn about moving in. It shouldn't matter how long we've been together. I love her and she loves me. You need to get used to me being in her life, because I'm not going anywhere." She flops down on the chair and crosses her arms. She reminds me of a young child throwing a tantrum.

"There's no need to be so romantic about it," Jess pouts.

I take a seat at the other end of the room.

"Look, Jess, we both care about Izzy and want what's best for her. It's my job to look after her and care for her. I can't do that properly while she's with you."

"You don't mind that she's still married?"

If she thinks Izzy's marital status would stop me, she really is delusional. In response I raise my eyebrows and stare at her.

"I only ask because she said something that suggested that you didn't like that she was still married."

"What did she say?" I rack my brains for anything that would have given her that impression.

"She said that you wanted more from the relationship and that you didn't like that she was still married."

I know what conversation that was—the one that crushed every part of me. Admitting that I wanted all in wasn't hard. The risk that she wouldn't choose me was the biggest gamble of my life, but Izzy didn't understand. I needed her to choose me and stop retreating back to her marriage. I wanted her to admit her true feelings and have the courage to stand up for herself.

"What I said was that I wanted more from our relationship than currently existed. I wanted her exclusively and

I wasn't willing to settle for the moments she could squeeze me in only to watch her retreat back to Phil."

"So you don't want her to get a divorce?"

"Oh, hell yes, I do. But her not having one isn't going to stop my relationship moving forward with her. She's made her choice and it's me." Jess has a lot of guts to challenge me. Not a lot of friends would do that.

I wonder what Natasha will say when she finds out. As my mentor, she's probably going to be mad as hell that I haven't spoken to her sooner. I'm going to have to tell her everything. At least she can stop trying to set me up with her 'take' on an appropriate sub for me.

"Look, Jess, I'm going to be completely honest with you. I've waited a long time for Izzy to walk into my life. She means the world to me, and I finally feel that I've found the right woman. I don't care that she's married. We started our relationship in an unconventional fashion. That doesn't stop me loving her or wanting to start my life with her." Things will be a lot easier if Jess just accepts that we're not on different sides. I can tell that the honesty has helped. Jess's body language has softened, and with luck, so has her opinion of me.

I sit and wait. I don't know what her game plan for tonight was, but if she thinks to drive us apart, she's going to have to change it. I won't change my mind about Izzy.

"You really love her. It's not just an affair?"

"Of course not."

"Okay then." She stands and starts towards the door, our conversation over and her mind made up.

"I'll be outside tomorrow morning for her. Make sure she's packed up," I say as Jess walks out.

She doesn't answer. I hear the bang of the door closing behind her.

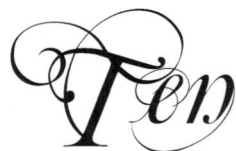

I hardly sleep all night, worrying about how I will leave Jess when she's clearly still mad at my decision. Being up at the crack of dawn means that I'm all packed and ready to move my suitcases.

I hear a gentle knock at my door and Jess's voice. "Knock, knock. Can I come in?"

"Of course." I drop a folded shirt into my suitcase.

Jess slips inside the room and waits by the doorway. She looks a little unsure of herself, which is completely out of character.

"Are you okay?" I say.

"Yes, I'm… I just came to say I'm sorry, and to ask if you needed any help packing?" She grins up at me from under her lashes.

"Really?"

"Really. I shouldn't have gotten so angry, and I might have been a little hasty with my judgement. I want you to do what is right for you. If this is it, then I'm good with it." Relief crashes over me and lifts my spirits. I should have been ecstatic about moving in with Seb, but my fight with Jess put a damper on my buzz.

"Thank you, Jess. It means such a lot for you to tell me that. I promise you that this is what I want. I'm just getting there a little quicker than expected." We giggle a little, relieving the remaining tension between us.

"For the record, you said you wanted to take control of your life by moving out on your own. The next thing, you're moving in with him. Try and see it from my point of view. I just want you to be happy. I don't want to have to see sad Izzy again."

"I know, I know. I don't think I could have done this without you. Thank you."

"Now come on. I believe Seb might be waiting outside for you."

"Already?"

"Are you packed?"

"Nearly. It didn't take much. When I turned up here I only had a couple of suitcases."

"Do you think he'll come in and get you?" Jess has a naughty look in her eye.

"I think if he could, he'd come in here and drag me out."

"You'd better finish your coffee and packing before he comes in, then."

* * *

"Do you have any more things you need to collect?" Seb asks when we get to his home.

"Not really. There will be some possessions and trinkets still at the house, but I'm in no rush." Seb has carried my cases into my room.

"You can unpack some of your clothes into your wardrobes, but I want you in my room. This will still be your room to have your own space, but I want you next to me." He's looking down at me with a half-smile on his face. He looks smug, which is a completely new look for him. "Do you remember the rules we first discussed?"

I cock my head to the side, a little unclear on what he means. "No tights. I prefer dresses and skirts. I'm sure I haven't seen all of the underwear you bought. Those rules." His smile has turned into a devilish grin now, which sets my heartbeat racing. I try to tap my desire down and process what Seb's asking.

"So, the underwear and clothes are permanent rules?" I can cope with the underwear. My dress and skirt collection isn't vast, though, and is usually reserved just for work. "What about jeans and more casual clothes?" My heartbeat is picking up, but for completely different reasons. I don't want to be dictated to about what I wear all the time. Wearing certain clothes for meeting with Seb was one thing, but keeping that up permanently...

"We'll take it a step at a time. Don't worry. If you have any questions then talk to me." Seb places sure hands on my shoulders and pulls me against his chest. I wrap my arms around him and breathe him in, relaxing against his strength. "We can talk more about this tonight. I want you to get settled in first. If we need to get you anything else then we can pop out."

"Alright, that sounds good." He leans down to kiss me, forcing my doubts from my mind.

I spend the next hour unpacking my clothes and arranging them in the wardrobes. Seb has explained that there is room for some of my things in his room as well, so I keep my wardrobes full of work wear. My 'good' underwear joins the lingerie that have been here since I bought them. I sneak a look into the drawer that held all of the toys Seb had me purchase. Everything is still in place, but I close that drawer quickly.

I pick up my anklet and sit down on the bed. I stare at it, as if it holds the answers to all of my problems. Admittedly, they don't seem significant at the moment. I can't shake the uncertainty that has set in since Seb talked to me about rules, though. I run the anklet around in my hands and think about the significance of the piece of jewellery. Seb gave it to me to signify my submission to him, to give him permission to take control and to tell him that I am his. *Does that still stand, even with us living together?*

Submitting to Seb is a craving I know I need more of, but we've grown past that. We love each other and want to have a life together. That doesn't mean I want to stop the sexy stuff, but I'm not sure how it fits into day-to-day life. Seb has told me we'll talk later. Perhaps I'm just getting myself wound up.

All of my toiletries are lined up next to Seb's and I've tidied away my last few items. I live here. With Seb. The realisation forces a smile across my face. I fall back onto his bed and snuggle against the covers. I'm going to wake up to him every morning. He's going to love me and I'm going to do everything I can to make us happy. *Happy.* Right now, that is the emotion I want to concentrate on. I block out the doubt and focus on the now.

I knew he would be cooking tonight—our first meal moved in. I walk back to my room and pull open the wardrobe to decide what to wear for dinner. Giving up my jeans on a Saturday is one thing, but making Seb happy by dressing up for dinner is easy.

I walk through into the kitchen where Seb is pulling a dish from the oven. He looks up and smiles, nods to the fridge and goes back to his preparations. A pang of disappointment that he didn't notice the effort I'd made in wearing something sexy for him turns my stomach. I chastise myself for my thought, though—I can't expect a compliment every time I walk into a room.

A bottle of wine is chilling in the fridge and I take it out and pour our glasses and move over to the dining table.

Seb serves dinner, but he doesn't seem his usual self. Our rhythm is off and it has butterflies fluttering in my stomach for all the wrong reasons.

I finish the scrumptious lamb noisettes, my appetite more than satisfied. There was little conversation through the meal, only the promise of a conversation and explanation from Seb later on. "Hmm, that was delicious. Thank you."

"You're very welcome."

"Where did you learn to cook? You seem to like it." My curiosity over this man is never far away.

"My father is a chef. He taught me some basics."

He's being very modest, but I've secured another piece of information. "In New York?"

"Yes, that's why they moved out there. He's the head chef at a restaurant in Manhattan." He holds out the bottle of sauvignon. "Would you like some more wine?"

"Please." I hold out my half-full glass and Seb tops me up. He puts the bottle down but stands and walks around the table.

"I can't tell you how much it pleases me to see you wearing that outfit for me tonight." His words immediately bring a flush to my cheeks. The disappointment I felt when he didn't say anything when I came to sit down is alleviated. "I know that we're both going to have questions, but I want tonight to be about us, and I'll explain what I'd like to happen."

"Okay." My voice is a little hesitant. Seb's body is tense, and I know that he's not been fully relaxed through dinner. The tension is swarming in the air between us and is beginning to charge. I sip my wine, disguising my fidgeting body.

"I had you as my submissive at home a few times, and that was restricted to the bedroom. I want to try more than that. I want for us to have a D/s dynamic out of the bedroom as well, starting with twice a week. See how we adjust and take it from there. On those days, I want you to submit to me completely. Wear your anklet if you need it to help get you in the correct frame of mind.

"You'll wake before me, get up and dress in your own room in the clothes I choose for you. You'll make coffee and bring it to me in bed. You'll wake me up with a kiss. It will be on weekdays as well as the weekend, but we'll discuss it to make sure it works with our schedules." His deep voice holds me in a trance, as if lulling me into a seductive state. "I'll want you home, waiting for me when I get in, like before, with a glass of wine and my kiss. Everything else is up to me. You will follow my instructions."

Oh my god. Seb's eyes never leave mine through his speech, and his scorching look, dripping with desire, has me panting. Who would have thought being told what to do would get my knickers so wet quite so efficiently?

He comes around the table and places his arms on either side of the headrest, caging me. "Oh, and Isabel, you'll call me Sir."

"Mmm," I squeak, turned on by his words and his actions.

"Open your legs for me, Isabel." I do as he says, although I'm slightly embarrassed. He hasn't even touched me and I'm drenched. His hand travels up my thigh, raising my skirt higher, and he slips his finger beneath the lacy fabric. "So ready." The gravel in his voice reverberates through my chest. "Do you like me telling you what to do?"

Yes! You know that. "Yes, Sir." My whisper solidifies something within me, centring me, and I can feel my physical reaction to the words as well.

"God, I've wanted you to call me that for so fucking long." He thrusts his finger inside me harder, curling it to hit my g-spot, and I moan in response. "You won't come this time, Isabel. I have something else planned for tonight, to push you."

As his words sink in, I try to hold off the torrent of pleasure that his fingers are causing.

"Please, Sir."

"Oh, you'll be begging me later, but right now, this is just my appetizer." He withdraws his finger and places it in his mouth, sucking all evidence of my arousal away. I nearly come at the sight of him. He smiles at me, his eyes dancing with mirth.

Seb stands and offers his hand to me. I try to accept graciously, allowing him to pull me up. He slowly leads me out into the lounge area, and with each footstep, trepidation runs through my limbs, forcing me to focus on each breath.

"You used to be nervous about this. I don't want you to be. I will tell you to do this often as it pleases me to no end. I am going to enjoy this and revel in the freedom that I didn't have before." I watch him, already guessing what he's going to tell me to do. "Strip for me, Isabel."

I can do this. I pull down the zip on my skirt and brush it over my hips. I don't rush like I used to, I take my time. My fingers move to the buttons on my shirt, slowly revealing myself to him, a flash of skin at a time. I pause when I'm standing in just my underwear. "Go on," he commands, his eyes drinking me in. I reach back and unclasp my bra, push my knickers off and then begin to roll down my hold ups. "Stop! Leave them on. You look stunning in just thigh highs and heels. This is something else I've been waiting for." I feel the blush cover my cheeks and I dip my head to hide. "Don't hide from me. You're beautiful." I nod my head and feel myself lifted. "We'll work on your confidence, Isabel, but thank you. Now, kneel down on the rug and spread your legs so I can see your pretty pussy. Good. You're glistening for me, Isabel. That makes me hard—so fucking hard." I swear his dirty talk has upped a gear and it's going to have consequences.

I try to remember if Seb ever spoke to me in quite such a dirty way before, and conclude he must have been holding back. It's hot and certainly makes me want him even more.

I take a steadying breath, trying to get comfortable. He hasn't asked me to lower my head but I have, instinctively. "Stay just like that. You're beautiful, Isabel. Open to me. Surrender to me. You test my control. God, I want to do so much with you." His words are lighting me up, and my pussy is aching and needy from his earlier attention. I hear rustling and start to raise my head.

"Don't!" His harsh command stills me and at the same time heats me further. *Please, don't leave me like this.* I know that begging won't work and that I need to relax and trust in Seb. I want to do what he asks and follow his words, but it can be so hard. I lower my head and focus on the patience I need. I wait. And wait.

My knees grow uncomfortable and my earlier arousal has slipped into nervousness. I can't see anything, but I know the hands on the clock are laughing at me. I shove the thought aside and close my eyes.

"Well done, Isabel." His seductive voice purrs in my ear and I'm suddenly right back to feeling needy. "Now, for what I had planned. I'm going to blindfold you and tie your hands. The only thing I want you to do is feel. Understand?"

"Yes, yes, Sir." *Okay, the nerves are back*. The cool silk covers my eyes and I relax into the comfort it provides. My little sanctuary. Next, my arms are drawn behind my back, a soft cuff wrapped snugly around each wrist. He pulls me to my feet and guides me to take a few steps forward.

"I want you to lie across me, Isabel. I'll guide you." Seb pulls me forward and I end up across his lap on the sofa, my hands still secured behind me. I'm positioned so that my chest and head are supported on a cushion, my legs stretched out behind me. The friction of his trousers against my naked skin makes me feel naughty, like he shouldn't be doing this, and it only serves to heighten my need.

"Very nice." His reassurance and praise melt my nerves. Seb starts to caress my skin, running his warm hands over my back and down my legs. It's almost hypnotic. "I'm going to make you beg tonight, Isabel. I want to hear just how much you need this. Don't be quiet."

"No, I won't be quiet, Sir."

"Good girl." Light kisses rain down on my skin from his touch, his fingertips dancing across me. First my back and then over my bottom and down to the tops of my thighs, he massages me again and again, and I purr.

Slap, slap, slap. I groan. Seb smacks me gently and the heat zings all over my body. I feel like I need to squirm, but know I shouldn't. More smacks, harder this time. "Ahhh!" All the attention Seb has given me, mixed with my restrained position, has me keening, and my pussy is shamefully aching. Two more hard smacks land and I gasp. I hear Seb's low groan as well. I'm relieved this is affecting him just as much as me. He hasn't said anything, but he continues to show me attention through his actions.

His warm palms squeeze and rub my bottom and thighs, relaxing my body further. As his hands wander, I move my legs apart, instinctively giving him room to play with me. He doesn't take the hint. Instead, he spanks me again. His blows are harder, more sure, his rhythm evening out and becoming a constant. I almost get lost within it. The smacks build, igniting some dormant fire within, before he calms me down with his caressing hands.

Each time Seb strikes a little harder and firmer it adds to my unravelling. My legs strain to open, enticing him to touch me, but I only feel wet and empty.

"Sir, please," I pant, shocked at my own voice.

"Yes, Isabel?" Even through the politeness I can hear the want in his voice.

"Please, touch me."

"How?"

"With your fingers." *Smack, smack, smack.* His strikes aren't stopping and I'm starting to feel panic rising inside of me. "Please, Sir, I need more."

"Tell me, then."

"Please, just… Sir," I beg.

"Tell me. Tell me how you want it."

"Fuck me with your fingers." The panic has turned into desperation. My inhibitions about asking Seb for what I want vanish.

"Jesus, you're soaked for me. I'll never tire of this." Seb doesn't hold back and thrusts several fingers straight inside my pussy. My muscles tense and convulse. *Yes, god, make me come!*

My mouth is open, and I can feel the scream building as my climax thunders forward. Seb withdraws as I'm about to fall and spanks me again. My scream of frustration erupts. "Yes, Isabel. Scream for me." He plays me, alternating between finger fucking me and spanking my thighs and arse cheeks until my throat is dry and I feel like I'm going to come apart.

"I need to come. Make me come, Sir, please."

"Fuck yes!" His fingers delve in and hit me just where he knows will settle my fate.

"Yes, fuck, please. Yes."

It's finally enough to spike my orgasm and I grind into him as my body takes over. The sound of my blood roars in my head and my heart beats an accompanying thud. I come down from my high and try to pull my hands apart, but realise they are still bound. My heart is still pounding and my bum is burning, but I feel soft and calm, like I've been sat in the steam room for too long.

"You back with me, beautiful?"

"Just about."

Seb unties my hands and helps me to sit up on his lap. He engulfs me in his arms and I nestle into the crook of his neck.

"How did you feel about that, Izzy? I know I've spanked you before, but this was much more intense."

"I liked it."

"Liked? Is that all? Remember, I always want you honest with me."

Liked. I mull the word over in my mind. It isn't the right word. It doesn't come close to expressing how I felt, but at this moment in time, it's the best my mind can come up with.

The way Seb built me up so gently meant I was blissed out before the smacks even started. That made it sensual and turned what should have been painful into something hot and erotic. I curl up in his arms and start to drift to sleep. I almost feel drunk.

Seb carries me from the living room back to the bedroom. He places me gently on the bed and then strips out of his clothes. He climbs over me, cocooning me with his body. He doesn't let me rest, raining soft kisses down my neck and chest. His lips gently tickle my skin. "I love playing with your body." His lazy caress does nothing to help my sleepy haze. He tugs at my nipple with his teeth, shooting my body back into overdrive, assuring my body is awake again. He rolls and pulls it with his tongue and teeth, and I'm helpless to do anything but answer with my body.

"You woken up now?"

"Mmm…"

"Good enough. I want you to kneel for me. I'm not done with you yet." *Oh god!* Seb drags my hips upright and pushes me down onto my front. I brace on my arms as he pulls my hips back toward him. Warm hands run down my spine and the

97

shivers send my nerves spiralling. *How can he do this to me again?*

He's careful not to touch my tingling skin, keeping his hands on my hips and thighs to position me. "Chest and shoulders on the bed, Isabel." His command is all but a growl, and I relish the feeling of what I can do to this man. I lean forward and lift my bottom for him. "God, seeing you like that, presented to me with your skin still blushed from my hand, makes me fucking crazy." I expect to feel his hard cock teasing my entrance, but his mouth covers my pussy instead, his tongue spearing me in frantic swipes. I grab the bed covers as I cry out while trying to remain in the same position. My climax is poised to be unleashed, and I'm quivering at the coiling and tensing of my muscles.

"Not yet, Isabel. I want you to come around my cock. Don't come yet." His order turns my moans of pleasure to groans of desperation. *How? No, please... I can't.*

"Sir, please."

"Just a little longer. I want my fill of you." I try to block it out—the soft, hot feel of his tongue as it strokes my sex, licking and sucking at my juices, the pressure of his fingers on my hips, and the sound of his throaty moans.

I'm right on the edge and I want to beg, to let go, but Seb's approval keeps me in check. I've disappointed him so many times by not being able to do what he's asked of me.

My breath is burning in my chest and my heartbeat echoes in my head. I hold my breath, trying to abate my mounting climax. "Please... please... please, Sebastian." His tongue stops its assault and I welcome the moment of reprieve while he grabs for a condom. His heavy cock thrusts into me until he's buried all the way inside me.

He pulls out and crashes back into me. "Come." He grinds into me so hard I feel winded. All my nerves go off at once. My pussy clenches around him, my body shaking and my chest heaving as my orgasm peaks and pulls Seb along with it.

"Yes, Isabel. Take me. Take all of me."

My hips are sore and my sex feels numb but attuned to every movement. I can't move.

Seb pulls out and releases me to collapse on the bed. "God, you're perfect. Well done." His praise only adds to the warm glow that's rooted deep in my chest. He rolls me towards him and hovers over me. "So, how did you feel about that?" His question mirrors his earlier one.

"I liked it." I grin at the humour in my identical response.

"Izzy, I let it go earlier. I need you to tell me how you feel." I inwardly sigh. I know this is what he does. It's part of his control, but it's still hard for me to vocalise my feelings. When I used to sit at his feet, it was less intimate, but just as special. It was easier. "You're going to have to get used to talking to me face to face. You can't hide from me."

I count to ten in my head. *I can do this! I can do this!*

"I loved the spanking. It made me feel helpless and sexy, and the way you did it, it didn't register as pain. I find it hard telling you what I want. I want to… I can in my head but I need to be absolutely desperate first." I don't look at him, but at least we're talking. He doesn't interrupt, so I muster my courage to continue. "I was worried that I'd come when you were licking me. I didn't want to disappoint you again." I close my eyes and try to snuggle into him.

"Izzy, please look at me." I crack my lids and I'm confronted with a radiant smile on Seb's face. "Baby, I'm so pleased with you. You can't begin to know how much you wanting and needing what I do to you means to me. Know that I'll only take you as far as I believe you can go. There is so much that is new to you, and I want us to play, explore and find the right balance for us. But you must communicate with me."

* * *

"What do you do?" We started to get to know each other over Christmas, but I want to know all about him. I can now. I'm not crossing a line that I've drawn in the sand about our relationship. I got a little bit at dinner, and after all the sex and the dozing in each other's arms, now seems like a great opportunity.

"I work for Phoenix Consulting. I've told you that."

"Yes, but what does that mean? What do you actually do?"

"Well, I work with companies who need help getting their projects and programmes done. They don't always have the right strategy. I help. I often go in and help 'on the ground', so to speak. Otherwise, I manage it remotely from the office. Sometimes the company can't work things out. Their financials or the board have other ideas and we have to step in to wrap things up and shut the company down. That's the worst-case scenario, though."

"Do you enjoy it?"

"Twenty questions, is it?" He squeezes me closer and I rest my head on his naked chest. I can talk to him when we're like this—close, but not as intimate.

"I'm trying to get to know the man I've just moved in with. I'm curious."

"Okay. Well, yes. I do enjoy it. I'm very good at what I do and get paid well."

"You wouldn't work for yourself?"

"Sometimes I'd like to, but I'd probably work myself to death. This is a happy compromise."

"Okay." I tuck this newfound knowledge away, happy that he's open and talking to me. Some of the old familiarity of our friendship is creeping back.

"I travel a lot for work. I'm in London and Manchester regularly and am often away. Not always for long periods, but overnight and long days. You'll have to get used to that." Seb adds a harder tone to this bit of information. I think about what it will mean for me. Phil was always working and used it to hide his affairs. Christmas taught me that I still have a lot of trust issues that I need to work on. *Will I be able to trust Seb completely?*

"You okay?"

"Yes, just…"

"Isabel, honesty, or this won't work."

Crap! I don't want to admit that I have doubts already. "I was just thinking back to all the times when Phil said he was working, and he wasn't."

"I understand that it's going to take some time, but you need to learn I'm not Phil. I don't want you to even remember Phil exists."

I'm no longer content in Seb's arms. I sit back on my legs and face him. I trusted Phil for a long time and he betrayed me. Seb and I hardly started under the best of circumstances. "Please don't blame me for thinking the worst."

"I don't blame you, but I want us to work on that."

Seb's fingers nudge my chin up until I'm looking into his eyes. There's no sign of anger on his face and I relax.

"Don't be insecure with me. You don't need to be." He curls my loose lock behind my ear and holds my face in his hand. I nuzzle into it, looking for the affection I crave from him.

"I'll try." And I mean it. I will try to remember these times when the shadows creep in as I know they will.

"I'm going to want to stay in contact with you when I'm away. Texts, calls—you'll tell me where you are and where you're going. You're mine now, and I intend to keep you that way."

Eleven

I triple checked the alarm last night before going to sleep. It had been a few days since I'd moved in and this was the first day when I was to follow his instruction and take my submission outside of the bedroom. There was no way I wanted to sleep in and forget to start the day the way Seb asked. I was too excited to sleep properly. I kept turning over all of the different scenarios I'd seen or read on the blogs I followed. Would he ask me to do something during the day, wear something new, not wear something, would he wait until the evening to play or would it start first thing as I wake him? It was like waiting for my birthday gift. I could see it already wrapped up. I just needed to rip the paper off. Turns out that I was awake when the alarm sounded anyway.

I creep out of bed and make us both a coffee, a gentle hum thrumming through my veins as if I've already drunk too much caffeine. As I take the steaming drinks back to the bedroom, my nerves begin to shake the mugs in my hands.

Waking him will start my day of total submission. I'm turned on thinking about it. My imagination and reality are two different things, though, and if I am being honest, I'm a little anxious about what will happen if I can't follow through with Seb's request of me.

Life used to be simple. I would make a decision and follow through with it. I didn't realise I had grown so reliant on the routine and order that went with that. I was comfortable there. Now that my actions aren't always in my control, my anxiety creeps in, clouding my judgement. I desperately want to please Seb. He makes it so easy for me to let go of all of the worry and concerns that I carry and just feel.

That's what I want. Now, I'm taking another step forward. My gut is telling me this is right.

I settle next to the bed and lean over to kiss him awake. He stirs and answers my lips with a swipe of his tongue.

"Good morning, Isabel. Mmm, I certainly enjoy waking up like this."

"Your coffee, Sir." I continue to kiss him, leisurely taking my fill of his lips. I'm waiting to see if Seb will take over and dictate the pace so early on in the day, but he's happy to receive my affection.

"As much... as I'd like... to stay here all day... you need to get dressed." Seb tries to talk around our kiss, but I've somehow forgotten to stop kissing him. "Down, sweetheart. There will be plenty of time for that later. Now, dressed. Everything I want you to wear is on your bed in your room. Don't cheat. Only the items I've selected." The fact that Seb thinks that I'm going to cheat shrivels my building arousal. When Seb first gave me tasks to complete when I wasn't with him it was exciting and seductive. *"You will. I'm going to give you homework, Isabel. You must make yourself come every day this week, finishing Friday. Do you think you can do that?"* But I failed at the homework so often that he already doubts me. I walk off to my room and try to hide my bruised ego. His doubt stiffens my desire to do better this time.

After I moved in, we agreed that I'd still have my own room to have as my own space. Several garments are spread on the bed. I approach cautiously.

It's a work day, which means that Seb has control over how I look walking into my office. It's a test of trust for me to allow him to do this. And it's my test, to see how comfortable I am with this—the reality of submission versus what I agree to under Seb's touch.

I pick up the black dress first. It's one of my nicer dresses, but I have no problem with his choice for work. The neckline is slightly lower than I'd normally choose, but thinking about Seb looking me over makes my skin tingle.

He's laid out my grey wool wrap coat, my short black blazer and my black boots. Black thigh highs are tucked under the clothes, and I breathe a sigh of relief that he's included a bra and knickers. *Scratch that!* He's picked my black push-up bra and the smallest thong in my possession. *I'd never wear this to work.* Tossing the clothes aside, I stalk into the bathroom and turn the shower on hot. The toiletries in Seb's bathroom are duplicated in here as well. I try to let the water soothe my knee-jerk response. It helps, and I can see that Seb is having his fun. Wearing sexy underwear is something I am fast getting used to. Well, if Seb wants to have me wearing sexy, I'll wear sexy.

I finish my shower routine and blow-dry my hair. Dressing in the clothes set out, I walk back into our bedroom. Seb's sitting in bed, reading on his iPad. He looks up at me, expectancy written across his face.

"I see you found the clothes." He leans back and smiles at me.

"Yes. Thank you, Sir." I crawl over the bed to kiss him. "I need to get going for work soon. Would you like another coffee?"

"No, you get going." He turns back to reading his screen and I'm deflated. I'd expected a bigger reaction from him. *I'm doing what he's asked. Why isn't he happy?* Putting the irrational thought aside, I finish getting ready for work.

"Bye then," I shout.

"See you this evening." I head out the door, waiting for something else to happen. I don't know what, but I feel like something was missing. I had expected... something else.

I send my text when I arrive at work and head for my desk. No one can see that I'm wearing different underwear, it's all in my head, but I can't help but feel self-conscious. *Get a grip, Izzy. They aren't going to say anything.*

The rest of the day is tedious and tiresome.

I jump at each text that Seb sends, hoping for some naughty instruction or dirty thought. Instead, I get pleasantries and general conversation. 'What would you like for dinner?' was not the type of question I was hoping for. 'Are you thinking of what will happen later?' 'Are you wet imagining everything I could do to you?' That is what I was expecting, and I can't prevent my disappointment that there isn't more of that.

When Seb and I were together, my submission always existed in a sexual context. Although I didn't know what he had planned for us, I understood that it would be sexual in nature. Today, I'd assumed that would be the same. So far, nothing.

I make it through the day and am home to make sure that the wine is poured and ready at seven. I feel like a kitten who's been left all day and is trying to wait patiently to be played with.

When I hear him walk through the door, I have to force myself not to run up and throw my arms around his neck. I do as instructed and wait for him. Then, I hand him his wine and kiss him his welcome.

"Mmm, thank you, Isabel." He smiles warmly as I linger with my kiss. "I'll get the food started." My heart drops when he moves to start preparing dinner. I suck my lip into my

105

mouth to keep from protesting. The bar stool has my name written all over it, so I get comfy.

Seb is proficient as ever with the preparations. The smell of the steak adds to the mouth-watering sight of Seb in the kitchen. It only causes my frustrations to grow.

Previously, when I met Seb at his apartment, I expected to learn what submitting to someone felt like, making my yearnings previously locked away behind a computer screen a reality. Even in the beginning, we both knew why I was there. Now, there's been nothing for me to focus on, nothing to occupy my mind or try to show that I want to do as Seb tells me. There is an air of uncertainty. It creates an anxiety that's new. The anticipation bubbling through me like champagne falls flat.

"Are you going to sit there and stew all evening, or will you share what's on your mind?" Seb breaks through my thoughts, and I try to right my frowning face. I know what will happen if I try to hide that I am preoccupied.

"I was just thinking about today, that's all."

"And that has had you scowling at me for the last five minutes?" His brows rise in question.

"I didn't realise I was scowling. Sorry. I just… well…" Seb's stance turns tense. He takes the pan from the heat and comes round to stand over me. His hands cup my face so I have nowhere to look but at him. His aqua eyes pierce mine, daring me to be anything but honest with him.

"Today was different from what I was expecting."

"Go on."

"I thought that there would be more of a challenge, something that I would struggle with so I could show you how much I want to please you. Or something that was naughty or sexy that I could do for you." I whisper my thoughts and search his eyes for his answer.

"There isn't always a challenge for you, Isabel. Before, I tested you and pushed the boundaries of your submission, sexually. It was the only avenue open to me given our circumstances. Now you're mine. My options have expanded." His lips draw back into a satisfied smile. "You made me so fucking happy this morning. The submission you show by dressing in the clothes I'd like you to wear, bringing me coffee in the morning, greeting me at night with a glass of wine—these small things all make up the days when you're submissive outside of the bedroom. It indicates to me your desire to please me, just as much as something that you may struggle with."

"You like the simple stuff? Not just the sexual submission?"

His hands slip from my face, no longer holding me to his gaze, and move to stroke my hair, soothing me as he answers.

"Yes. For me, the control is part of who I am. I've not found a woman who could meet my... wants. You do. In every way. We'll learn together. That will need communication. Do you understand?" He pulls my hair back, sending shivers of expectation down my spine.

"Yes, Sir."

"Good girl." He crushes his lips onto mine, punishing them with his force. His grip on my hair is tight and adds to the edge of pain that mixes with the delicious pleasure of his tongue. Deep, sensual thrusts have me whimpering with need. He pulls back, and only his grip on my hair keeps me from sagging like a rag doll.

"Tell me how you feel, Isabel. After talking to me, I want to know what you're thinking."

Thinking? Don't stop kissing me. I clear the lust that's invaded and think back to the words he spoke to me.

"I was... relieved that today wasn't too hard. I didn't want to disappoint you like I always managed to before. I can do this. I want to, but I expected more. It felt like something was missing. I was frustrated."

107

"Sexually?"

"Mmmhmm." Heat flashes to my cheeks, proving I can still blush for Seb.

"You associate submission with me dominating you in bed. I like that. It will certainly make my life easier when I want you wet and waiting for me all day. Having you follow my instructions, be mine to control, that soothes a part of me, and I'll look forward to the next day that I can control you." He inches my legs apart and runs his hand up my thigh to skim the damp fabric of my thong.

"Sir..." My plea is past my lips before I can stop it.

"Not quite yet. I've almost ruined the steaks but we still need to eat. I'm very pleased that you opened up and talked, eventually. Thank you, Isabel." Seb releases me and steps back to the kitchen to rescue the abandoned steaks.

"We're just going to eat?" I can't keep my disappointment from my voice.

"Oh, sweetheart. We're going to eat first, then I'm going to get you *really* comfortable in our bed. I've been thinking about you all day, and I have a few ideas that you might be more contented with than just wearing the clothes I've selected for you." Seb's sexy smile shows the promise to his words. The bubbles return, fizzing through me in excitement for what Seb will do to my body.

* * *

"Ms. Fields, it's Mr. Osbourn. Your husband has failed to acknowledge the divorce petition, so I'll be seeking it to be served to him by a court bailiff."

"Can't we simply proceed?"

"Not without proof he's received the petition."

"But he has. He came to my house and threatened me."

"I'm very sorry, Ms. Fields, but we need to be able to prove it. If he has threatened you, I can look at filing for an injunction against him."

"What would that do?"

"Depending on what injunction you apply for, it can help protect you against harassment or threats. Especially if you think he might escalate to violence. If he breaches the injunction he can be arrested." I think about what Mr. Osbourn says and remember the look on Phil's face when he was about to hit me.

"Can I think about it? I just want to get the divorce over with. He can't actually stop me from divorcing him?"

"No, but he can make it a drawn-out process that will likely cost you both a lot of money."

"Will you... Will you keep me posted?"

"Of course."

"Thank you." I end the call feeling defeated already.

"That didn't sound fun. Everything okay?" Jess asks, concern clear in her voice. We arranged to meet over lunch as we've not seen much of each other since I moved out.

"Not really. Phil hasn't returned the acknowledgement of receipt. It's a form that tells the court he's received the divorce petition. I now have to prove he's received it before we can move proceedings along. God, why is he doing this?"

"Oh, sweetie, I know he's being a dick. Have you heard from him since the other evening?"

"No. And I don't want to after what he said. He threatened me, and if you weren't there, I'm sure he would have hit me." I grit my teeth and force the tears back down. I want to be strong, but right now, it's difficult to remember that. "He's going to make leaving him so much harder. He doesn't want to split the house, either."

"He can't do that, can he?"

"He can object to what I proposed. He can't stop the divorce, but he's going to do everything he can to hurt me. I just want it to be over."

"It will be. How's Seb?"

"He's good. We're good. He hasn't said anything about it, but I know he wants me to be finished with Phil as soon as possible. I think that's why he wanted me to move in so quickly. It's his way of tying us together."

"Well, that and he adores you."

My cheeks heat at her reassurance of Seb's feelings. "Thank you for meeting me for lunch. I needed to get out today. Plus, I miss being able to talk to you quite so freely."

"Hey, that was your doing. Nothing to do with me." Jess holds up her hands in mock protest.

"Don't let me get lost, okay?"

Her playful expression falls from her face. "Hey, you won't. I don't even know what you mean by that, but it won't happen."

"It's just that there's so much I'm unsure of, it's daunting. The new relationship with Seb is moving really fast. Yet I'm not even divorced. I want to close that part of my life, but Phil's not making it easy. I don't feel in control of how my life is progressing. I feel adrift, like I've lost part of me, of Izzy."

"It's just new to you. That's why you're feeling lost. You aren't, trust me. If you feel like you might be, then you call and we'll talk it through, okay?"

"Thanks, Jess, for being there for me. Again."

"Always." We hug and my throat clogs with the relief that Jess is in my life. Despite my fears or my worries, she's always there for me.

"Right, I need to go. You have a report to finish for Mark and an ex-husband to divorce. I'll see you soon. Stay strong."

Jess heads out of the restaurant and I try to absorb her words. I feel anything but strong at this moment. I'd hoped, at the beginning of this, that Phil and I could work things out between us, amicably, like adults—acknowledge what we had, and decide to move on. He must have been unhappy. Why else would he be seeing other women? That's the reason I ended up finding Seb.

We'd loved each other, once upon a time—I thought. His lack of cooperation makes me think the last twelve years has been a sham.

As if he knows I was thinking about him, Phil's name flashes on my phone.

"What is it, Phil?"

"I want you to stop this divorce bullshit and come to your senses. Why are you doing this, Izzy?"

"Well you should have thought about that before cheating on me and treating me like crap. I want a divorce and you can't stop this."

"Well, I disagree."

"You can't just ignore the paperwork. You will be served the petition and then whether you respond or not doesn't matter. I will divorce you." I hang up and tear my way through the reception area and up to my desk.

Phil's attitude makes my blood boil. Frustration radiates through me and I want to scream. *Why is he doing this?* My phone vibrates, and I nearly hurl it across the office. Looking down, I see it's just my alarm to text Seb. He's been very clear on keeping him updated as to my whereabouts. I don't mind. I thought it was nice to start with; we'd text back and forth and I'd feel connected to him. Now, I have to text him regularly and it's just a check-in, no back and forth. It makes me feel small, and I don't understand why they've stopped being personal.

111

I pull up the files that I need to complete the report Mark has been asking for, and focus back on the familiar work in front of me, the area of my life I know inside and out.

The weekend arrives, and Seb and I relax, sleep in, eat and become accustomed to living with each other. So far, it's heavenly, and it helps that he's a wonderful cook who likes to spoil me. Our bubble lasts until Tuesday morning when Seb has to go to London.

"I'll be back Friday night, but not until late." Seb is still in bed, but I am rushing to finish getting ready for work. Lucky for me, I am busy and it will keep my mind off the fact that Seb is leaving.

"I know."

"And don't forget, I want you to keep checking in with me. We agreed. I might be in London, but that doesn't mean I don't need to know what you're doing and that you're alright. Regular messages, every other hour, and phone me if Phil so much as sends you a text."

"Yes, I've got it." I grab my blazer from the wardrobe and my black heels, sliding my feet into them before I lean over and kiss Seb goodbye.

"Is that all I get? I'm not seeing you for three days and all I get is a quick peck?" His sexy smile and hooded eyes betray the intention behind his comment. I walk back to his side of the bed and kiss him properly. I draw myself back before we get carried away. If I let myself, I'll get sucked into my own tailspin about Seb going away. Keeping busy is my key. Lucky for me, that isn't going to be a problem this week.

"What's wrong, Isabel?"

"I'll miss you and I'm trying not to think about it. Now, I need to get to work. I've got a client presentation at 1:00 p.m. today and one tomorrow. I'm nervous." He looks at me and cups my cheek in his hand. My reaction is automatic; I nuzzle into him, happy to take the affection.

"I'll miss you, too, sweetheart. Get going. Good luck with your presentation. Remember to text me when you get to work. That's not optional. I want to know you are somewhere safe. I'll see you in a couple of days."

"Okay, I will. But I can't when I'm with clients."

"That's fine."

"Thank you." Any more talking and my nerves and fear would have gotten to me. Since the weekend, I've felt so much better, and I need to get through this separation without any drama.

"Drive safely. I love you," I throw back as I leave the room and pick up my bags. *I can do this.*

I get into work a little earlier than usual. It gives me the much-needed time to get my head together for the client presentation later on. It's the first one I've done with Mark, and I want it to go well.

He's been impressed with the strategies I've pulled together, and since Christmas, he has been giving me more projects to look over. The next few days couldn't have come at a better time with Seb being away. I text him before firing up the computer and getting myself a much-needed coffee.

"All ready for later?" Mark startles me as I'm pouring my liquid caffeine.

114

"Um... I think so."

"Don't worry. You'll be fine. They like the work we've been doing, and the new campaigns have seen a positive spike in ROI." I know all of this because I've been the one to run the analysis.

"I know. I'm just not looking forward to the presenting part."

"I'll be doing most of it. They are due in at 1:00 p.m. so let's meet at 12:30 p.m. to run through. Beta conference room, okay?"

"Okay." I turn back to my coffee.

"You're doing really good work, Izzy. I'm glad I got you to look at the client portfolios." Mark's praise is very welcome.

"Thank you." Training people is one thing. Running their campaigns to effect significant impact on sales is something very different. I love my job, and I have found comfort in the knowledge that I'm good at this. Hearing Mark confirm it really helps.

I've drilled my campaign slides to death. I know all the figures, and what's behind them, by heart. I'm ready.

"Izzy, slight change of plans." Mark is standing over my desk looking flustered. "The people from Sportletic are here early. Something about a miscommunication about times. We need to present now. Come on." Mark's words make my stomach turn at the prospect of going through this without a final briefing with Mark. I see my phone on my desk. I'm not going to be able to let Seb know.

"Are they here already?"

"They are in the welcome room, giving us a few minutes to get set up. Come on... we need to do this." I grab the files from my desk and scurry after Mark.

Going through all of the information in my head is one thing. Repeating it aloud, with conviction, to a bunch of strangers who could pull their business from us is quite another. Three suits in their mid-thirties walk in and sit on the opposite side of the conference table. They've built a successful sports company, Sportletic, and are expanding to launch a new fitness app. The initial campaign we managed for them has performed well, but Mark needs to sell the next phase to ensure they stick with us. My palms are sweaty and my heartbeat has quickened. I take a final glance at my notes and my phone. There's a text from Seb, but it will have to wait. I didn't have time to text him my change of plans.

Mark makes the introductions and starts the presentation. As per plan, I provide my input regarding the social media campaign strategy. All three suits pay attention, nodding along. The youngest of the three makes copious amounts of notes but doesn't ask me any direct questions.

It turns out that the men from Sportletic were saving their questions until the end of the presentation. Nearly two and a half hours later, we finally shake hands, confident that we will be putting our plans into action.

"Oh god, I didn't think they would ever stop with the questions."

"I know. You did really well, though, Izzy. You really showed you knew the account. You should be working the client pitches more often." My knees feel wobbly and I collapse back into my chair, exhausted from the grilling we took. "We have the same again tomorrow with Everlyn, but hopefully that will be more relaxed. They aren't going anywhere. They just need to see a shift in direction." I knew tomorrow would be the easier of the two.

I peek at my phone. Two more texts from Seb.

Good luck with the presentation later. S

Text me back when you get this. S

What's going on? We agreed on this.
Please text me. S

I'm fine, the presentation got moved at the
last minute and I didn't have time to text. Love you
Izzy

I take my notes and head back to my desk. Before I
reach it, my phone starts vibrating in my hand. I know who it is.
"Hello."

"Isabel, can you talk?"

"Quickly, I'm at my desk."

"What happened? I was worried when you didn't
respond. Did the presentation go alright?"

"Yes, it went really well. They asked lots of questions,
though, and it was a little off-putting having no time to go over
it with Mark first."

"They moved up the time?"

"Yes, I told you that." I know I have to bring up my
feelings about these texts. The pause on the line screams tension
and I hate that, after only a few hours, we've lost what we had
over the weekend.

"Seb... these texts, checking in with you, it makes me
feel like a child. Like you are literally checking up on me."

"Izzy. It may seem intrusive to you, but I like knowing
what you're doing and where you are. I also like that I'm
keeping myself at the forefront of your mind. Think of it as
another form of submission, doing something you know will
please me. If that's not enough of a reason, it's a way for me to
keep you beside me wherever I am, and with your situation with
Phil... Izzy... when you don't respond, I'm afraid he's cornered
you somewhere and the next call will be from Jess."

"I'm sorry," I say in a soft voice.

117

"I think we need to talk this through when I get back."

"Okay."

"Do you have any plans for tonight?"

I haven't, but I suddenly need to see Jess. "I'm probably seeing Jess. I'll let you know." The tension drips with every word we speak. It's clear that neither of us wants to leave the conversation where it is.

"Stay in touch."

"I will."

"I'll see you soon."

I leave the office early and head straight to Jess's with a quick text to her as I get in the car. It's a weeknight so the likelihood is that she'll be in.

"Jess, it's me. Are you home?"

"Kitchen. You alright?" I walk in and join her. She's sitting at the kitchen table with her laptop open in front of her.

"Working? Sorry, I didn't mean to barge in. I just needed to talk, and to see you, of course."

She grins up from behind her screen. "No, I'm just checking some emails. Put the kettle on, or the gin is in the cupboard if you need something stronger."

"I think we'll start with tea."

"Okay then… spill." She shuts the laptop and gives me her undivided attention.

"Hear me out before telling me that I'm crazy."

"No promises. If you're being really stupid, I'm going to cut you off and tell you. I'll be gentle, though." She wags her eyebrows at me. I bring the steaming mug of tea over to her and collapse next to her, my arms bracing my head against the table. "Oh, hun, come on. I'm only playing. Tell me. I'm sure we can figure it out."

"I know we can. I'm being stupid." My voice is muffled from trying to speak while still hiding.

"Will you at least tell me why you're being stupid so I can help you fix it?"

I sit back up and heave out a breath.

"Seb's away, and we have this agreement where I'm supposed to check in every other hour via text. He worries about me, especially with the Phil thing. He's been quite clear and I've agreed. I was at work and the presentation I was delivering got rescheduled and I missed a couple of texts. He got mad because I didn't tell him I would be late with the texts." My summary is as basic as I can make it, providing enough information that Jess can help, but without explaining everything else that goes on between Seb and me.

"Okay, he asked you to do something. You couldn't. You're mad because…?"

"Because he was being unreasonable, and it's ridiculous that he needs me to text that regularly. We used to have fun text conversations, but now it's just… Get the gin. I'll grab some ice. I need a drink." Jess looks confused by my sudden energy, but quickly follows along.

Armed with large drinks, we curl up on the sofa.

"Right, I need to explain a few things about our relationship. That way you might see where I'm coming from."

"Okay, I'm listening." The playful Jess from earlier seems to have disappeared with the addition of alcohol.

"Do you know anything about D/s—Dominance and submission?"

"Uh… in principle." Her brows pinch together as if I've said something that she disapproves of.

"Right, well… I've always had this urge or want to give up control in the bedroom, to have my partner look after my needs, not have to make any of the choices. I make nothing but decisions all day, every day. I longed to give it up in the bedroom." I feel my own cheeks pink at my confession. Jess doesn't bat an eyelash, so I continue. "Well, after I first met and

119

got to know Seb, he saw that I had some submissive traits. Turns out that he has some dominant traits and that's a big part of our connection."

"Go on." Jess is now eager to hear my words, her focus locked on me.

"Well, that was what I wanted—to give over control in the bedroom. But since I moved in, Seb wants to see if we can have that same dynamic outside of the bedroom as well, to see if I am naturally submissive to him at other times, and find out where my balance lies. We agreed to two times a week where I'll submit to his control. I'll do as he instructs or asks, completely. It's what he wants."

"This is outside of the bedroom now?"

"Yes. The other day he chose what I wore to work, what we'd do. Little things like that."

"Okay, so where does the text stuff come in?"

"Well, he wants me to text him and keep him updated in general. All the time. I have to let him know what I'm doing and where I am. At first, it was nice. It made me feel like he was watching out for me. Now…"

"Now, what?"

"I feel stifled, like I need to report to him. It makes me feel like he's in charge of me. Which is fine in the bedroom. I like that, but I don't like the idea of giving up all of my control outside of it. I've been self-sufficient for so long. Relying on Phil was never an option. I've gone from one extreme to the other. I wanted our relationship to pick up where we started. When we were together, it was so good, so natural."

"And you don't feel that way now?" Jess goes back to nursing her drink.

"No, I do. It is, when we're alone. But the submitting stuff is hard. I'm constantly wrestling with my feelings. Phil won't let me move on. Seb made the choice for me to move in. I have to do what he says. Alone, each of those things is fine.

All together, it's all… It's all too much. Everything's changing and I'm feeling lost."

"But you wanted change? You certainly didn't want to stay with Phil."

"No, I most definitely didn't want to stay with Phil. It's just… I'm worried that I'm no good at the submissive stuff outside of the bedroom and that Seb wants that. What if I'm not enough?" My lips tremble at the thought. I don't let the tears fall.

"Oh, hun. Look, I know that Seb adores you. He is head over heels for you. There is a lot going on for both of you. It's only been a few weeks. Don't rush things. Take it slowly. You won't lose yourself, but I think you need to be open with Seb on how you're feeling. Seb forced the moving in thing, despite your gut reservations. You love him. Give yourself some time and have some patience. Isn't this new for Seb as well?"

"Yes, it is."

"Then don't be so hard on yourself, or him. I think you're expecting to walk straight into an established relationship. You should be enjoying this time."

"Says the girl with commitment problems." I take a long draw of my drink, glad of the momentary break.

"Hey, don't deflect. You came to me. I haven't even called you crazy yet."

"Am I being stupid?"

"I think you have a lot of things to deal with. You've left your husband, and he's being a dick. You've started a relationship with the man you had an affair with and have moved straight in with him. Then there's all the dominance and submission stuff." She puts her drink down and whispers to me, "We're going to talk more about that when we've had another drink, right?"

"Yes, Jess." I burst into laughter. "If you want, we can talk."

"Good, because I'm trying to stay focused on the relationship crap. Iz, you really need to stop freaking out over everything. You're not going to lose him. He moved you in, for God's sake."

"I know. I told you I'm stupid, but it's really hard."

"Give it some time and talk to your man."

"That simple?"

"Hell, I don't know. I'm Miss No Commitment, but it sounds like you're trying too hard."

I think about everything Jess has said. She's right. I might have some fears, but isn't that normal at the start of a relationship? Aren't my concerns normal for any new couple, but with a few minor variations? We're both adjusting and there is a huge amount to contend with.

"So, more drink?"

"I can only have one as I've got another presentation tomorrow."

"You'll still spill about the bedroom stuff, right?"

"Do you fancy it, Jess? Handing yourself over to a man to do whatever he likes to you?" I grin, knowing just how good that can be.

"No, I don't think so. I'm more of an in-charge kinda girl in the bedroom." We both giggle as she heads to top up our drinks.

After last night's girl time, today starts out much better. I stayed over at Jess's as I'd had a drink and didn't want to be up too late. I called Seb and told him that we needed to talk on Friday, but that I'd try harder with the communication.

I text Seb at regular intervals but try to put more effort into them. If I change my view of the texts, stop thinking of them as a check and frame them as just keeping in touch, I feel more comfortable. Not forgetting the scenario of yesterday, I warn him that I have another client meeting and that it could run over. I explain that I'll text as soon as I get out.

Seb explained this to me during our heated words yesterday, but it wasn't until today that I could understand and use it to help. Instead of these being restrictions and control placed on me, I am doing something to please Seb—something that he needs. It's a simple flip of motivation but it helps a great deal.

By the end of the day, I am buzzing. The Everlyn presentation went better than expected. They increased their budget with us, and Mark wants to meet with me first thing on Monday. Not even arriving home to an empty apartment can dampen my smile.

I soak in the bath for far too long. My toes have pruned and there's no room to top the tub up with more hot water. I reluctantly step out and get ready for bed. It has been a long week.

Walking around the apartment, I try to look at everything through new eyes. I considered this place Seb's when I moved in. I still do, but I want those pictures to go. Pictures of beautiful, half-naked women only serve as a reminder of my insecurities. If I am going to make my relationship with Seb work, then I need to overcome my self-doubts, but that doesn't mean I need to live with artful reminders of what I'm not on the walls. Seb has asked that I don't compare him with Phil, and I'm not. They are worlds apart, but that doesn't mean that I can shake my little demons. A shudder racks my body as I think back to all of the times that Phil lied to me. In the beginning, I didn't notice. I still trusted him. By the end, I didn't care.

With Jess's words from last night still fresh in my mind, I relax and try to see our relationship objectively. I am allowed to have concerns and fears. That doesn't mean that the relationship won't work.

Seb has moved me in. My bags and coat are in the entrance hall, my toiletries in the bathroom and my clothes in the wardrobe. He is serious about me. He wouldn't do that—fight for me to move in—if he wasn't. Can I adapt and learn to accept all the elements of the submissive relationship that he wants? I need to give myself time to find out.

I head to bed and move to Seb's side, inhaling his clean scent that clings to the pillow. So many of my actions echo those of my past visits, but they seem so far removed from how I feel now.

I need to talk to Seb, communicate properly with him and stop being afraid. He couldn't have stressed the importance of being open and honest more vehemently, yet I've shirked every opportunity. Not purposefully, just out of habit and fear. I can't do that any longer. I won't. I want to try harder for Seb.

I can't wait until you're back. Love you. Izzy

I can't wait to be back, sweetheart. S

I'm looking forward to our talk when you come home. I have done a lot of thinking. Izzy x

He doesn't respond straight away, but it's just past nine in the morning. He might be busy. I push the fleeting doubt from my mind and get on with my day. I'm finally feeling positive. The doubt has finally eased and allowed the good to blossom.

I've promised myself I'll talk to Seb tonight before we go any further, and I need to apologise. That's my game plan. I just have to stick to it for the rest of the day.

I know it's only been a few days since I last saw Seb, but the last few hours seem to pass slower than the first two days combined. Keeping up with my texts helps with the countdown, but it also increases my nerves about our talk this evening. Each text sets off my mind and I keep going over what I'm going to say. Rationally, I know that I shouldn't be nervous. I am doing something that Seb wanted from me from the start. My stomach doesn't seem to get the message.

There are no plans for tonight other than our talk. Our text messages seem fine, but our last few phone conversations have been less than happy. I want the tension between us gone.

I leave the office at five and head home. I know Seb will be home late, but that doesn't matter. I'd rather pace and work myself up about how I am going to apologise at home than stay at work.

125

After trying to distract myself with my Tumblr page on my iPad, I change into a dress that I know Seb will approve of and head to the kitchen. It's late enough to start some food, and I want to make my favourite go-to dish. I used to eat this at least once a week. Garlic, peppers and olive oil make a quick and simple sauce for spaghetti, topped with basil and parmesan. I get everything ready and leave pulling it together until I know Seb has parked.

I pour the wine and wait, nibbling at the crumbs of cheese ready to coat the pasta.

I'm just parking. I'll be up in 5. S

Finally! I jump into action and make the final preparations for the food, setting it on the breakfast bar.

I hear the click of the door. When he enters, I throw my arms around his neck and hug him as hard as can. With everything going on in these three short days, I didn't realise just how much I missed him. As soon as I feel his touch, a part of me eases and I relax, the tension evaporating on its own.

"Miss me?" I hear the sexy smile in Seb's voice.

"Yes. You know I did." I pull back and look at his handsome face. My eyes drop to his lips, my hunger for pasta instantly replaced by a hunger for Seb. I pull my lip between my teeth, fighting the urge to kiss his lips. I pull out of his grasp and reach for his hand, taking him toward the kitchen where our dinner awaits.

"You cooked for me?"

"I can cook, Seb."

"Sorry, I know. It's just unexpected. Dinner will be a lovely treat. Thank you. It smells delicious."

"This is one of my favourite pasta dishes. I hope you like it."

126

"I will. Can I wash up first? I've been in a car for the last five hours."

"Yes! Of course. Sorry."

"Relax. I'll just be a minute. Then we can eat."

A few minutes pass and he comes back to the kitchen and turns me on my bar stool.

"If I wasn't starving, we'd be in the bedroom before we got to the food. I've missed you." My cheeks blush and I'm struck by how such a simple compliment has given me such pleasure. I hold on to that thought and gesture for Seb to sit down and tuck in. *The sooner we get through food, the sooner we can talk.* I know if Seb takes me to bed, I'll lose my courage and focus. We can spend all night in bed. After we talk.

Seb's appreciative moan adds pressure to my swelling heart. This. This is what I want. To please Seb.

"Mmm, this is delicious."

"Thank you." I pick at my food, my appetite non-existent. The time for talking is upon us.

"You're not eating. Is something wrong?"

"No, I've just... I need to talk to you and I'm a little nervous about how you'll react to what I say." I twirl my fork in the pasta, keeping my eyes focused away from Seb's.

"Would you feel more comfortable talking as I eat? Then we can go to bed." He tilts my chin until I meet his gaze. It both calms and stirs my emotions.

"Yes, please. Is that okay?"

"Talk to me, Izzy." He lowers his lips and brushes mine, encouraging me to talk. He turns back to his food, giving me space.

"I want to say sorry first. I didn't think about how my reaction to moving in together would affect you. I was also feeling uncomfortable about how often you wanted me to text you."

127

"Thank you for acknowledging that." I wait for him to finish, but he goes back to the pasta and takes a long draw on his glass of wine.

"I think, with everything that happened between us and the changes in my life, I was feeling unsettled. Jess told me I needed to be patient and not expect everything to just fall into place. I think she's right. I should allow us some time to work things out. So I'm going to try harder." I seem to have glossed over the control part and my doubts around the submission, but I've been clear on wanting to try.

"Anything else you want to add?" He's still not looking at me. It helps my ability to get the words out. He's encouraging me.

"I may have some doubts, but that's just my insecurities talking." I try to brush off my worries. "Do you want some more wine?" I jump off my seat and head to the fridge. After I top up both our glasses, Seb pulls me towards him, the bottle of wine still in my hand, and begins to nuzzle my neck.

"If you've finished with food, I want us to go to bed. Now." The change in Seb's tone sends ripples of excitement through me. I nod my response, setting the wine bottle on the counter top before Seb pulls me through to the bedroom. He makes short work of my dress, revealing my naked skin beneath. Seb pulls the covers back and gestures for me to climb in. I turn and watch as he efficiently strips out of his suit. He stalks to the bed and scoots under the covers with me. Seb turns me so my back is pressed up against his chest and he links our legs, connecting us from shoulder to toe.

Strong, sure arms hold me in place and his lips rest on the shell of my ear.

"Now, I want you to tell me everything that has been going through your head. You're safe. I've got you and I'm not letting you go. Talk to me."

So much for keeping a few things to myself!

I know I have to do this, so I steel myself for what's coming. At least he isn't making me tell him face to face.

"What more do you want me to say?"

"I need you to tell me all of your feelings and not just what you think is enough. This relationship is new for both of us. You're right. I need to know what you're struggling with."

"I feel like I'm losing my independence. Like I said before, everything is happening so fast and I'm trying to find my feet." Seb begins lightly tracing patterns on my skin, coaxing me to open up further to him. "I used to enjoy the texts, but I don't want to feel like a child checking in with a parent. I didn't understand your point."

"Go on, sweetheart."

"I know you want to see me as your submissive outside the bedroom, but it's the bedroom stuff that I long for. The rest of it, I'm not sure. I seem to fight with myself over what I want and pleasing you. And I'm not sure if I'll be enough for you if I'm no good at it." I release the tension I've been holding, racing to get the final words out. Now I've said them, they are still scary, yet being wrapped in Seb helps to ward off the worst of my fear.

Seb pulls me back even closer to his body, if that's possible.

"Why didn't you tell me any of this earlier?" His voice is soft and soothing.

"I didn't want to disappoint you. Plus, it's something that I'm only just grasping myself. You know how I struggled with the homework you set for me. I want to please you. That hasn't changed. I'm just... I don't want to give up all of my independence. I never had to check in with someone else all the time. I made my own decisions, and I don't feel comfortable letting that go."

He turns me around so we're face to face, and I risk looking up to his eyes. "Don't you know how I feel about you?

You are all I will ever want or need. I want to push you, test your boundaries and find out what you're comfortable with. Your trust is a gift to me, as is your love. I love you, Izzy, and I won't do anything to jeopardise us."

He said he loves me! He said he loves me!

I can't help the smile that cracks across my face in response to those three little words. Three little words that have cemented my heart as Seb's. They dissolve my doubts, and I'm left with a shimmer of expectancy for what will happen next.

"Let's pull back on the submissive days. Take it one step at a time. I still want you to try for me." It's not a question, but his eyebrow rises, seeking my agreement. I nod, elated with his words. "Good. Now, I'm going to worship your body with my tongue and you're not going to come until I'm buried inside you. You're going to feel just how much I love you."

I love you. Those three words have been a soothing elixir to my woes. The last two weeks have been brilliant. Work is going better than ever. Seb's only been gone for the odd overnight stay, and I know that the solicitor is moving the divorce forward. Balance has resumed, and with it, my confidence.

Since the argument with Seb, I've tried to be more open with expressing my feelings. In return, he's not pushed me past what we've already done. I'm happy and I'm in love. It's been a long time since I woke up in the morning and felt those things.

Even on my non-submissive days, I've fallen into the habit of getting coffee for us in the morning. Since I'm the one with the greater need for caffeine, it suits me just fine.

I bring the coffee back into the bedroom and place it on Seb's side of the bed. He walks into the room behind me and I turn to watch him hovering.

"Do you trust me?"

"Of course, Seb. Why?"

"In your room, I've put out a garment bag containing some clothes. Take the bag with you to work. Change into the clothes at the end of the day. Wear only what I put in the bag. I'll pick you up."

"I don't understand. It's not Tuesday or…"

"Trust me, Isabel. I'm going to show you something that's important to me. You'll wear your anklet. Do you understand?" His voice has dropped. He's serious about this.

"Where are we going?"

"It's a surprise. You'll have to trust me."

"Yes, I'm sorry."

"Good girl. Come here." He pulls me in to his side, softening the bite from his words. Logically, I know he's pushing me. We've had a few weeks of taking it steady. This is all new for him as well. I'd hoped that things would remain as they were, at least for a little while longer, although I've never told Seb that. "This evening will challenge you. It's more than I've expected of you when we've played together previously, but it's something I'd like to try and explore with you."

I'm caught in that heady mix of nervous excitement, amplified by my growing arousal at Seb's words. As much as I may have encroaching doubts over how much of the time I want Seb to be in control, it still sets my pulse racing when he is. My breathing, for one, is a giveaway that he's sure not to miss.

"Doing what I tell you turns you on, doesn't it, Isabel?" His warm hand travels down my body until it's resting on my hip. I surrender to the look of craving in his eyes and lie back on the bed. He continues drawing little patterns on my skin, inching one way, then the other. His patterns strategically hitch my cami-top higher on my stomach and his wandering hands peel my knickers from my hips.

He finally brushes against my clit. He presses harder, stroking through my pussy. "Fuck, I'm never going to get tired of feeling how wet you are for me."

I open my legs to him, giving him the access I want him to have. The tension is building in me, and right now, I'd love

132

for Seb to take over and make me forget my concerns. *Well, isn't that a contradiction?*

"You want me to make you come, sweetheart?"

"Yes," is the only reply in my mind right now.

"Good girl. But tonight is going to be very intense for both of us. Thinking about having you spread bare for me is going to be torturous for me all day. Spread your legs as wide as you can and keep them there. Don't move." Seb quickly repositions himself in between my legs, his intentions now very clear. I hold my thighs, forcing myself to keep my legs wide for him. He doesn't want me to move. Determined to keep to his command over my body's need to move, I squeeze my eyes shut and breathe deeply. *I can do this. Concentrate.* Seb's gaze rakes over my flesh, his eyes dazzling, and he locks with mine as he leans down to tongue my clit. He sweeps slowly up and down, so softly it almost tickles. He assaults me with his mouth, lapping and sucking and coating me with his saliva. My gasps and moans ricochet around the room and my hips press his mouth into me harder. My orgasm is spiralling, along with the desire to keep my legs wide and ride his face.

I will him on, desperate to feel the release that will soothe my nerves. Seb's tongue goes exploring, not leaving any part of my pussy alone. *Yes, just... a little...*

His pause interrupts my panting breaths. His cock thrusts inside of me hard and fast, and it propels me over. I cry out and grasp hold of Seb. He continues his punishing rhythm and I'm swept along with it, giving in to him. Seb has mastered me and it's exactly what I want and need. He continues his rhythm, carrying me along with him.

"God, yes!" Seb stills, releasing into me, and I slump back into the bed.

Since leaving Seb this morning, I've not been able to settle or master my growing apprehension. The bubbly anxiety, not the dread that sits in the pit of your stomach. My fingers take the brunt of the nerves, drumming on the desk every few minutes.

Finally, the clock hands move and I hear a bing from my phone.

I'll be waiting outside in 5 mins. S

Reading the words sends my pulse into orbit. The unknown is both exciting and terrifying. Seb wants to push my boundaries, so I know it won't be something we've done already. A shiver creeps up my spine. I walk to the bathroom to change. I lock the cubicle, unzip the bag and pull out the dress that Seb wants me to wear. *Holy shit!* I'd never buy something like this. I rummage at the bottom of the bag, looking for the underwear that will accompany the dress. Of course, there isn't any.

I stuff the dress back into the garment bag and head down to the reception bathroom. There is no way I'm walking through my office dressed in this. Once safely inside the ladies room, I pull the offending article back out. I lift it out, and a swathe of deep red fabric drapes against my body, not even close to skimming my knee. The length isn't the problem. The lack of fabric is. Backless is an accurate description, and it's far more revealing than anything I would ever wear.

Seb chose this for me with very clear instructions. I close my eyes and flex my ankle feeling the bite of the tiny chain against my skin, signifying my submission. *It's just a dress.*

I quickly change out of my appropriate work wear and slip the silky material over my head. It drops to my mid-thigh, with wide shoulders allowing the material to drape open and expose my back. The back plunges so low that the top of my knickers will be clearly visible. There's certainly no way a bra is possible. Seb's instructions were very specific. I wear only what he set out for me. *That means no underwear. Crap!*

I can do this. I've sat at a bar without my knickers before. This is no different. It's just a little bit more revealing. I diligently lose my bra and shimmy out of my knickers. To my shock, they're damp, betraying my body's pleasure at following Seb's instructions, despite my reservations. *Perhaps it's my reservations that are making this so naughty.*

Easing into my sky-high heels, I pull myself up and stand tall. My nipples peak under the fabric, clearly on display, and I will them to soften. At the bottom of the garment bag is the jewellery box containing my anklet. My already stuttering heart pounds harder as I hold it in my hand. When I put this tiny piece of jewellery on, I give myself to Seb. I agreed to that and it helps to ground me—giving me a sense of purpose that helps my mind relax. By asking me to wear it, he knows that I'll need the reassurance that it brings.

I sweep some gloss over my lips, add a little mascara and shake my hair to add some volume. The self-consciousness halts me as I turn to exit. *I can do this. I want to do this for Seb.*

Burying my anxiety, I walk out into reception. The chill doesn't help make my breasts any less visible under the dress. Before I open the door, I can see Seb parked up outside, standing against the car. He spots me and I hurry out to meet him. The January air bites into my exposed skin as I rush to the car. He blocks my path. His eyes roam my body and it takes a moment for them to reach my eyes. Stepping aside, he opens the door and I do my best to slide in without flashing anyone. Seb rounds the car and joins me, adding to the already toasty temperature of the interior.

"Good evening, Isabel." Seb greets me with a deep rumble, and despite the warmer atmosphere, goose bumps trail over my skin.

"Good evening, Sir."

135

He pulls out into traffic and doesn't continue with the conversation. My adrenaline spikes again at his silence. He's building the tension—or at least the tension in me. "Am I allowed to know where we're going?"

"Of course you are." He doesn't elaborate, though.

"Will you tell where we're going?"

"I might if you ask me properly." His lips twitch at his response.

Fine.

"Please, Sir, will you tell me where we're going?"

"Thank you, Isabel. Yes. I'm taking you to dinner."

Dinner? Dressed like this? I nervously pull at the hem of my dress, which has risen to indecent heights now that I'm sitting down.

"Stop the nerves, Isabel. I asked you to trust me." With his words, Seb places a hand on my thigh and gently squeezes. It stills my nervous twitch and I draw strength from his warmth.

Seb's contact doesn't break for the rest of the journey. We drive past the outskirts of town and into the country. The roads narrow and turn more twisty until we turn into a driveway and stop at a large iron entry gate. Seb waits for a moment and the gates open. The gates tell me to expect a grand mansion house at the end of the driveway. Instead, a large, modern, cottage-style house sits there. Two outside lamps illuminate a bay for several cars and the way to the entrance. Ivy covers most of the outside stone work, but I can't tell much else in the shadows. The small windows are camouflaged in foliage.

We drive up and Seb parks. He hands me out of the car and leads me closer. I see shadows of what must be extensions to the original building. I can't help but hope that I will get to see it in the light of day. It must be stunning.

The exterior of the cottage holds my attention until we're standing at the solid oak door. Seb presses the buzzer and I'm brought back to the present. I shift toward him, seeking reassurance. His arm snakes around my back, brushing against my flesh, and draws me closer. The heavy door swings open and we're greeted by a tall, slim gentleman dressed in a tidy suit.

"Good evening, Mr. York. If you'd like to follow me, your table is waiting." Seb ushers me forward and I follow the gentleman into the cottage. Once inside, there is no evidence of the cottage-style house or ivy running rampant over the outside. Smooth marble flows from the doorstep out into a reception area. Swathes of thick, rich material curtain the back wall and seclude us from anything that might be beyond. The room has a warm glow, a radiance about it. It makes me want to stand up tall and be confident walking into such a place.

The gentleman leads us towards a frosted glass door, decorated by more furnishings, and opens it for us. We enter a room set with a dozen small, intimate tables, the only light being cast from the candles on the tables.

Several other couples are already seated, and I stiffen in Seb's arms.

"Shh, you're doing fine. You look amazing, and if they stare, it will be because of that and nothing else," Seb whispers to me, and the words cast a magical trance over me. Even though Seb chose the dress, hearing him tell me that he thinks I look good helps my confidence to no end. Breathing in, I take a sure step onto the hardwood floor, my heels clicking loudly as I walk towards our table. I take the seat the gentleman is holding out for me, but Seb doesn't let our contact slip and keeps my hand in his as we sit down. We're at right angles to each other at the small round table.

"The specials tonight are line-caught sea bass with mushrooms and oyster foam, pork tenderloin with salt-baked celeriac and apple sauce or hazelnut gnocchi. Can I get you anything to drink?"

"A bottle of sparkling water, please."

"Of course, sir."

I rearrange myself on the chair, wiggling to try to conceal more of my legs with the skirt of the dress. His gentle rub on the back of my hand is soothing, making me forget that I'm not wearing anything that would be classed as decent in my book. The ambience is intimate—a secret rendezvous between lovers. I can't help but respond to the surroundings and the fact that I'm here at the wishes of Seb.

Embers of desire spark to life as I look at him across the small table. Candlelight warms his face and illuminates his shining eyes. He looks pleased. I can't control my answering smile.

"I want you to know that tonight is going to be as much a test for me as it is for you. I wanted to bring you here to explain certain things. About me, and about us. But you'll have to be patient. Trust me. Do you understand?"

"Yes, I understand. I think. Are you going to tell me where we are or what we're doing here? Besides having dinner?"

His lips harden and he huffs out a breath.

"Sir, are you going to tell me why we're here, *Sir?*" I don't mean to forget, but with the circumstances as they are, and not being in the bedroom, it keeps slipping my mind.

"We're here to enjoy an evening together, and to press the previous boundaries of our relationship. I told you I would. I love having you as my submissive and I want to explore it further. It's what I've always wanted."

Those few words melt my heart, and I know that whatever happens tonight, I can give Seb something he's always wanted. *Why is pleasing him so important to me?*

"Excuse me, sir. Your water. Are you ready to order?" My thoughts are interrupted by the gentleman waiter. I haven't even thought about the menu or picked it up from the table.

"I'll have the sea bass, please. My guest, the gnocchi."

"Very good. Thank you, sir." He disappears as silently as he approached. As my eyes follow his retreat, I glance at the others around the room. Three other couples are engaged in quiet conversation. I look a little harder and notice that all the women are wearing a minimal amount of clothes with plunging necklines or raised hems. The men are all dressed in smart suits. My dress fits in perfectly. I turn my attention back to Seb and catch him watching me. Intently.

"Your emotions flit across your face. I love it, but I'd like you to tell me how you feel." He reaches for his water and takes a measured sip. I am learning that talking to Seb is important. It helps us and I shouldn't be frightened to share. *But it is so hard sometimes!*

"Well, I wanted to look around the room, try and feel more comfortable as I'm not sure where we are. All the other women are dressed like me or similarly—lots of flesh. It made me feel... safer. Less on display."

"Good girl. You don't mind me ordering for you." I don't miss that it isn't a question. I like that Seb takes control of the small things. It makes me feel important, special, that he knows me well enough to order for me.

"No. I like it when you do."

He beams at my response.

"Have you been here before, Sir?"

"Yes, but not for a little while." Seb only ever gives small crumbs of information to me, and I'm desperate to lick up every single one of them. I raise my eyebrows and look expectant.

"The sea bass, and the gnocchi."

Seb grins as the waiter sets down our food, knowing that I would have pressed for more. It smells delicious and I remind myself of the jewellery adorning my ankle. Today is not the day to press him.

* * *

139

At the end of our meal, Seb stands and offers his hand to help me rise. He gently leads me from our table to the other end of the restaurant. Frosted glass doors seal off the dining room from the room beyond. Several more couples arrived during our meal, and their attire forms what amounts to a uniform—the men in well-tailored suits and the women in barely-there cocktail dresses. As we approach the door, another suited staff member pulls it open for us.

We're back in a reception area of sorts. There are open areas branching off from this main space, also adorned with fabric and curtains, making them seem more private. There are a few leather sofas and wooden drinks tables to one side. Seb pulls me closer to him as he moves me to one of the areas. As it opens out, it appears to be a bar. A few plush sofas are scattered in the corners, creating cosy areas. The lighting is soft and minimal, helping the ambience from the restaurant to follow into the larger space.

Two tall, elegant ladies walk past and I battle my instinct to cower against Seb. Their beauty stirs my insecurities about other women. We don't go into the bar but steer around to another alcove room. This one is more secluded and has opulent floor cushions and pillows scattered around several winged back chairs. A man sits in one of them with a curvaceous woman at his feet. The scene reminds me of the times I sat at Seb's feet. *I want that!*

I feel the pressure of Seb's hand against my flesh but I want to resist it. I want to watch these two. My embarrassment is overcome by my own curiosity. Something about this couple makes me want to stay. The room isn't closed off, nor are they hiding behind any curtain or screen.

"Come on, Isabel." Seb's hushed voice doesn't hide the command behind it. My feet start moving forward, although the destination isn't clear. We appear to be touring all of the rooms that are connected to the reception. I think back to the 'cottage' that I thought I was entering when we arrived. Where has all this space come from?

"What is this place?" It certainly isn't just somewhere to have dinner. I would guess it to be an exclusive club.

"It's called Solace. It's a place that caters to Dominant and submissive needs. I want to show you part of this lifestyle." My feet are able to keep moving although my mind has completely tuned out. I think it stopped working when I concluded that this was a club. Seb's been here before—likely with other submissives. *Now he wants me to do what I thought was private between us observed by others?* My mind is racing and I'm suddenly scared to obey him. *What if I don't like what's on the other side of the door?*

For the first time, I seriously consider saying 'Black', my safeword.

"Don't tense up on me. I can feel your body's reaction. I need you to trust me. Nothing is going to happen that you're not happy with." His words take the edge off. Seb grabs my hand and turns me to face him. "Trust me." Hot, sensual lips meet mine and I take refuge in his attention. I kiss him back, telling him that I will try. For Seb, I will try.

"Follow me, sweetheart." Seb pulls me protectively close and we walk swiftly through the rest of the reception area. He sets us toward a stone archway with a marble pillar running down one side of the arch. It looks like an entrance, with steps disappearing out of view. Trepidation seeps inside of me and I cling to Seb.

"Remember your reaction to the couple you saw earlier? You liked what you saw. Keep that in mind."

The staircase spirals down and is lined by black, iron railings which I use to steady my steps. My heartbeat echoes the loud click that my heels make on the polished stone. When we reach the bottom, we enter a small waiting area of sorts.

Corridors lead off to the left and right. Seb pulls me to the right along the hallway.

The lighting is much darker. What I thought of as intimate in the rooms above has been replaced by shadows and intrigue. Another frosted glass door blocks our path. Seb pulls me towards it, and out of the shadows, a suited employee opens our entry. His attire is more casual than upstairs—an open collar shirt with his sleeves rolled up. The doors open and the heavy bass beat drums in my ears. My eyes adjust to the lessening light and shadowy forms take shape. Dotted around the room are couples in various stages of undress and activity. Seb's hand urges me to follow him deeper into the room. I recognise the sounds of hands slapping on flesh and the passionate moans that accompany them.

I don't want to look, but my traitorous body is warming to the feeling of being here. My eyes drift to each area as we pass. It's not busy. Many of the 'play areas' are empty. A man is gently spanking his partner over his knee in a small nook halfway into the room. We don't stop and I tear my eyes away from the woman's pert bottom, open to whatever her partner wishes.

The same feeling from earlier washes over me. *I want that.* My head might be reluctant, but my body's eager. As my thighs sweep together, I feel moisture with every step.

Benches, metal racks and PVC-covered tables make up some of the other equipment in the room. Seb slows in front of a wooden X. It towers over me, restraining the writhing woman who is cuffed to each corner point. I've seen images of a St. Andrew's Cross, but I hadn't expected the reality of it to be so... daunting. A shirtless, burly man distracts my view of the woman. He's pacing in front of her like a lion, the flogger in his hand twitching with every step. My breath catches as I look back to the woman. A sheen flushes her skin. Her mouth hangs slack.

142

Is this what I look like when Seb spanks me? Do I look as erotic, as hungry as she does for the strike?

The man trails the fronds of the flogger over her skin as he paces around his vulnerable prey. Her gasp doesn't reach my ears, but I don't need it to. I can see her ribs heave and her lips mouth words. She silently begs for relief. Her desperation is written on her form.

"More," I murmur. She needs more, like I do, every time I'm with Seb. My own need blooms in the pit of my stomach, and my clit longs for the friction of my thighs, my dress, my fingers.

"You should recognise this, Isabel. I've done this to you. I'd like you to watch this evening. Look at what the Dominant does and how his sub reacts. Let yourself enjoy it. Understand?" The deep tones of Seb's voice stoke my growing need. I melt into him.

He's right. I do recognise this. The sensuality and carnal nature of the scene steal my curiosity. I see her, but I also see me. I feel her arousal as my own. The lion stops his stalking. The flogger rises and descends. *Thud, thud, thud.* Each strike matches my heartbeat as the fronds fall to her back.

The man covers her body with his. He traces the shape of her slender body with his hand before his palm slaps. He pads back a few feet and swats her again with the flogger in his hand. The muscles in his upper torso transfix me. They tense before each strike, a snap in his arm to deliver the next blow. My eyes follow his movements and I see the sub relax into her restraints after each hit. A rhythm ensues, their exchange mesmerising.

Minutes merge together until I pant with frustration. The steady beat of Seb's heart pumps against my back. He presses our bodies close, shielding me from any stray eyes. *I want more.* I want his touch. I want his affection. The sub's desperate moans mirror my desire.

"Do you like watching the power exchange, Isabel? Do you see what the sub gives to her Dom? She surrenders her body and her control over what happens to him. She puts her trust in him not to hurt her and to bring her pleasure. That exchange is the first step in this scene." Seb's words drip with sensual command. With nothing other than his voice, Seb could make me come on the spot while watching this show.

"Yes, Sir. I like watching them." My husky words sound sexy even to me.

"Continue to watch. Don't take your eyes off them." A shiver runs over my skin at the command. I doubt I'll have any trouble obeying.

Seb's hand snakes under my dress and teases a path up my inner thigh. His touch promises the relief my pussy craves. We're in a public club, anyone could see Seb's hand between my legs. I should stop Seb's public fondling and protest. My legs shift in response, widening so that Seb can find my aching clit.

My eyes fix on the couple in front of me. The Dom flicks long, sensual, suede tails over her back and thighs before moving towards her. I watch and I feel. Seb's fingers rest tauntingly close to my labia. I'm desperate for him to touch me. He skims a finger over my wet seam and I sag back into his body.

"Someone is very wet. Do you want to be flogged? Do you want me to tie you up and flog you?"

"Yes, god. Please, Sir." His finger drives inside of me, my reward for begging. Seb slides in and out, slow and steady.

"Keep your eyes open and on the couple." My hooded eyes fly wide at his warning. The Dom has turned the woman around so she faces us. A blush rushes over my cheeks as she looks right at me. With one hand clamped around the sub's neck, her Dom whispers in her ear and spanks her sex with a small flogger.

"That sub is going to come when her Dom tells her to. I'm going to finger fuck you and I want you to come when she does." I don't answer. I'm lost in my own fantasy. I hear Seb's words and I want nothing more than to do as he says. My nerves, fears, *everything* from earlier is forgotten. Nothing else matters but watching the woman in front of me submit to a man controlling her pleasure—controlling mine.

Seb's fingers grow urgent, and keep time with the smacks of the flogger. Her muscles are tight and her chest rises on every deep breath. The sub is desperate to release. My orgasm coils in my stomach, my legs tense in the restraints of Seb's body. *Just... a little... more.*

"Come!" a deep, gravelly voice barks and the sub contorts wildly as her orgasm fires. Her release and Seb's fingers force my own climax. My knees give and my spine stiffens as I ride crashing waves of pleasure. I close my eyes and sink back into bliss.

Soft, wet lips cover the column of my neck and I regret that we are in a room full of people. I want to be hidden away where Seb can make love to me until I come again. His erection jabs into my back, and I wonder what his plans are now.

"Come with me." Seb pulls me back through the room towards the doors. After leaving the room, Seb stalks down the corridor, past the archway and along the other hallway. There are a series of doors to one side, evenly spread apart. He stops, enters number eight and pulls me inside.

A king size bed dominates the room bare of little else. My stomach drops at the click of the lock, but I'm glad of the privacy. I drag my eyes from the bed and search Seb's face. He looks hungry, and I'm his perfect treat to taste. I wait patiently for instruction.

"I'm going to strip you and then I'm going to suck your gorgeous breasts into my mouth. I want you to be loud. Tell me how I make you feel. When I can see your wetness trickling down your thighs, I'm going to lie down and you're going to ride my cock."

Oh god, I want to come! "Yes, Sir."

"Good." He closes the distance between us and I brace for his assault. From our dirty talk I expect a passionate embrace, but Seb takes his time. He's gentle. He slides the fabric of my dress from my shoulders. The bodice slithers to my waist. He sucks my nipple into his mouth before lowering his knees to the floor, pulling the rest of the fabric from my body. Sparks travel down to my clit. He's still in his suit while I'm standing before him naked, submitting to his fantasy. *My fantasy.*

He pops my nipple from his lips and circles my belly button with his tongue. I convulse and bend my body in pleasure. Pressure registers deep inside me and I grow unsatisfied with his tease. I want to ride him.

"You like that?"

"Yes," I pant, holding onto his shoulders for stability. The ends of my hair tickle my bum as I throw my head back in pleasure.

"Are your thighs wet yet, Isabel?"

"I hope so. Please, Sir. I want you." His tongue pauses in its stimulation of my body. *Please, please, please.*

"On the bed." I turn and crawl onto the bed. On any other occasion I'd admire the silk sheets, but I want Seb under me. He walks around to the side of the bed, divesting himself of clothes. He lies down and I eagerly climb onto him.

"We do this my way. Understood?"

"Yes, Sir." This is what I crave. This is what makes my heart dance with joy. Seb takes control and doesn't allow me space or time to worry or think. I can relax and just feel.

"Straddle me."

"Yes, Sir."

He leans up and guides me to the position he wants. My pussy is open to him and grazes his firm cock. I barely avoid grinding down on him.

"Keep your hands behind your back. Hold onto your wrists. I'm going to move you." I do as he says. He lines up his hard, straining cock with my entrance and thrusts in. We both moan in pleasure. The gentle pressure of him filing me sends pulses of heat through my body. I fight the urge to move my hands and grab his shoulders for support.

Each of his fingers digs into my hips, anchoring me to him as he begins a gentle rock. He slides in and out, rubbing deliciously against my exposed clit. My eyes roll back and I let heat, love and lust consume me.

The gentle motion doesn't last. He picks up pace, thrusting me down onto him and spiking my arousal. I'm not going to last long, but he said nothing about holding my orgasm back.

"Yes, oh yes. Sir, you're going to make me come."

"Good. Just a little bit longer." Seb's hands move and he wraps my body in one of his arms, pulling me closer to him. We're so close. The shift in position adds to my pending rush.

"Sir, I'm going to come…" As I shout the words, Seb's free hand snakes over my bottom, and his finger presses at my rear entrance.

"Good. Come."

I'm so focused on my climax that the unfamiliar pressure only adds to my release. As his finger breaches my tensed muscle, his body contracts and he erupts inside of me. I want to escape the intrusion of his finger but that would require me to stop milking his cock.

Finally, when the tremors have subsided, I slump forward onto Seb's body. He falls back to the bed, taking me with him. His finger pulls out and I shift to let his cock slide free. We're too spent to do anything more and I rest against Seb's chest, listening to his pounding heart.

I wake to a chill and take a moment to orientate myself. We must have dozed off. I head to the other door in the room and hope it's a bathroom. It is and I clean up and sneak back to Seb. He's stirred, too, and is holding the covers open in welcome for me. I snuggle under and resume my comfortable position against his chest.

The soft trailing of his fingers over my shoulder relaxes my tired body, but my mind is awake. I have so many questions about this place, but I'm not sure how much I want to ask or even which questions I want answers to. I know that Seb learned what he knows from somewhere. Perhaps this was the place. Maybe this was where he took women and spent evenings dominating them.

"Will you tell me some more about Solace? Why you brought me here?" My voice sounds small and unsure. I'm still not sure how to be on the days that I give over control to Seb. The rules are fuzzy in my head. When it's just the intimate sex stuff, it's easy. I've always wanted that. It's natural. Outside of that...

"I've been coming here, on and off, for several years. A friend of mine recognised some of my traits, similar to how I recognised the submissive in you, and suggested I give this a try. Of course, I loved it. It was something that had been missing for me until then. But I didn't like the public element of the club scene. There is an expectation to play with other submissives, casually, nothing past the scene or evening. That wasn't what I was looking for."

"You wanted a relationship?"

"Yes. I wanted to meet someone with matching interests, someone who shared my desires and my hunger for a D/s exchange."

"And they didn't? The women in your past?" I can't help sounding nervous, but Seb just holds me tighter.

"If I wanted a submissive for one night, I could play at Solace. If I wanted a long-term D/s relationship, I had to risk finding a submissive woman through dating. A pattern developed. The women I got even remotely close to feigned interest. My date would pretend that D/s was what she wanted and submit just enough that I believed her. I began to hope I'd found an honest submissive. The woman would tell me how much she wanted to please me and make us work, but as soon as we got past a few sex toys and kinky underwear, pleasing me went out the window. These women found no pleasure in my more stringent desires, so I learned to guard my true feelings."

I remember back to the beginning of our relationship, to his task to buy a number of sex toys to play with that filled certain criteria. He gave me the instructions, but it was my

149

choice what to buy. He always said that he was impressed with my choices.

"What are you thinking, Isabel? I need you to communicate with me."

"I'm just thinking about what you've said. About this place. I'm not sure… It's a lot to take in."

"You were doing fine until I told you about why I brought you here."

"Was it a test?" I voice my biggest fear—that Seb was testing me like he was the other women in his life.

"No, sweetheart. This wasn't a test. Not like that." He rolls to his side so we're facing each other and tilts my head up with his finger. "Isabel, look at me." My eyes jump up to his. "I already know that you're perfect for me, that we match. You want what I want from a relationship and you submit beautifully to me. I wanted to explore your boundaries to see how you liked the club environment, to see if this interested you. I'm going to continue to do that, explore and find out how far I can take you. It's how we'll grow stronger, by exploring our mutual pleasures. We have our own rules that work for us. You submit to me totally for a couple of days a week. I've never had that before and I fucking love that you want to please me.

"I've told you before that I've taken you further than I ever thought possible," he says. "I want to see where else I can take you. I'm drawing from my past experience, but you need to talk to me. If you don't like anything…"

"It's not that I didn't like it."

"Then what?"

I steel myself to be strong and just tell him. "I'm experiencing a part of your past and it raises some of my insecurities. A part of me wants something new for us, that's special, just for us."

"Oh, sweetheart. The women in my past are exactly that—in my past. I might have learned technique, how to flog, how best to spank, but there was never the intimacy that we share. I was never a regular here. Many of my visits were to catch up with friends in a mutually convenient and interesting environment."

"Okay." After listening to his words, I feel lighter.

"Okay, what?"

"Okay, Sir."

"Better. I know you have insecurities, but we both have a past and you need to learn to trust again. Understand that I'm not your ex-husband."

"I'm sorry."

"We'll get there, sweetheart. Tell me what you thought of the club."

"You mean you couldn't tell from my reaction? I thought that would have been obvious."

"Oh, your reaction was perfect. How did you feel about the rest of it—upstairs, the restaurant, the nooks and the playroom, the other people?"

"I loved the restaurant, but I was nervous about what else was coming so I found it hard to enjoy the special details. I felt anxious and wasn't comfortable in the dress. I didn't know what was going to happen next. Yet the whole set up was very sexy. The intimacy of dinner, together with the anticipation of what was to come. It was a lot to take in. I did want to, though."

"I know. Thank you for trusting me today. I know the dress was the first stumbling block for you, but you look fucking gorgeous in it. Now, I want to take you back to our bed and make love to you."

Just like that, my heart swells with love for this man.

Lying in our bed at home, you'd have thought I'd be able to sleep. Especially after all of the sex and excitement. *Wrong!* It's Friday tomorrow, today... I glance at the clock. 3:50 a.m. I have to be up for work in a couple of hours.

Seb sleeps soundly next to me, but I can't stop going over what happened this evening. I never imagined I would allow myself to do what we did. I didn't even know places like Solace existed. The club was everything that my fantasy could have designed, and not as intimidating as some of the blog and Tumblr posts made it out to be. My body certainly didn't put up any objection.

I know I like to submit to Seb. That's never been in question. My growing fears over my independence don't feel so big anymore. *Could I give over more control to him?* My frustrations are building, along with my confusion at my own feelings. My emotions have been an ever-changing hindrance.

Slipping from the sheets, I pad quietly out to the kitchen. I pull a pan from the drawer and warm some milk while I pull the cocoa powder from the back of the cupboard. I haven't resorted to hot chocolate to help me sleep in years. As I stir the chocolaty goodness, I stare vacantly.

I take my mug and curl up in Seb's chair. If I'm not going to sleep, I may as well try to unravel my feelings. Although he agreed to take things slow, tonight was a much bigger step than we've previously taken. But I did it. Sure, I had some wobbles, but at no point did I want to stop. The desire to please Seb outweighed the anxiety of not knowing what was going to happen, or my initial reluctance at following through. Perhaps I can be everything that Seb hopes I am.

Trusting my feelings and putting faith in them again is still a big step. Added to that is my fear that I'm not everything Seb needs. That thought is my biggest downfall. Perhaps all I need is more time. We are taking it slowly, properly. Things are falling into place. The world doesn't end when my experiences expand.

My head nestles into the side of the chair and I curl around myself, thinking back to how it felt while Seb made love to me earlier tonight and how my feelings for him have grown over these last few months. *I will be enough for him.*

"Izzy? Izzy, wake up, sweetheart." Seb's voice calls to me in my dream. It's a nice dream. "Izzy, wake up. Time to get to work." His voice is louder now and I blink. "Good morning. When did you sneak out here?" Seb crouches down in front of me, a hot cup of coffee on the table next to him.

"Umm, about four this morning. I couldn't sleep." My eyelids feel like they have weights attached to them, dragging them closed. I force a few more blinks and try to hold my eyes open. All I want to do is go back to sleep. My eyelids slip closed.

"No, no, you have to get up. It's Friday. You can sleep in tomorrow." Pulling my arm up, Seb drags me from my slumber and walks me straight to the bathroom. Water droplets are already running down the side of the shower. Seb had his.

"What time is it?" I utter behind a stifled yawn.

"Just before eight."

Shit! "I'm going to be late!" I try to move my body into gear, but it's simply not cooperating.

"Relax. I'll drive you to work and pick you up this evening."

"That's going to be no quicker than me driving myself," I shout from under the shower, frantically wetting, washing and rinsing.

He doesn't answer, so I assume he's leaving me and my bad mood to get ready. In record time, I'm out and rushing to gather the first suitable clothes I can find.

Ten minutes later, I walk toward Seb, who sits leisurely at the breakfast bar.

"I'm ready. Let's go."

"How are you feeling?"

"Like crap. I need more sleep."

"Why couldn't you sleep?" Seb asks once we're heading to work. My head tips back and I take the opportunity to close my eyes for another few minutes.

"It was a busy night, Seb. Lots to think about." As soon as the words are out, I want to take them back. They sound like a brush off and I know Seb will see them as such. "I'm sorry, I didn't mean to snap." He doesn't say anything else for the rest of the traffic-riddled journey into Bath.

"Call me when you're ready to leave and I'll come and collect you." His tone holds none of the warmth from this morning. I curse my tired brain for not choosing better words.

I make it to my desk only thirty minutes late, but Mark isn't anywhere to be seen. I head for some much-needed coffee and text Seb.

> I'm sorry. I wasn't thinking about what I was saying. I'll see you later. Thank you for driving me. Love you. Izzy

Seb's been quiet all day, and I can't escape the thought that my dismissive retort this morning might be the cause. He's acknowledged my check-ins, but only just. I'm glad my brain isn't functioning, otherwise I'd be right back with the issue of turning something that used to be fun and comforting into a chore.

I pack up and head down to reception, and he's waiting on the curb outside, his face still in profile, emphasising his gorgeous features. He doesn't turn to me as I approach the car. After I've settled myself in, he pulls into the traffic and the car fills with the silence from this morning. I don't want to fight. I'm too tired, but I hate when there is clearly something between us. I want to fix it, make everything right.

Resting my head back and closing my eyes, I try to find the energy and the strength to talk to Seb openly and honestly, without reservation or hesitation.

"I couldn't sleep because I was trying to figure out how I was feeling after you took me to Solace. I was confused. I didn't know what I should or shouldn't be feeling. So I went to make myself a hot chocolate. It helped. Everything that was familiar to me has gone. Everything is new, which is exciting and brilliant, but intimidating, too, and that means that I retreat and let my insecurities get the better of me. I'm sure of myself, and of you, when you take control sexually. The full day yesterday led up to that, but I did find it hard. Finding it hard doesn't mean that I don't trust you. It's just me trying to get used to all of this." I peek to see Seb's still focused on the road. The distance is helping me to talk. "The way you take control is sexy and comforting and makes me want to do as you say, but when you're not with me, my head comes into play and that's when I doubt what I'm doing." I don't want to say any more.

"Was that so hard?" Seb's voice is soft and soothing. Now he has me on the verge of angry tears.

"Yes. Yes, it was. You know I struggle with being open about my feelings. I am trying. I've tried so hard today, when all I wanted to do was shut everything out and switch off. I didn't. For you. I know what I said this morning was stupid but I'm shattered."

"Shh, sweetheart. You've done so well. Thank you. You even opened up to me without me prompting you. That is a great step for you. Don't be upset." His words send my tears welling over my lashes and my lip won't stop trembling. I stare out of the window, shielding my face so Seb won't see that I've cracked.

I think back to this time yesterday. We were on our way to Solace. Now, I feel emotional and raw.

Seb pulls me from the car, cocooning me as he walks me up to the apartment. I'm in a zombie state. My eyes are scratchy and dry, despite the tears, and I can barely lift my legs. He leads me safely into the bedroom and tucks me up into bed. I relax back on the pillow and fall straight to sleep, exhaustion overwhelming my body and mind.

I wake and peek at my phone. It's just after 8:00 p.m. There's no sign of Seb so I assume he's left me to rest. I stretch and climb out of my nest. I change and put some comfy PJs on then go in search of Seb. He's not in his office so I venture to the kitchen. The apartment is quiet and dark, and I wonder if he's gone out. My heart sinks.

"Are you feeling better?" Seb's deep voice shocks me and I reach for the breakfast bar in fright.

"Jeez, Seb. You scared me."

"I'm sorry." He comes out of the shadows to stand next to me.

"Are you hungry? You've not eaten." Seb moves past me and into the kitchen, opening the fridge and pulling out some leftovers.

"A little. I'm sorry. I've slept the evening away."

"You needed the sleep, and I don't mind. You've been through a lot. Are you feeling better now that you've got your feelings out in the open?" His question draws a frown to my face. I don't feel any better. My worries are still there and I take a deep breath.

"What if I'm not enough? What if I can't be the submissive you need?"

"You are, Izzy. I don't know what else to say. You need to start believing in us." He's not cross, but his tone tells me that he's exasperated with me.

"I do. I'm trying."

"Then what's the problem?"

"Can't you understand that this is happening really fast for me and I'm struggling to adjust to the changes? They might not seem like much to you, but they are for me. The small piece of independence I regained after leaving Phil is evaporating. I don't feel comfortable with that. I want to be the woman and the submissive you need, yet I want to keep my self-sufficiency as well."

Seb's quiet for a while. Something has shifted. He heaves a deep sigh and I hold my breath at what he's going to say next. "Come on. I'm going to run a bath for you. You need to relax before going to bed. I don't want you up all night again." He disappears into the bathroom and I hear the water begin to fill the tub.

I follow after him and wait in the bedroom. I'm not sure if he understands my point, but at least we're talking. He walks back from the bathroom and places a gentle kiss on my forehead. Tucking a lose strand of hair over my ear, he cradles my face in his palm. His soft smile tells me he's not mad anymore.

Slowly and sensually, Seb pulls my pyjamas off and leads me into the muggy bathroom. The tub is filled with bubbles and the scent of citrus lingers in the air. Seb takes my hand and helps me in. I lie back and relax into luxury.

"I'll be waiting for you when you're out."

"Thank you."

Seb leaves and I tap down the twinge of disappointment that he didn't join me. I should have asked him. Years in a bad marriage where it was easier for me not to express my feelings or desires have made it hard for me to voice my wants. I want our connection, his touch and his control to help me gain an understanding of my feelings, to help me understand him. I sink under the bubbles and dunk down into the deep water. The quiet swamps my senses and clears my mind. I concentrate on letting go of all my doubt and fear, to look for the positives and move forward. I emerge and let the water splash around. *Be positive. Don't let fear and doubt in.*

I leave the bathroom and towel dry my damp hair. The fluffy bath robe calls to me, so I slip it on and head out to Seb. He sits in the lounge with the lights on now. There's a small platter and two mugs on the table.

"All relaxed?"

"Yes, thank you."

He lies back on the sofa and pulls me between his legs. I snuggle into his chest. Being close like this immediately soothes me and I repeat my mantra from the bathroom—be positive. Don't let fear and doubt in.

"I've got an overnight stay in Manchester this week. I think the space may help you, ease the pressure you may be feeling."

He's right.

"But I don't want you to stop keeping in touch. That won't change, Izzy. You know that it's as much for me as you."

"I know." Seb leans over to grab a few grapes and feeds them to me. It's too late for a meal, but a few bites are very welcome, especially from his hand.

"You may feel this is too soon, but I've been waiting for you for a long time." When he says things like that, I feel like a stupid girl. Why can't I relax about all the changes that he's introducing? Why can't I go back to how I felt when we only had a few stolen moments together?

"I know, but please… Please try and see it from my side as well. My entire world has changed. The routine I'm used to,

159

what I can and can't do, having someone who actually cares for me. It feels overwhelming, Seb. I love you—so, so much, but perhaps we can slow down?"

"We'll find our way, Izzy. Talk to me, and tell me your fears. It's the only way I can remove them."

"It's not just about my insecurities. I have to learn to be the Izzy I want to be with you. Being with Phil was all I knew. Please be patient with me."

"Let's focus on communicating with each other. I know you've learned to bottle up and not speak your mind. You don't seem to have any problem when I dominate you at home so I'll continue to do that."

"That sounds good." He rewards me with a bite of chocolate.

* * *

"Izzy, this report makes for great reading. You've made some great percentage increases from the stats six months ago. Well done."

"Thanks, Mark."

"Keep up this work and I'll talk to management about making you a senior account manager."

"Really?" I'm scurrying to pack my bag. At his words, I stop and look at Mark.

"I'm serious, Izzy. Well done. Your added hours and effort haven't gone un-noticed."

"Thank you. I know I've been a little… inconsistent."

"As long as your work doesn't suffer, I'll put up with your inconsistent attendance. Now, go home. I'll see you tomorrow."

My smile is completely genuine. Mark wanders back across the office and I continue to straighten my desk. My phone vibrates with a reminder to text Seb. I hastily fire off a quick message, eager to get home and tell him the good news. I stuff my iPad and a few files into my bag and nearly run out of the office. It's about time I had some good news to tell Seb.

The last few weeks have been a mix of trying to find the right balance between us. While he's been away, I've had to focus hard and not go to my dark place. Seb's been aware of that and has helped by phoning me regularly. Work has been a fantastic distraction and my hard work has paid off.

I can't stand the checking in via text message. I understand that he's concerned for me and my texts reassure him I'm safe, but it doesn't help. All of the personal detail, the cheeky and often blatant sex texting has dried up. I miss it.

I march down to the car park, eager to get home. Being away from Seb always exaggerates my feelings. His presence grounds me and offers the reassurance that other forms of communication can't.

"Izzy, can we talk?"

"Phil!" I'm startled, dropping my car keys as I approach my car. "You scared me." My eyes search the car park, looking for witnesses.

"Sorry, I didn't mean to." He sounds defeated, sombre even. His change in mood sets off every suspicious fibre in my body. He was shouting his demands the last time we spoke. *What's changed?*

"What do you want, Phil?" I grip the keys in the palm of my hand, feeling certain his anger will show any minute.

"Please, Izzy. Hear me out. I'm not here to fight. I promise." Him saying he's not here to fight doesn't help my nerves. In a matter of weeks, he's gone from someone I shared a house with to a man that I'd cross the street to avoid.

"I need to get home, and I'm not happy about you just showing up like this at my work."

"I'm sorry. Look, I've been thinking and I've made some bad decisions. I wanted to apologise." His face sports a five o'clock shadow of scruff and the bags under his eyes rival

161

mine at their worst. Despite his sorry appearance, I can't let him talk his way out of everything he's done.

"I don't have anything to say. You refused to talk to me, to hear me out when I wanted to do this amicably. My solicitor told me you've acknowledged the divorce petition and that you'll be defending it." He can't expect me to just forgive and move on.

"I'll withdraw my defence, or whatever I need to do. I won't fight the divorce, but I hope that it won't come to that. I want another chance. I want us to work. I miss you, Iz. I've been a wanker." His outright apology floors me. *What? Why couldn't we have had this conversation months ago, when I needed him to listen to me and admit that things were broken?* I stare in shock, not sure what I can say. "Iz, will you give us another go?"

"Another go? Are you serious? After everything you've said and how you've treated me? I wanted us to end as friends. We've spent nearly half our lives together, but you couldn't respect that enough to come clean to me. I needed you to be there for me and you chose to give up." My forgotten hurt and disappointment at the failure of our marriage is now vibrating through me. "I'm not innocent in this either, Phil. I'm seeing someone and I'd like to be able to move on. I should have asked for the divorce a long time ago, but I didn't have the courage."

"I don't care what you've done. We've both been bad, but I need you, Iz. I love you. Please... I'll do anything."

"No, Phil. Stop. I don't love you anymore."

He's getting agitated, desperate to make me listen to him. "I'll do the bedroom stuff. I'll tie you up and spank you. I'll make it good, for both of us." He grabs for my wrists, pleading with me. I shake him away and back up against the car.

"No! This isn't going to work. I won't change my mind."

"Please, I'm begging you. I love you. I've been an idiot. Come on, just think about it. We love each other."

"I'm sorry, Phil, but it's not that easy. I don't want to be with you anymore. I want the divorce."

"That's it? It's over?"

"It's been over for a long time." That I've not backed down seems to stump him.

"Please, don't do this. Give us some time. We can work it out."

"No. I'm not backing down. Are you still going to fight this?" It will be a hell of a lot easier if he doesn't defend the divorce. We can both move forward. I wasn't looking forward to having this strung out in court.

My question hangs in the air and I hold my nerve.

"No, I won't continue to defend it."

"Thank you." I release a sigh, relief draining me of all my nervous energy.

Phil creeps backward, tentative in his steps, as if he's unsure of what to do next. I watch him turn and leave without a backward glance. For the first time in months, I feel lighter. Things are finally going the way I want and I have some semblance of control over my life.

I slump into the car and lock the doors. Adrenaline from my confrontation with Phil makes my body tremble. This face-to-face might have ended on a calmer note, but I've not forgotten how angry he was the other day. I text Seb to say I'm heading home. I don't mention Phil. That information is better handled in person.

The tremors finally cease as I pull into the parking space at Seb's building. Phil's behaviour didn't show any of the aggression that I had come to expect from our previous confrontations. His lack of anger is unnerving all on its own. I've learned not to trust his word and I know I should take his visit with a pinch of salt.

"I'm home," I call as I push the door to the apartment open. It's been a long and tiring day and I'd like nothing more than to soak in a bath under a mountain of bubbles.

Seb's sitting in his chair in the lounge as I walk into the apartment. He's holding a tumbler of amber liquid and looks as tired as I feel. Seb doesn't usually drink, so seeing him with a glass this early is different.

"Good day?" I ask in a hopeless attempt to lighten the mood. I can already feel the tension sparking in the air.

"Not particularly. You?" He doesn't look at me and proceeds to sip his drink.

"As a matter of fact, yes. I have some good news and later I'm going to reward myself with a long soak in the tub." Seb's eyes flash to mine at my suggestion.

"That sounds like a great idea. First, I want us to talk. Come." He beckons me over to sit by his feet. It's the place that I've always found comforting, and I know that I won't struggle to talk when I'm there.

I lower myself to the floor and let the familiar feeling at being in this position calm my nerves. As soon as I stop fidgeting, he starts to smooth my hair. His touch sweeps away all of my tension and stress. The gentle caress lulls me into a dreamy haze. My eyes drift close and my breathing slows. His touch is hypnotic.

"I know you like this. Tell me your good news."

"Well, Mark is really happy with my work. I told you I've been doing more client work, and it's paying off. He said if I can keep it up he'll make me senior account manager." With Seb's relaxing caress and the good news, I feel blissful.

"That's fantastic news. I know how hard you've been working recently. Congratulations." He places a gentle kiss on the top of my head. My body lights up with shivers. "Why didn't you let me know earlier?"

"I didn't want to share the good news in a quick text. Plus Mark only told me as I was rushing out the door."

"They don't have to be quick, Izzy. You're choosing to see them like that because you feel you're checking in. We've been over this before."

"I'm sorry. I know we have, but I still feel the same way about them. Texting used to be nice, and sometimes it still is nice, but not when I have to stick to a schedule." My happy mood fades into the past.

"I've been thinking about what will help you feel more confident about my feelings for you. I thought that telling you I loved you would be enough, but I know you still have doubts."

"I know you love me. I don't have any doubts about that." I'm quick to reassure him. I don't want him to think I don't believe him. I turn and pull myself up on to his lap. "I love you and I know you love me."

"But…?"

"Does there have to be a but?" I look at his chest, hiding as I know what's coming.

"But you still don't think you're enough for me. You still worry. So…" He pulls me into him and wraps me tightly against his body. "I think we should move, get a new place together that's just for us. It can be our home. We can build it together."

I look at Seb, the concern now gone from his face. It's like him asking me to move in with him all over again. I'm trapped between screaming at him and hugging him. My voice is trapped inside my throat. I don't think I'd be able to speak, even if I knew what to say.

"Are you going to say anything or just stare at me?"

"I'm not sure what to say at the moment. We're already living together."

"I know. But I want us to start building our future together. I understand that you have insecurities and I want to help ease these for you. I want to show you that you're it for me. Having our own home will help. You can stop worrying if you know you'll be enough for me."

"I can't commit to something as significant as buying a house with you, just like that. Besides, I don't have any money and I won't until the divorce becomes final and the house I owned with Phil is sold. Hopefully, I can avoid a court date now and things will move a little faster."

"Oh, why's that?"

My heart stops and my stomach lurches. I try to sit up on Seb's lap but his arms have turned to steel bands, locking me to him. "Have you spoken to him?" Seb's voice has gone eerily soft.

"Yes."

"When was this?"

"He caught me as I was leaving work." I know that I should have told him this first, but I wanted to have the good news before the bad.

"I've been quite clear that you're to tell me every time you have any contact with him. Fuck, you were cowering behind your door when I came to pick you up at Jess's." He jostles me from his lap and starts pacing round the room. Guilt assaults me as I realise how badly I screwed up, even though it was unintended. *Stupid Izzy!*

"I just wanted to come home and tell you the good news."

"Well, that's what I was hoping for as well—to share something with you to help you. Us!" He fists his hands in his hair and I can't escape from feeling like a silly little girl. "I've tried time and time again to get you to be more open with your feelings and communicate with me. It's the first rule we had. After everything we've been through, I'd hoped that you could at least talk to me now. Clearly, I was wrong."

No, no, don't... I can.

"Seb, please. I wanted to have some good news to share with you today. I've been better at talking."

"Yes, when I push you. You offer less now than you did when we were first together. Despite everything, I can't get through to you." I stand still, watching Seb pace like a caged animal. "I hate that he was anywhere near you, Isabel. I know you can't do anything to speed up the divorce, but that decree absolute can't come quick enough." Seb heads over to the kitchen, pours himself a drink and swiftly downs another. He walks straight past me and heads towards the door. "I'm going to go out for some air." He doesn't turn around and slams the door as he leaves.

I've had too much alcohol to drive. I smash through the lobby doors and start along the pavement. I need to get my frustrations in check. Izzy doesn't seem to understand my feelings for her; as much as I try to show her, she doubts. I'd hoped that being together, her confidence would grow, like it did when we first started seeing each other. Being connected to that shit of a husband keeps crippling her self-confidence, no matter what I do to help her. Fuck! My mood is darker than it has ever been, and I know that unless I get this ache, this pain, out of my system, I won't be able to go back to her tonight.

My phone vibrates in my pocket and I pray that it isn't her. I slow my pace enough to dig my phone out of my trousers and see Natasha's name on the screen.

> Hey, stranger. Do you fancy a drink? Or I could meet you at Solace. Nat.

> Drink. I'm walking into town now. We can meet. S

I should have known that would warrant a call from her. My phone rings in my hand before I get a chance to put the damn thing away.

"Hello, Natasha."

"Don't give me that tone, Sebastian. Why are you walking into town? It's a forty-five minute walk."

"I've already had a few drinks tonight and I need to clear my head." I haven't slowed my pace. I drive my excess tension into every step.

"Where are you?"

"I'm about five minutes from my apartment. I'll wait for you outside the Costa."

"I'll be there in a few minutes. Do you want to go for a drink or to Solace?"

"Drink. I'm in no state to be at Solace." I know that she's not going to let that comment slide, but right now, I don't give a fuck. She might be able to shed some much-needed light on the unresolved issues I have with Izzy.

Twenty minutes later, we're sitting in a quiet bar of a boutique hotel that Natasha loves, on the outskirts of the city. I turn the heavy glass tumbler around in my fingers, watching the amber liquid ripple in the glass.

"You don't often brood. It's unbecoming." Natasha has allowed me the time on our journey here to compose myself before her scrutiny begins. I knew it would be coming.

"I've never been in a position like this before."

"So why are you brooding?" She sits back and waits.

"Isabel is challenging every part of my self-control and I am struggling with how to deal with that." She lifts her perfectly shaped eyebrow, offering a disapproving stare. No words are needed. I know that she's waiting on the full story. "Isabel and I had a fight. I've set some expectations regarding how we communicate and she's struggling with them, to the point of being disobedient."

"You're being purposefully vague. I've been away for two weeks. We don't see each other regularly, but who the fuck is Isabel? I swear, Seb, if she's another vanilla sweetie playing at being a sub just to screw you…"

"No." My tone leaves no room for question, and even though Natasha is a Domme, she understands when to stop.

169

"She is a beautiful submissive. Vulnerable, yet strong. Sexy as sin and everything I want."

"So why are you here with me and not with your sub?"

I take the next half hour explaining how Isabel and I got together—our initial friendship, the coincidence of meeting again, her first trusting step into my world. It brings all of the feelings we had—our story—back to my mind, and the frustration and anger ebb away. Natasha listens dutifully. The murderous look she gives me when I gloss over the point where I went up to Manchester tells me that she certainly doesn't approve.

"You abandoned the woman you love?" This time it's her tone that leaves no room for question. "Not only do you love her, she is your submissive. You effectively scened with her and then left her aftercare to no-one. You fucked up, Seb." My opinions on the events before Christmas are different to Natasha's, but they still hit a nerve.

"I don't see it like that. I told her I wouldn't continue our relationship as an affair. She needed to hear it. It was her choice what to do next. I made my intentions very clear to her." I down the scant inch of liquid left in the glass and head to order another from the bar. I bring back two filled glasses and sit back down, steeling myself for the rest of this conversation.

Natasha has been my mentor, if you will, from my first foray into BDSM. She introduced me to what being a Dom meant and brought me to Solace. She's helped me to navigate my way through the world that I've always wanted to share with the right person. We have, on many occasions, locked horns on what's right for me. She doesn't understand my reluctance to play with a different submissive each week. She's happy being a Domme and isn't looking to settle down. I constantly battled with finding the right woman who didn't scare at the first show of handcuffs.

"So, you fucked up, in my opinion, but you still have her. Explain." She won't back down on her opinion on how we ended. For now, I'll let her have it.

"She left her husband. I wasn't about to wait for her more than I already had, so I moved her in. I wanted to push to see how far her submissive streak went, so I proposed a TPE on two occasions a week." That's what I want. Total Power Exchange. Natasha picks up her glass of water and lets me continue. "As well as that, I imposed some rules around keeping in contact. It was to keep us connected, especially when I was away for work and so I knew if her idiot of an ex came near her." Thinking about Phil brings out my possessive streak like nothing else. Izzy is mine, body and soul.

"So why are you brooding?"

"Izzy is struggling to find her way with the TPE I introduced, as well as some trust issues. She's fighting against what she wants to do and what she believes she should."

"And as her Dom, it's your job to guide her."

"I am. I've backed off. I know I can't press her too hard, but at the same time she needs reassurance, consistency. She needs to believe that she's it for me."

"Is she?"

"Yes." I look at Natasha, daring her to challenge me on this. Surprisingly, she doesn't. She smiles.

"So…"

"She lied to me about why she came home late. Her dick-wad of an ex showed up, and instead of telling me straight away, she told me the other news about her day. I told her that I think we should get our own place. Something for us, but she doesn't want that, which is fucking ridiculous because we already live together." I don't mean to sound so much like a petulant teenager, but I can't help myself.

"You're frustrated."

171

"No shit." I down my drink and nurse the empty glass on the table.

"Why are you frustrated?" I think about her question. It's lots of things; that Izzy and I are struggling, that we haven't found that perfect balance that seemed to come so naturally when we were seeing each other before. I'm frustrated at myself and at the fact that Phil is still in the picture. I want her to be mine and she won't believe in that until she's divorced. I'm all in with her, mind, body and fucking soul, and I'd marry her tomorrow if I could.

I don't answer her question and instead grow more agitated with my own thoughts.

"Okay, so why did you ask her to move? You said she's already living with you."

"She's moved into my place, yes, but I want more than that with Izzy. She's a beautiful woman who, at the moment, needs my reassurance. I thought that we could start afresh with our own place. Somewhere for us to build memories, not tainted by the circumstances in which we met or the women in my past. I hoped that she would see this as a step forward together."

"This is new for you. You've found 'your one' and now you're rushing to cement that relationship the only way you know how. By control and force. What about the TPE? How is she responding to that element?"

"I started light. I explained that I wanted to explore it with her. She would light up from within when she submitted, like she could let go of all of her worries and finally be who she wants to me. I want to see more of that Izzy."

"Good. But you need to remember that she's vulnerable, sensitive, and probably more so coming out of a marriage. You may be doing it in your ever-so-caring way, but you're still pushing her. Hard. Give her some time."

"I'm doing everything I can to offer her what she needs, to show her how much I love her, but it hurts that she doubts that."

"Do you think she really doubts your love or that she's struggling with her emotions?"

She raises that eyebrow again, challenging me.

"Fuck." Natasha's words make a lot of sense.

"Yes, indeed. What's she telling you? Communicating to you? Why did she not tell you about Phil right away? Why is she struggling with some aspects of her submission and not others?"

I let out a huge sigh. This has been a barrier for Izzy since the beginning. She struggles to express her feelings.

"She's not the best at keeping me informed about how she's feeling. I've been working with her on it and been straight from the beginning. She knows the importance of being open and honest with each other."

Natasha considers my words before issuing her advice. "You're giving her time and space. Maybe some of these issues are Izzy's to conquer and not for you to slay."

Natasha's words sink in, but they don't provide me with the same confidence that they usually do. Natasha has always been into the temporary relationship element of D/s. This is out of her sphere of experience just as much as it is mine. I stare into my drink, considering the benefits of one more kick of alcohol through my system. It will certainly help me to sleep in my empty bed tonight.

"Are you going to drink that or go home?"

"Home." I stand, a solemn weight hanging around my neck. As Isabel's Dominant, I should be able to anticipate her needs, be there to comfort and protect her, build her confidence and trust. Right now, I'm not, and Izzy isn't helping the situation. I need to look at why she's struggling and try to help her. I need her open to me. No more barriers.

The car ride back to my place is filled with silence. Natasha pulls up outside my building and I hesitate when leaving the car.

"Thank you."

"Don't wait so long next time. Just because you're a Dom doesn't mean you aren't allowed to ask for help or guidance. Will you bring her to Solace?

"I already have." I can't help the wicked grin that spreads across my face at that memory.

"Oh, I can't wait to see that."

I shut the door and let her pull away. I decide on two things before I make it back to the apartment. One: I will get Izzy to talk to me, and I'm going to show her that it can be a very pleasurable experience. And two: I know that Izzy loves me. She needs time to trust in our love, and I'll give it to her.

Eighteen

It's past ten when I finally hear the front door open. I've stayed in my room all night, not wanting to risk being in sight when Seb finally comes home. All I've had for company are the sad and disappointed thoughts of what led to this.

My body tenses and I strain to hear whether Seb will come and see me.

Soft steps grow louder. They stop and I hold my breath, hoping with everything that I have that the door will creak open. Painful moments tick by. Pressure crushes my chest as the door remains closed. His steps sound again, passing my room. He doesn't want to talk with me. *Where has he been?* No! I force that thought away and reach for my phone.

Jess, I've messed up. Help! Izzy

What have you done? I'm sure it's fixable.
Jess

I hope that she's as optimistic once I've explained.

Are you still up? Can I call? Izzy

Sure.

"Hey, so tell me what's happened?"

"We had a real fight."

"Honey, don't take this the wrong way, but couples fight."

"I know, but I did something stupid."

"What, and you think that Seb's just going to end things? I know what you're like, woman. You jump to the wrong conclusion every time. Did you not listen to me last time we spoke?"

"I did and I know that we'll need some time."

"Then what's the problem?"

"I didn't tell Seb that Phil was waiting for me by my car at the end of the day. Phil told me that he wanted another chance. I told him it didn't change anything."

"Serves him right. He's crazy, Izzy. You need to stay clear of him."

"It's not like I asked for him to scare me half to death as I was trying to get to my car."

"Alright, calm down."

"Seb wasn't very happy that I didn't tell him straight away."

"You lied?" she says. "But you know Seb is, like, super freaky on the Phil front."

"I didn't lie. I was going to tell him when I got home, but I wanted to share some good news first. Mark is going to put me up for a promotion. I wasn't keeping him in the dark. Then Seb mentions getting a house together." I let my sentence trail off.

"Izzy, why are you struggling so much with this? He wants to keep you safe and keep an eye on you. Most women would be over the moon if their partner showed that much attention. You do the control thing in the bedroom. I don't understand. And what house stuff?"

Jess has summed up my quandary. I'm not even sure why I'm having trouble, but I am.

"Seb asked me to move in with him."

"What do you mean? You're already living with him."

"He means buy a house together, or rather him buy something for us."

"Wow! What's wrong with the apartment?"

"Nothing. He said that he wanted this for us. He thinks it will help with my worries over being enough for him, but it just makes things worse."

"You're going to have to spell this one out for me, Iz. I'm not sure why you had a fight about this. I can understand the Phil thing, but you're already living with him."

"I'm struggling with everything that is happening. I've gone from Phil not caring about what I do, to Seb who wants me to check in every other hour. Seb loves me fiercely, but that's not enough to make a relationship work. I thought I loved Phil. I thought we would be together forever, and look where that got me. Plus, there are aspects to our relationship that I'm not yet comfortable with. It feels like I'm losing a part of myself when I agree to submit to him when we're not physically together. Like I'm losing the independence I have. I didn't realise the extent of control I would need to give up to have a relationship with Seb. And what if he's not happy unless I can do it all?"

"And the house thing?"

"I can't let him buy us a house. I have nothing to put into it until the divorce is over. Then, maybe, but Seb has everything on fast forward. I just want to slow down and build on our relationship."

"Have you told him that?"

"I thought I had. We talked about taking the submission a step at a time. We were doing that. Now this."

"You need to talk to him. Properly. Pretend that you're talking to me, like you just did."

"I know. He hasn't come in to see me, but I know he's back."

I'm quiet for a while, trying to put all the pieces of my muddled brain in order.

"You still there?"

"Yes, yes... I was just thinking."

"Talk to him. He loves you. You love him. Don't make it harder than it is."

"Okay, thanks. How are you, anyway?"

"I'm fine." Her voice is nonchalant, clearly brushing off my concern.

"Really? And Greg? How are things with him?"

"Fine. Nothing much to say." I know that Jess doesn't offer up details until she's ready to talk. She'll tell me in her own time.

"Thanks, Jess. I'll let you know what happens."

"You better. Good night."

After I finish with Jess, the room is deathly quiet. I tiptoe to the door and press my ear against the wood, listening for any signs of life. There are none. I grasp the handle of the door but stop. *Should I go to him?*

I open the door and creep into our bedroom. Seb is lying in bed, half propped up, his arm draped across his forehead. I attempt a stealthy approach, wanting comfort from him above anything else now that I see him. With his free arm, he lifts the covers, and I grab on to his invitation, snuggling up against his chest. He drops the covers back over us.

"Tomorrow, we talk. Now, I need to sleep," he groans to me.

"Thank you." I can talk to him and I'll be open and honest. I'll tell him everything I told Jess.

As soon as my alarm sounds, I wake up and head to the kitchen to make coffee. Seb is still asleep in bed and I can wake him as I would on one of my submissive days. The kitchen is dark and quiet as I enter, and I make short work of the task.

I tease the bedroom door back open, determined not to wake him, and place the cups down as quietly as possible. Stripping my cami-top and shorts off, I slip under the covers and up to Seb's warmth. I slide my hand up his back and over his shoulder, pulling him back against me, then I lean over to place a kiss against his lips.

He stirs and opens his mouth at my request. As I deepen the kiss, his arms wake and pull me down to him. We're lost for a moment, the events of last night firmly in the past.

"What are you doing?" Seb mumbles behind the kiss.

"I'm kissing you awake." I look down and offer a small smile, suddenly nervous that my plan to offer my submission isn't what he wants.

"You have coffee?"

"Yes."

"Is this because you're giving me control today? Please be clear with me."

"Yes, Sir."

"Do you have your anklet on?"

"No, I don't need it. I want to show you how serious I am and that I know I messed up yesterday." I sit back on my heels and lower my head, waiting to see how Seb will respond.

"Are you sure? You've been hesitant and I've been taking things gently these days. Today, I'm not in a soft frame of mind." His veiled threat sends a shiver through my body. His voice resonates deep within me. Nervous butterflies dance around my stomach, adding to the tension coursing through my limbs. Like this, in a sexual way, I have no concerns over submitting.

179

"Yes, Sir." I breathe the words, confirming that I'm handing myself over to him. I know he'll want me to communicate and I know that I need to.

"Good," he growls. He lifts my head and places a soft kiss on my lips. "Put on your robe and nothing else. We're going to talk over breakfast. I'll cook." He pulls on a t-shirt, boxers and jeans and leaves me. I grab my robe from the back of the en-suite door and follow him, bringing the coffee with me.

I take a seat at the breakfast bar and watch him go about preparing breakfast. My stomach grumbles in appreciation, having forgotten food last night. Seb doesn't start the conversation, and I'm left anticipating what he'll ask or say.

A plate of scrambled eggs and toast slips under my nose before he makes eye contact. I can't tell if his eyes hold the warmth I long for or the ice from last night still. His body language leaves no doubt that he's in charge. He's commanding. He holds the power.

"Have you thought about what happened yesterday?"

"Yes."

"Yes, what?"

"Yes, Sir. Sorry, Sir."

"I want you to tell me what happened yesterday."

"Okay, I was at work. Mark caught me at the end of the day to say well done. He said he'd put my name up for promotion. I was really happy. I finished packing up for the day and wanted to get home to tell you when my alarm sounded to text you. I sent the text and then went to my car. Phil approached me at my car and wanted to talk. I didn't really have an option. He asked if we could try again. He said he'd been stupid and wanted me back. I told him it was too late. I asked him if he'd change his mind about defending the divorce. He agreed. I picked up my keys, got in the car and texted you to say I would be late." I lay the facts out as simply as possible.

"Go on."

180

"I got home and came up to find you drinking. I was worried as you seemed to have had a bad day. You wanted to talk so I told you my news and that's when you suggested that we buy a house together. I was concerned that we're moving too fast and suggested that we should wait until I was divorced."

"Good." Seb tucks into his food, forking several mouthfuls of egg, and gestures for me to do the same. I pick at the edge, not wanting to have a mouthful of food when I know Seb will want me to talk in a moment.

"Now, I want you to tell me, in exactly the same way you just told me about yesterday, why you are struggling to keep me informed by text." He goes back to his food, waiting for me to continue.

"I… I don't mind texting you. I used to enjoy it." I drop my head and pick a vacant spot to focus on while I try to open my feelings to Seb. "When you used to check in on me, I found it comforting and reassuring. Now I need to check in to a schedule, all thought and feeling has been lost for me. I know that keeping you informed shouldn't be difficult, but I don't like that it can interfere with my day and that I'll be in trouble for it. I don't see why I have to be so strict. You don't always reply back and that's fine, but if I don't check in, you act like I've made this huge mistake. I know we talked about it, but nothing has really changed for me. At the moment, the small things show me that I don't want you to have so much say over me when we're not together. It's different when we are, but it worries me that there might be bigger things I don't want to do and I'll end up like those other women. What if I'm not cut out for this?"

I've broken through my block. The words are coming more freely. Trying to keep to the facts and being calm and logical is helping.

"Well done." He leans over and runs his hand over my thigh. "Why didn't you tell me about Phil?"

"I just wanted to get home to you. I knew if I texted you about Phil, you'd worry. Phil seemed different this time. He was defeated. I've never seen him like that, and for once, I wasn't scared of him." Seb's finished his breakfast and turns to face me. He's watching all of my movements. He picks up on every shift or fidget.

"Okay. Have you finished eating? You've hardly touched it."

"My appetite seems to have deserted me."

"Alright. Come." He stands and walks into the bedroom, and I trail in his wake. At the edge of the room, I watch as Seb positions a large pillow in front of one of the posts at the foot of the bed. "Take off your robe and kneel upright on the pillow. Face the bed." I slip my robe off, move to the bed, and sink into the cushion. "Hold onto the post. Don't let go." As I wrap my fingers around the wood, tension steels my body, keeping me in position. "Do you remember when I used the crop on you so you'd tell me why you didn't want to sleep with Phil?"

"Yes, Sir."

"I'm going to use it again." My stomach drops and my skin awakens with goose bumps. "I'm not going to blindfold you. I want you to look straight ahead. Don't turn around. Understand?"

"Yes, Sir."

Seb's feet are quiet against the carpet but I know that he must be going for the crop. I do as I'm told and try to relax against my racing heart. He's done this to me before, but that doesn't settle the anxiety fizzing through me.

My palms are sweaty, and I struggle to hold my grip of the post. I try to think back to how it felt before, knelt down and anticipating what Seb would do. The same growing ache has surfaced, drawing my focus and raising my temperature. The first flicks tickle my back. Seb slides the popper down my spine and proceeds to flick soft bites across my lower back. My nerves crackle under the gentle caress. He moves his focus up my back and across my arms before hitting the tips of my nipples.

My breathing falters and I struggle to rein in shuddering breaths. He starts bringing the crop down faster and harder, careful not to hit in the same place. Seb covers my back, breasts and down to my bum with stripes, but he hasn't asked me anything. I'm panting now. The ache in my stomach is burning hotter than any other part of my skin.

"Why don't you want to get a place to call our own?"

"I do, just not yet. I want it to be a proper place for us. It can't be if I don't feel like I've given my part, Sir."

"What do you mean by given your part?"

"I want to help out with bills. That still stands. If you want us living together then don't make me feel guilty or kept. I need to contribute, have my own independence."

"Are you still worried about submitting to me on the days that we agree to?"

"Yes." The word is out before I can think it. The caress of the crop has focused my mind on the pleasure, making my answers automatic. A heavy 'thwack' sounds and then registers on my bum. *Oww!* "Sir."

"Why?"

"Because I'm not good at it. I struggle and want to question it as soon as you're not there. I don't want to disappoint you."

"And...?"

"I kept failing at the homework before. I don't want you to be upset or disappointed."

"And...?"

"And what?" He hasn't stopped the action with the crop. Pain, heat and pleasure morph into a lust-filled haze, lulling me into a rhythm that makes it easy to answer. The crop continues to fall relentlessly.

"What are you afraid of?"

"That my insecurities will take over and you'll get sick of having to reassure me all the time." My arms shake with the effort of keeping them in place. I want to wrap myself up. I've already closed my eyes, finding comfort in the dark.

"I love you, Isabel. Isn't that enough for you?"

"Yes, it is."

"But it's not." He pauses in his strikes and hits my bum harder than ever, as if he's encouraging me to speak the words.

"It wasn't enough for my husband. He said he loved me and still cheated. How can I be sure when I know I can't do everything you ask?"

He softens the crop, falling back to light kisses. "You are more than enough for me, Isabel. You are everything that I've ever wanted. You submit beautifully to me. You're beautiful and sexy. You challenge and inspire me. I love you. We're finding our own way, our story, remember. You let me take you to the club and you were so turned on I could barely see straight. If you're only comfortable submitting while we're together at home then that is more than enough." The crop finally rests, but I'm left with a buzzing from my skin. "Open your eyes for me, sweetheart." I slowly blink them open, but resist the urge to turn and find him with my eyes. I don't need to. He pulls my chin to the side so we're looking at each other.

"As much as I love using the crop on you to allow you the headspace to talk, I wish you'd open yourself up to me more freely."

Tears flood my eyes at his sweet words and I let them fall. No matter my fears, Seb is there trying to lay them to rest. He scoops me up and heads for the bed. "Do you feel better now?"

"Yes, Sir," I sniffle.

"Did you still get wet for me?" I look up at him, shocked and embarrassed at the same time. His sexy grin spreads across his face and he leans down to devour my lips.

184

* * *

We've not escaped the bedroom all day. It's been wonderful. Seb will be away for several days again next week, but since the episode with the crop, I'm not feeling the same sense of worry.

"Come on. I need to feed you."

Seb drags me out of bed and covers me in the thick bathrobe. He dresses in his jeans and t-shirt and heads out to the kitchen.

"Sit." He indicates the breakfast bar.

He quickly busies himself pulling ingredients from the fridge and setting water on to boil. Pasta is a go-to meal and right now that is exactly what I want.

"So, if you don't want to buy a house unless it's equal between us, how do you feel about looking for somewhere that we can rent together until we find the right house for us?" I thought we'd been over this already, but apparently not.

"Why do you feel that we need somewhere new? I like your apartment."

"I like my apartment, too. But I'd like a home with you. I want you to see that you are all that I want. Having something permanent like a house together might help reassure you." He doesn't look at me, just carries on chopping vegetables to put into a sauce.

I ponder the idea. Yes, it might be something to look to in the future, but I don't want him to just buy a solution to my worries. The fact that he wants to is part of the problem. The plus side would be a place that doesn't have half-naked women draped over the walls in the form of art. *This would work, but not just yet.* I can't help but feel bad that Seb is trying to do all of these things to support me and I don't want them. Getting free of Phil is what I need.

"Izzy? You alright?"

"Yes, sorry. I was just thinking. I've been horrible to you."

"Isabel, you have to work on your self-confidence, there is only so much I can tell you. You need to believe in us. You need to believe in our love for each other." He comes around the breakfast bar and holds my face in his palms. *Why can't I trust my love for him?*

He doesn't break our connection, and tears prick my eyes. "Tell me why you are crying. Talk to me."

"I love you. I want that to be enough. I'm just..."

"Phil has a lot to answer for. We need to focus on communication. If you can't talk to me, it doesn't matter if you satisfy all my sexual needs. We won't make it."

My heart clenches in my chest at his damning words. They stab pain right into my soul. More tears spring to my eyes and my breath stutters. *No, that's not what I want.*

"What do you say?"

"Loving you isn't enough at the moment. I loved Phil. We were married and it still ended badly. Horribly. I feel like you are trying to take control of my life, which I love when we're in the bedroom together. Outside, it feels like you're crowding me. I need time to come to terms with our relationship and the failure of my marriage. Moving into a new house isn't going to solve it." Hot tears stream from my eyes. Communication has never been something I'm good at, but I have been trying with Seb.

"That's better, sweetheart." Seb kisses me and wraps me in his strength. "We can wait on the house, but I do want us to have our own place eventually. I'm so pleased that you opened up." He begins to worship me with his lips, and it melts away the fear that I would be rejecting him by saying no.

186

Nineteen

"Hi."

"Hi, so, how did it go?" Jess is straight in with the questions. Seb is working in his study, so I'm taking the opportunity to talk to Jess about the developments.

"Good. We talked. Properly this time. We're going to wait on the house idea, and then I think I'd rather rent than buy something straight away."

"That makes sense. Was it so bad?"

"No. He told me I need to work on believing in us."

"I could have told you that. I don't understand it. He loves you and is determined to make you see that."

"Yes, I know."

"Well?"

I can see her giving me the eye through the phone.

"Hey, you know I find it difficult. Phil and I were meant to be forever. Even at the end it was a huge deal for me to move to get a divorce. Moving on and putting that much faith in a new relationship… it's frightening. How do I know it won't all happen again?"

"Is that what you're afraid of?"

"Amongst other things. Seb's going to be away for part of next week. Fancy doing something?"

"That sounds good. Anything in mind?"

"We could go shoe shopping and then grab something to eat. Nothing special, just some time together. You can spill the beans on Greg."

"I've told you, there's nothing to tell."

"Well, you've been seeing him a couple of months. That's good?"

"We'll see."

I hear Seb come in to the bedroom.

"Okay, I'll phone you about details for this week."

"Sure. Behave, and try not to get into any more fights."

"I won't. Bye." I finish the call as Seb appears in the doorway. He saunters over to the bed and perches on the edge. I crawl over to him and wrap my arms around his neck. "Have you finished your work?"

"For now. I've been thinking." Seb brushes my hair off my face and pulls me to sit on his lap. "I still want you as my submissive. I'll always want that, but I need for you to be confident and comfortable more than I need a submissive. I think you'll adjust once we're together with no baggage or worries, and then I can see how far we can explore the sexual element to us. You'll still submit inside our house, or when we're together, like at Solace. Everything else can wait." A concoction of relief and disappointment floods me. I tilt my head and rest it in the crook of his neck.

"We will get back to you being at my beck and call. Right now, I need you to believe in us, and in me."

"Promise?"

"I promise. Now, I know I said that we can wait on the house stuff, but if you get bored on your iPad, you can always start having a look at what you'd like." Without the pressure of having to move, the prospect of window shopping seems good.

188

* * *

Seb's busy in his study for part of Sunday, so I take the opportunity to look online to see what's on the market in the form of a potential new house. I don't even know what we should be looking at, so I just type in 'Bath' and '3 bedrooms' and hit search.

Dozens of pages of results are returned, but seeing the first few 'student' types, I quickly add some numbers to my search criteria. I know how much Seb's apartment must cost. This part of Bath isn't cheap, and the space is amazing. I don't even know if he rents this or owns it. *He must own it, surely.* Too many questions bubble through my mind so I set about quieting them. I pick up my iPad and walk towards Seb's study.

I haven't been in here since the first time he showed me around, and he hasn't been in here a lot of the time since I moved in. I slow my approach as I reach the door, my heartbeat picking up pace as I wonder if I should knock. Playing it safe, I tap softly on the wooden door.

"Izzy, you don't need to knock." Seb's answer is immediate and a relief. I crack open the door and slip inside. His laptop is open in front of him with a few sparse papers littered over the desk surface. The study matches everything else in the apartment. "You okay, sweetheart?" Seb looks at me, a hint of concern in his voice. I clutch the iPad to my chest and fidget at the door. There isn't another chair in the room and the desk dominates the space, situated dead centre in the room. Seb seems to understand my hesitance and nudges back from the desk. He pats his lap, telling me exactly where he wants me.

Once I'm settled, I begin my quest for answers. "What kind of place did you have in mind for us to look at?" I start with a general opener, knowing that Seb will have some clear parameters to work with.

"Do you mean in terms of the number of bedrooms or the type of house?"

189

"Well, both. All of it really. We haven't talked about what we'd like."

"I thought you didn't like the idea."

"I haven't changed my mind, but I wanted to take a peek at what we could rent when the time comes. I've only had the house I had with Phil."

He pulls me closer so his lips rest against the pulse in my neck. "Right now, I want a bigger study so I can lie you across my desk and eat you up." His tongue snakes out and licks my throat. Sparks dance down my spine and straight to my pussy. *How does he do that to me?*

His grip tightens around me, but his trailing hands and tongue move no further. "As much as I want you on my desk, I have to get through a lot of prep before I leave. If I get it done now, I won't be away for more than a couple of nights."

I try to keep the frown off my face, but my lips seem to be pouting of their own accord.

"Did you want to ask me anything else?"

Seb gives me one of his sexy smiles. Mischief flashes across his eyes, glinting blue and green.

"Would you be okay selling this place?"

"Sweetheart, we don't need to sell the apartment. I don't intend to sell it even when we buy a house together, let alone rent. I own this place outright. Look and see what you like and then we can talk details later." He eases me from his lap, signalling the end of this conversation. He's replaced my questions with more unanswered ones.

I leave and head back to the lounge. I close the search down and busy myself with my social media playground for the rest of the afternoon.

* * *

Sunday creeps into Monday and I'm kissing Seb goodbye. He'll be back Wednesday so it's only a few days at work to suffer through.

Despite all of the concessions he's made, the check-ins still stand when he's away from me. This time, I'm determined to make it fun. Despite not wanting to commit to something so big as a new place together, I see my future with Seb. So the idea of working out what he would like, what I would like, in a future home seems fun. I use the search I started yesterday and start sending him some options. As well as getting some much-needed information from him for the future, it is a way to keep things light between us. I'm excited, and for the first time, I look forward to our text talk.

By 2:00 p.m., I'm out of saved searches. I've also been un-productive, not something that I want to replicate. Mark is giving me more and more responsibility, and I don't want to let him or my clients down. Campaigns move so quickly you can't afford to be distracted. I allow myself today, sternly telling myself that tomorrow will be a better workday.

I pull up my search history from my iPad and refresh the search, pulling only newly listed properties. A beautiful sandstone townhouse sits in my results. With three bedrooms, it's close to work and has a floor plan that will work. My smile betrays my own excitement as I pull up the photos of the property. It has spacious rooms, and it's newly refurbished with all the room we could need. The layout is across three floors and would be ample for us. I look at the price and wince. It's in a 'stupid money' bracket. I send it to Seb anyway, although my excitement has deflated.

Seb has responded with quick, sharp texts to all of the houses I've sent him so far. I wait for his incoming message but it doesn't come. I click back through the images, picturing us in the rooms. *Would this be what I want?*

I call Seb, wanting to explain that the last house was a joke and that I can't see us spending that much money on a property that we're only going to be in temporarily. It rings through to his voicemail and I'm stabbed by disappointment.

"Hi. Will you call me? Speak later." I hang up after leaving my short message, close the iPad and try to concentrate on work. My phone vibrates and I snatch it up.

> Where do you want to go tomorrow? Addisons OK? Jess

> Sure, I want to shop first though. So 5?

> See you then x

Before I lock my phone, I fire off a message to Seb.

> Are you busy? I'm sorry if I was silly with the last house. Txt me back. Izzy.

An hour later, I finally hear my phone again.

> I'll call you later. In a meeting. S

I fight down my disappointment and get on with what's left of the afternoon.

* * *

Two glasses of wine on an empty stomach have not helped my disappointment and frustration that I've still not talked to Seb. It's past 7.30 p.m. and I've had nothing back since the text stating he was in a meeting. If the situation were reversed, he'd have dragged me out of my meeting by now and probably spanked me until I was sobbing. Finally, the phone I'm holding with a death grip vibrates to life in my hand.

192

"Hello?"

"Hi, Izzy, I'm just calling to say it's going to be a little longer before I can talk to you. I'll call you later." I can hear muffled voices in the background, but above them all, the unmistakable sound of a woman's voice calling for Seb. "I've got to go."

"Seb…" The line disconnects before I can say anything.

At least there were other voices. My mind is thinking positively for now. I pour the remnants of my glass of wine in the sink and make myself a quick sandwich. *Why is he still in a meeting? Who's he with?* Are these the thoughts of every woman who's in love, or just the ones who started their relationships with an affair?

After this afternoon, I've only texted a couple of times. Rationally, I know that he's busy at work, but he knows how I hate having to comply to this rule. We really need to discuss one another's expectations for when he's away. *One step forward, two back.*

I'm just leaving. I'll call you in 5 minutes.

Seb

It's just past nine. Although every single scenario has gone through my mind, I know that I'm being foolish. Seb loves me and I need to learn how to trust again.

"Hello?"

"Hello, Izzy. I'm sorry about today. I got stuck with a client."

"Okay."

"Are you alright?"

"Not really."

"What's wrong? I'm sorry that I've been busy, but you know I have to be away."

"I know, I do… who were you with this late?" I hold my breath for his answer.

"Samantha is the FD of the company I'm working with. I've been in back-to-back meetings all day." He doesn't elaborate, and I know I have let my past suspicion cloud my belief in Seb.

"Did you get my messages? I wanted to explain that the last one was a joke."

"I did, but I didn't think it was a joke. It has potential."

What? "Really? But it's so much money."

"I told you that doesn't matter."

"Yes, it does. I can't afford anywhere close to that, even after the house is sold."

"We'll talk more about this when I'm back, but please trust me on the money front."

"Are you a secret millionaire and haven't told me?"

"No." He chuckles. "I do have some significant investments, though, and I'm more than comfortable. Please, just look for a house that you think you could call home. And thank you for looking for options."

"I might not be ready to commit to moving in, but I will one day. I feel like I'm getting to know your tastes better. You really like the one I sent?"

"I think I'll want something more open plan for our real house. I want us to be together in a home that we can call ours. That's my goal."

"Okay."

"I promise I'll be available whenever you call tomorrow. I love you. I'll see you Wednesday."

"I love you, too. I'll try and keep you posted."

"Good night, sweetheart."

* * *

I order two take-away coffees and wait at the table by the door. Jess is running late, but we have plenty of time to browse for shoes. And by browse, I mean Jess trying to convince me *not* to spend a week's wages on a pair of shoes.

After speaking with Seb last night, I started looking on a few other sites to find a house that Seb would like as well. There was one, still with a stupid price tag, but the townhouse had an open plan feel on the ground floor thanks to some recent renovations. I sent it to Seb this afternoon and he's been positive about it. He's hardly a smiley face kind of guy, but 'that's more like it, space to have my way with you' was definitely a move in the right direction.

"Oh, sorry I'm late." Jess bustles into the coffee shop, sits down next to me and grabs the coffee waiting for her.

"Bad day?" I ask.

"Not especially. Well, partly. Doesn't matter."

"What's up?"

"Just work stress. I'm looking forward to getting some time with you, though. Come on."

We get up and start walking towards Milsom Street. I've made Jess my shoe shopping partner on many occasions and she knows the drill. We browse windows before heading swiftly to the Selfridges shoe department, search for a pair that catches my eye and then weigh the pros and cons. The cons usually consist of the cost.

"Seriously, Izzy. Don't you have a million pairs of heels?"

"That doesn't mean I don't need another pair. Come on. Why don't you try some on? There is nothing better than finding the perfect pair of heels. It's like unlocking a magic box of confidence and sprinkling it all over you." I turn my heel this way and that in the mirror, trying to decide if the Alexander McQueen court shoes are the ones for me.

"I like shoes, just not enough to spend hundreds of pounds on a single pair."

"You just haven't found the right shoe. Come on, Cinderella. Let's find you your magic. You never buy any when we shop."

"Izzy…" She groans at me as I pull her along behind me, surveying the options on display.

"Okay, let's start small. Black patent leather. Look, not too pricey and they go with anything." I wave the classic under her nose and her eyes brighten a fraction. *Gotcha!*

* * *

I order two gin and tonics as we're seated at the table. It's just past 6:30 p.m. and the restaurant is still quiet. We nestle our newly purchased shoes at our feet and start looking over the menu.

"So, Seb's away. How are you doing?"

I smile at her, unable to contain my grin. "We're having fun texting."

"So everything's back to normal?"

"I wouldn't say that. More like we're acknowledging that it's not going to be smooth and happy all the time. We're finding a few bumps."

"I told you that's fine. Don't panic."

"I know, and I think that I can see that now. It's alright that we're finding our feet. It doesn't mean that we love each other any less. He keeps reminding me that we didn't have a conventional start but that it doesn't matter." I smile at her and really feel the meaning behind those words. Finally, I can see it's alright. Our story will play out like it should, but the point is that it's *our* story.

"Well, I'm really happy for you. You deserve it. And he's alright about putting the brakes on the house?"

"Yes, although I did start looking at what options we had. I'm thinking of it like window shopping and looking is actually quite fun." I can't help beaming at her. I jump to the

196

edge of my seat and lean in towards her. "I found this one house, it's a renovated townhouse in the centre, just off of Pulteney Road. Jess, it's gorgeous. Open plan on the ground floor with an immaculate kitchen, a massive master bedroom on the first floor and two more upstairs."

"Wowzers, that's got to cost." She raises her eyebrows and proceeds to down her gin.

"I know, it does and we'll have to talk properly about bills and stuff once the divorce is settled. It's actually got me feeling excited, which is stupid because I didn't think I was ready. Can I get excited? I can, right?" The yearning is clear in my voice.

"Of course you can. It should be an exciting time for you. Don't hold back because you're not sure what you should be feeling." Her words pull on the torrent of feelings that have been plaguing me over the last weeks.

"Sometimes I don't know which way is up. My emotions and feelings have been going from flat and predictable to a rollercoaster. It's not that easy, Jess. My cheating husband has turned into an abusive stranger. The man I love moves me in, imposes rules which I struggle to follow despite wanting to please him, and I have yet to learn how to trust Seb being away when all I can do is think about all the times that Phil said he was working. There's been a lot. Sometimes I wonder why Seb puts up with me at all."

"He loves you. Hold on to that. Yes, it's complicated and scary and you have a shit ex to get rid of, but boil it all down to the fact that you love each other and are moving forward."

"How are you always the voice of reason?"

"I can spout it. Doesn't mean I have to follow it."

"Talking of, how's Greg?"

"Like I said the last time, fine. There's nothing to say. We've been on a few dates."

"Okay, I'll leave it. Do you want another?" I look at her empty glass and signal to a waiter. "I'm starving as well. Can we order?"

"Go for it."

We settle into our usual girly chitchat and talk the evening away. I text Seb on my way home.

> How was your evening? S

> Jess and I had a good time. It was nice to catch up. Izzy

> Thank you for keeping me in the loop. S

> I know we're trying to find our feet, but you said it helps you not worry. I would never do anything to spite you. Izzy

As the taxi pulls up outside the apartment, my phone rings and I see Seb's gotten fed up with the ping-pong.

"Hello?"

"Hi, where are you?"

"I'm just walking up to the apartment building."

"Good." I let myself in and call the lift.

"I'm in the lift now. I'll be inside in a minute."

"Understand me, Izzy. I know you'd never do anything to upset or hurt me. You want to please me and that causes you a certain amount of confusion. Don't worry, I'll be patient. I'm out of my depth with how I feel towards you sometimes, and it's not the most reassuring place for me. I like being in control, and when I can't be, I don't handle it well. It's not an excuse, but as you're trying to be honest, I need to as well." His words spear my heart and I struggle to hold back the tears that threaten. Seb has validated everything I'm concerned about and I feel safe and reassured.

"Thank you," I whisper, my emotions closing my throat and making it hard for me to speak. I dive out of the lift and rush to the front door.

"Izzy, are you still there?"

"Mm-hmm." I close the door and slump into Seb's chair, curling in on myself. I clutch the phone to my ear, suddenly desperate for any contact with the man I love.

"Talk to me, sweetheart. I can't see you or hold you."

"I'm relieved," I choke out. "Hearing those words... It really helps."

"I'm looking forward to talking when I'm home tomorrow."

"Okay. I love you."

"I love you too, sweetheart."

It's been a long week. Work has been crazy busy, and Mark is encouraging me to take on even more client projects. I love the additional responsibility and control that Mark affords me with the team.

I park in my usual spot and make my way up to the apartment.

The heavy wood door shuts behind me and I move to switch the lights on, but the switch doesn't work. I wiggle it a few more times, trying to force them into working and hoping it was just a fluke the first time, but no. They aren't working.

My sigh echoes in the dark hall as I pull out my phone to use as a torch. I walk tentatively over to the kitchen and try the lights, but still nothing. When I walk down and into our bedroom, there is a single candle burning on the side dresser. Beside it, there's a handwritten note.

Drop everything and strip. Kneel in the centre of the rug.
Sebastian.

I immediately drop my bag to the floor. I take off my coat and boots, followed by my dress, shirt and underwear. My heart beats fast and sends quivers of excitement through my body, making me wet. His command, his control over me, is a complete turn on, and despite everything, my submission sexually has never wavered. I now know how good it is when I let go, what giving over that control can release inside of me.

The rug is positioned away from the candle and I walk to it and kneel down patiently. Sebastian won't rush this, so I try to relax. This will play out how Seb wants it to. My acceptance will make it better.

"Very nice, Isabel. I want you to wait for me, just like that." His voice is distant, but his command is solid. I have butterflies in my stomach as a result of the adrenaline building in my veins. I try to relax once more, to block everything out of my head, but I'm finding it hard. My imagination is running away with itself. All the experiences Seb has shown me fire through my mind. "I know how you like the dark, Isabel. Do you like my surprise?"

"Yes, Sir." My breathy voice sounds sexy, matching how I feel.

"I'm going to try something new with you tonight. I've always wanted to do this, but I need you to relax for me, sweetheart." His words hit the pit of my stomach and I try to stop the anticipation winning. I feel his words on the back of my neck. He kneels behind me and brushes the hair off the back of my neck before kissing along my shoulder. He replaces his mouth with the tips of his fingers and caresses my skin. He lays a large bath towel in front of me. "Crawl onto your front for me and lie down on the towel." I lean forward and do as he asks. I turn my face to the side. I can't see much. The only light in the room emanates from the candle, which throws shadows of grey flickering shapes over the walls.

His palms start at my shoulders and run down each side of my spine until he reaches my bum. He squeezes and moulds me, instantly making me needy. "So beautiful, Isabel." With his lovely words, his hand smacks down on my flesh.

I gasp, but the initial sting fades quickly, replaced by the warming of my skin. He continues to spank me and I begin to squirm. He knows how much I like it when he does this to me. The reaction is guaranteed. I start to relax, the heavy hits sending pleasure coursing through me with each strike. "Lie on your back and stretch your arms over your head." I moan as I roll onto my back, unhappy about giving up one of my favourite treats. Sebastian is kneeling over me, his chest bare, with just his trousers on. I can see he has something in his hand but I can't make out what it is. "Don't move." I'm excited about what he's about to do and the anticipation bubbles through my veins. I've learned that the greatest rewards come when I follow his commands.

He pulls my right ankle to the side, then repeats with the other, so that he's kneeling between my legs. The object he holds comes into focus now, a flogger, the fronds falling around his hand. He sweeps the tassels slowly and teasingly across my stomach, up to my breasts and down my arms, back across my stomach and down my legs. I know the fronds will connect with me—my body is tensed, ready—but I don't know when. The wait is as exciting as it is nerve wracking. He continues his slow torturous trail across my body again and again.

"Please, Sir, please." I need to feel more than this light caress. I want to writhe under his touch, but he hasn't asked for that. I want to please him, and that means I must control myself to show him I can obey. Oh, god, I'm going to snap soon if I can't move. The tension in my body makes my legs shake. "Please, Sir, let me move."

"Not yet, Isabel. Keep still." With his words comes the first strike of the flogger across my breasts.

"Ahh!"

"Shh, sweetheart. I want to hear the flogger against your skin." I moan, but as Seb continues, I keep the erotic sounds of my pleasure in my head. The flogger warms every inch of my skin. Sebastian isn't punishing me, he's loving me with each strike. My body begins to pulse with his rhythm. "You're a beautiful pink all over. Now, are you ready?"

Yes. God yes. Please fuck me, touch me. Make me come!

"Yes." He's not touched me, yet the flogger has melted me.

"So eager, Isabel, yet you don't know what I have in store for you." A sliver of fear ices my blood. I'd assumed that this was what he was planning—commanding me to restrain myself, to keep still and quiet. He slowly rises to his feet and leaves me on the floor. My heart is beating a fierce staccato, but I trust him.

I can't make any shapes out, but I do see a change in the light. Sebastian returns and resumes kneeling between my legs, holding the candle in his hand. It lights his face and I can see the dark intent in his eyes. "Do you trust me, Isabel?"

"Yes," I whisper.

"Good girl." With that, he tips the candle and the first drop of wax hits my chest. The heat spreads out as soon as it lands, the initial pain giving way to a warmth that is soothing. He tips again, more wax this time, creating a line down the centre of my chest to my navel. Panic blooms and I cry out, not able to contain the pain from the heat. Just as I get used to it, the heat dissipates into my skin and the panic recedes. The added danger to what he is doing has my palms sweating. My mind is battling over the knowledge that Seb would never do anything to hurt me and the potential pain that he holds in his hand. He pours more wax onto me. Different places each time—my hips, my thighs, my chest again. My body is ridged and tense, getting used to this new feeling of being bound by my own will and fear. It makes me feel naughty and sexy and desired.

203

Each drop makes it easier to enjoy the pleasure that is left burning on my skin. The hot wax registers but makes my pussy ache and tests how much longer I can hold still.

Just as I'm expecting another flash, Seb pauses. He puts the candle next to me and gently traces the lines the wax has made with his fingers. It multiplies the bliss and stirs tremors through my muscles. The wax has cooled now and my skin feels tight. His touch is light and gentle, ramping up the growing need for a release within my core. Watching him makes me want to beg for more.

"I love your skin, Isabel. I love watching what you will do to please me, to obey me. Do you like the wax?"

Do I like it? His question makes me think, and I don't want to. I just want to feel. "Yes, I do," I purr and my reward is a punishing kiss. I'm trapped between him and the floor and I feel small and delicate, completely at his mercy. I surrender to his assault and let this new sensation fill me up. He's tied me and bound me in so many ways, but he's never restrained me just by his command before. It's heady. "Please, Sir. I want to touch you."

"Not yet. I'm not quite finished."

I groan, but try to focus my body. He straightens on his knees and picks up the candle. He drips wax along a similar path as last time. This time, it's less shocking and more pleasurable. Each drop spikes a pulse through my body ending in the centre of my core. I close my eyes and surrender completely to Sebastian, no longer anticipating or judging the pain.

The drops get bigger, splattering my skin again and again. The flash of heat forces me to cry out at the edge of the pain. *Is this too much? When is he going to stop? I need to slow down.* I open my mouth to say 'yellow' when Seb thrusts two fingers inside of me and I almost convulse on the spot.

"Yes. Oh god, yes." I'm already on the edge, the building of my orgasm suddenly on fast-forward to the crescendo. Hot wax drips over my nipples just as my pussy clenches around his fingers. The pleasure and pain mingle as my body shatters. I come violently. My hips buck and grind into Seb's hand. "Yes... oh, yes."

I feel weak, drained, my body still shuddering from the orgasm. My mind is shaken from the sweet torture. Seb withdraws his fingers and blows the candle out. I relax on the floor, a happy sigh escaping my lips.

"Oh, Isabel, I do hope you're not too comfortable there? I'm rather pleased with you. Seeing you come for me, welcoming the mix of pain and pleasure, has made me fucking hard. I'm going to fuck you. I don't think we've christened the carpet yet, have we?" Before I know it, he's pulled my legs around his waist and sunk himself to the hilt.

I moan in pleasure, my oversensitive clit and pussy giving in to his desire. He starts to thrust, hard and smooth, pulling my hips closer into him. His weight presses down into my shoulders. He pushes harder and harder. His hands grip me forcefully. My body begins to quake and my pussy tightens with each stroke. I need to let go.

"Isabel. I. Want. You. To. Come."

I bend to his will, my body surrendering to him. It doesn't take long for my climax to peak, sending ripples through my body. I reach my crescendo, heat flooding through my very being. He follows me and cries out my name before he stills.

"That was amazing. I've wanted to play with wax for a long time and you responded so well." We both take a moment, coming down from the high.

"Come on, we need to clean you up."

"Can we put some lights on?"

"Maybe. Later we can light some more candles." I can't see him, but I can hear the smile in his voice as I break out in giggles.

* * *

Everything is perfect.

Work is going really well, although Mark hasn't come through with the promotion he mentioned to me. I'm still working on the client side and progress is good with the campaigns he's already handed across. The strategy behind the social media campaigns is more exciting and interesting to me, and I'm showing that I'm good at it. I certainly would welcome the increase in pay.

Seb has been home the last few weeks and hasn't had to go away for work. We've established a slightly less intense means of staying in touch, and he's backed off the 24/7 submission for now. He is making up for that in the bedroom, but I would never complain about that.

"Hmm, what's for dinner? It smells wonderful."

"Pasta pescatore. It should be ready in a few minutes."

"Shall I set the table?"

"Sure." I start setting out the placemats and find an open bottle of wine in the fridge. "Izzy, your phone's ringing," Seb calls.

I rush through to the lounge to grab my phone.

"Hello?"

"Hi, Ms. Fields, this is Mr. Osbourn. Do you have a minute?"

"Um, sure. Is everything alright? It's rather late." Well, it's 6:30 p.m., so at least it's after work hours.

"I'm afraid that Mr. Fields hasn't withdrawn his defence of the divorce. I've received the full details of his answer to the divorce petition. I'd recommend that we still apply for the decree nisi and ask for a case management hearing for the court to decide if it should be granted."

"He told me he wouldn't object." My heart sinks.

"I'm sorry, Ms. Fields. He's sought legal representation. At this point, I can only tell you that a court date is likely soon and I'll be in touch regarding the preparations.

206

There will be some forms to sign as well as some additional information required to proceed with the decree nisi. I'll email you the details."

"Thank you." That's all I can muster. After I hang up, *Why?* Fat, ugly tears spill from my eyes as I contemplate the battle ahead of me. I wanted to be free. I thought I'd be able to start my life again with Seb.

"Izzy, I'm dishing up." My appetite for food has gone.

"Sweetheart, dinner… What's wrong?" Those words, in his concerned, chocolate voice, make the tears fall harder. I hold my breath and brush my wet cheeks, hiding my tears before I look up at him. He immediately drops to the floor in front of me and wraps me in his arms. "Baby, you need to talk to me. What's happened?" His voice holds an edge that wasn't there a moment ago and it's what I need to pull myself together.

"Phil is still defending the divorce and I'll have to get the court to get the decree nisi and that's if they agree with my case," I muffle, holding back more tears. Seb's body freezes around me before relaxing back and pulling me tighter. "I'm sorry. I know you don't want me to still be married."

"That does not matter. I fell in love with you while you were married. I've waited for you all my life. A little longer won't hurt. I want to help, though. Who have you got looking after the divorce? I'm happy to put you in touch with my legal team who can help you with any preparations for court."

"No, it's fine. Mr. Osbourn is good, he can't help that Phil's being a vindictive snake. I just wanted this to be over. " I take a few deep breaths and blink away the last of my watery eyes. As much as his words help, I need to resolve this myself. I should have been brave enough to get a divorce before starting things with Seb. I move out of his grasp and sit back in the chair.

"You don't have to do this on your own, Izzy. Let me help you."

"What can you do? He's contested the divorce and I need to wait for a court date. Mr. Osbourn didn't state on what grounds he's contesting, but he's going to send me all the details."

"Okay, but please, let me help you if you need it."

"I need to do this, Seb. This is my burden and my way of getting closure. Don't you see? Until I'm divorced, he is still in my life, and I hate that."

"I know, but that doesn't mean you have to fight it alone. We're a team, a partnership."

"Yes, but this should have been over before I started anything with you. Let me put it right. I need to make it right."

"It doesn't matter that you're still married. I know you love me and you'll be mine soon enough."

Fatigue grips my body and I can't face arguing anymore.

"Come on." Seb pulls me up and leads me to the kitchen. "Eat. It should still be warm. We can talk later." He sits me down and I proceed to poke at my food.

After a few bites, I put my knife and fork down on the plate and gulp down a large glass of wine. I know that's the last thing I need, but at the moment, I don't care. Seb is silent through our meal, but I don't miss his eyes trained on me.

I'm already in bed before Seb joins me. He's been quiet for the rest of the evening and my mood hasn't improved. Seb walks into the room and stands by the door. His posture is tense and I can tell, just by looking, that he isn't going to come to bed and sleep. He closes the door and leans back against it, making sure to make eye contact with me as he does. It sends a slight shiver through me, like an unspoken word between us.

After everything that has happened this evening, this was not what I had in mind. However, within these four walls, I am at ease with my submissive nature and want nothing more than to please Seb.

"Take off your nightdress and lie on top of the covers with your arms stretched above your head. Hold them there. Don't move. Understand?"

"Yes, Sir." I hurry to move into position, my heart kicking in at the tone of Seb's voice. I relax into the bed, letting my worries of a moment ago sink away. My breathing is the only thing I can hear in the room, and it further adds to my building anticipation. I keep my eyes on the ceiling, refusing to let my curiosity win over Seb's command.

"You've had a lot to think over tonight. I'm going to take that away from you. Stay in this room with me. Keep your mind on me and everything I'm going to do to you. Do you understand, Isabel?" His words are hypnotic.

"Yes. I understand."

He takes that as his cue to wrap his hand around my ankle. He pulls me down the bed and then pushes my legs wide, bearing me to him. I cling to my wrist, keeping my arms above my head. This will be my focus. My own self-restraint is what Seb will be testing, I'm sure of it.

His hands roam up my legs, forcing my legs wider apart. I look down my body, past my rising chest, and watch as he focuses on my waiting pussy. He's not gentle. His lips close over mine and he sucks hard before releasing and starting his assault with his tongue. He presses it along my seam and licks until he finds my clit. He flicks, then stops. Flicks, then stops. He only gives me a moment's pleasure before taking it away, but it still has the desired effect. I lift my hips as he pulls away, trying to keep our contact.

"Stay still. I won't tell you again." I groan at his warning. Seb's already brought me to the level where I want to thrash and pull against my self-imposed bonds.

Seb moves his attentions up my body, trailing wet kisses across my stomach and up to my breasts. I immediately feel my orgasm fade away. He bites down on one nipple while pinching the other. The pressure sends pulses of tension through my limbs, but I resist arching off the bed. My breasts grow hot and sensitive as Seb continues to lavish them with his version of pain. I can feel my pussy weeping in protest, feeling desperate for attention.

"You're beautiful, Isabel. So responsive to me. Your submission is such a precious gift." He stands to shed himself of his clothes before pressing his body against mine. He's flush against me, his erection pressing into my thigh. He bites my throat, licking and sucking at my pulse, and pinches my nipple. Everything he knows will get me to move—to break my self-imposed bonds—he's trying.

My whimpers grow stronger and the sound of my pleasure is echoing around the room. My legs are ram-rod straight, tensing to keep from moving, and I'm sure I'll have bruising around my wrists as I hold my arms in place. *Do not move, Izzy. Show him.*

Finally, Seb lifts up over my hips and positions his cock at my wet pussy. "The only words I want to hear from you are 'yes' and 'sir', understand?"

"Yes! Yes, Sir."

Seb thrusts into me and I continue to shout 'yes'. He pulls back before thrusting again and stilling while he moves his hand down to find my clit. He rubs the pad of his thumb over my swollen flesh and I have to fight to stay still. I want to let go, but Seb has given me control over my submission. He's finding ways to explore my sexuality within the comfort of my own rules.

His slow rocks start to build a wave of pleasure within me, ready to crash over and pull me under. When we're like this, I don't want to do anything but give in to his pleasure.

210

Seb's pace quickens and my pants match in pace. He shifts position and lies down, smothering my body under his. I stare into his clear eyes and force mine to focus. Tears prick my eyes at the intimate connection.

"You're mine. If only in body and soul. Nothing will change that for me. You need to believe me. Trust me." He emphasises his point by driving his cock deep into me, sending ripples of delight throughout my body. "Trust me. Trust us. I want all of you, Isabel. I'll wait, but I want all of you. Mine to cherish. To love. To adore."

My orgasm sparks and Seb continues his rhythm, driving me higher and higher. "Yes, yes, Sir. Yes," I scream as the wave finally hits. My body can't hold it all in and spasms pulse through me. I thrust my body against Seb, forcing him deeper and harder inside of me. My arms and legs stay put, never breaking the imaginary silk. Seb's hips piston back and forth, driving me to delirium with pleasure.

"Fuck, Isabel. You still want more of my cock. Come. With. Me. Be. Mine."

"Yes!"

We lie in a sweaty tangle of limbs as we both float back to earth. We're both quiet, the only sound in the room that of our deep breathing. My body twitches as Seb finally moves off me, sending little shivers across my skin as the cooler air chills my flesh.

He quickly pulls back the cover and we scoot under it, immediately seeking one another out.

"I've been thinking about us, Izzy, about our future. If I proposed, would you say yes if you weren't married?"

What!

"I don't know… maybe." My words are soft and betray the doubt in my mind. *Marriage?* The thought hadn't even crossed my mind, but clearly Seb's been thinking about it. If I don't want to get married again, will this be something else I won't be able to do for him?

I swallow down the tears that are strangling my throat. They burn and my eyes begin to blur. Seb's arms come around me to offer the comfort they usually provide. Today, I don't feel the reassurance or strength I've come to rely on.

"Do you need more time?"

"Yes… I love you, I love you so much. I hadn't even considered marrying again. Look at what happened the first time, I failed, and breaking my vows… well, being married wouldn't hold anything significant to me anymore. I'm sorry." My answer is strained. My first marriage was meant to last forever. Now, Phil's dragging out the divorce just to spite me.

We sit in silence as the enormity of Seb's question sinks in. I don't know what I can say to him.

"You remember that I'm away tomorrow for a few nights?"

"No, I don't want us to be apart. Do you have to go?" Panic courses through me. I sit up and face Seb.

"Yes. I do." He pulls away from me and heads to the bathroom.

"Seb, I'm sorry." He pauses in his steps but doesn't look back.

Twenty-One

The last two days have been miserable.

It's like I've lost all confidence in my own ability to make a good decision. Seb's been away, and even through our talks, I can hear the hurt he's trying to hide from me.

I keep talking myself around to being able to agree to marriage. I know it's what Seb wants. I can give him what he wants by saying yes. I just can't say that magic word.

How can marriage mean anything if I can disregard it one moment and agree to forever the next? I rub my ring finger where my wedding bands used to be. I took them off for Seb. I broke my vows for Seb. He's the one I love, but there is still so much for us to figure out.

Seb is so sure, so confident, but I can't even think about marrying him until I know that we're on sturdier ground. I have too many insecurities and doubts. I need to believe it as much as he does. I can't go through this again.

On my way home. See you in a couple of hours. S

Drive safe. Love Izzy

I pull myself off the sofa and head for a shower. The last thing on earth I want to do is hurt Seb, but I need to try to make him see my point. As much as I love him, I need to consider if marriage is something I want in my future.

Piling my hair on top of my head, I let the spray wash over me and hope it takes the tension with it. Things should be easy between us. I don't want to fight. I want to get lost in our passion and shut out the world. I scrub and lotion before towelling off and heading right to bed. If Seb's going to be a few hours, it will be past ten o'clock before he's home. I pick up my iPad and make a nest, content with waiting up to see him. Despite knowing that he'll want to talk and probably ask me if I have an answer, I can't wait to feel his arms around me again. I miss the comfort they bring.

"Izzy... Izzy, sweetheart." Seb's rich voice pulls me from sleep. "Hi, you don't look particularly comfortable in bed." I'm slumped at a jaunty angle, having fallen asleep.

"No, I must have dozed off."

"Well, you're awake now. Kiss me." I reach up and grasp his neck, pulling him to me. Our lips collide and I let myself get swept away. The feeling is still there. The heat, the excitement, the love. Everything I want and need from Seb is there the moment we touch. The relief is palpable, but I need more.

"I'm going to make love to you," he murmurs against my lips.

"Yes. God, yes."

* * *

The bed is empty when I wake. The alarm is blaring at me, but I'm holding out for five more minutes before I have to start the day.

We didn't talk last night. We made love. We poured all of our emotion into showing each other our love before falling asleep. Now, I need to face Seb and see how he's dealing with all of this. I get dressed and head out to the kitchen. Seb's back is to me. He's cooking breakfast, so I stand and admire the view. His broad shoulders and back make a distracting sight for first thing in the morning.

"I made you coffee. It's on the side." He doesn't turn to face me, but clearly he knows I'm watching.

"Thank you." I take a seat at the table and continue to watch as he makes an omelette. He places it on a plate in front of me before turning back to his.

I pick at the food, looking for the courage that I need to start any form of dialogue with him today. He joins me at the table and tucks into his breakfast. He hasn't made eye contact and isn't in a hurry to speak, either.

"Please don't do this. Don't shut me out."

He puts down his fork and turns to face me. "I'm not shutting you out."

"Then why won't you speak to me?"

"I don't want to upset you, so I was hoping we could just have breakfast."

My heart breaks at his words, understanding that he's hurting as much as I am. I reach for his hand and squeeze it. "I'm sorry, Seb. I love you with everything I have, but I'm not ready, and I don't think I will be anytime soon. You know how much marriage means to me and what Phil took from me. I'm not saying never. I'm saying I need more time."

"I'll give you all the time you need, Izzy, but please start believing in our future. You need to start seeing things past your divorce."

Seb gets up from the table and leaves me to breakfast. Maybe he's got a point. I have been putting so much faith in getting the divorce, assuming it will be this magical moment when I'm finally set free and able to move on. What if that's not what I get?

215

I grab my coffee and go back into the bedroom to get ready for work.

The day drags but I manage to stay on top of my work. I've got to take one of the other team members through my training slides as she'll be delivering any future presentations. It won't take long, but it's a reminder of how fate brought me and Seb together. Lucy is a bubbly girl who's so keen to present, she'll be a natural. She's not as knowledgeable as some of the others, but she'll deliver the content well. The one constant through all of the changes and trials has been work. I've been able to hold it together and actually prove that I'm better than I thought I was. I'm doing really well. Mark is giving me more clients to look after and we're meeting next week to go over his vision and, hopefully, my promotion.

I make my way down to the car and fire off a quick text to Seb to say I'm leaving. I dig through my bag to try to find my keys.

A heavy weight slams into my back, knocking me against my car and holding me there.

"You had to do it, didn't you? I've just received my invitation to court. You're divorcing me on grounds of my affair and you're going to parade it through the court." Phil sneers into my ear as he leans all his weight against me. My stomach rolls and my head starts to pound. I close my eyes and think about Seb. I struggle against his weight but he has me pinned.

"You are simply dragging this out, Phil. You can't refuse to divorce me. You've contested it. The court will decide now. Why don't you just save us both the time and the money and stop this now." My voice betrays the fear gripping my body.

His weight lifts from my body and I take a much-needed breath before he twists me round. Pain flares across my cheek in a flash. I recoil from the force he uses, cradling my face from his assault.

216

"Get in the car," he growls at me, the pungent smell of stale alcohol on his breath. The point of a kitchen knife is levelled at my stomach. I look back to his face. Fury fills his eyes as he stares me down. I dig in my bag with shaking hands for my keys. As I fumble, I tap out a cry for help to Seb.

Phil, help

"Hurry up!" I find my keys and open the door. He shoves me down into the seat before rounding the car and sitting in next to me. "Now, drive home. We have some things to discuss." He rips my bag from my lap and dumps it in the back seat before pressing the knife tip against my ribs.

I fight the hysteria threatening to take hold of my body and will my arms and legs into action. My clammy hands grip the wheel and I set about driving back to Phil's house. He watches me the entire time, but I refuse to glance his way. *Seb knows I'm in trouble. Seb knows.*

The journey back to my old house is the longest of my life. Every time I try to look at Phil, he squeezes my neck with his fingers, keeping me looking at the road. The knife is a permanent pressure turning my stomach to lead. I contain the panic that has seized my body, the only outward sign, my trembling lip. My death grip of the steering wheel only lifts as Phil hauls me from the car. Painful fingers dig in to my neck as he forces me up the drive. He shoves me through the door and I stumble and fall to my knees. The pain in my cheek throbs in time with my quickening heartbeat. As I gather my senses, I hear Phil's chuckle as he sets the latch on the door.

That sound, that single little click clears my muddled mind. I will not let Phil tell me what to do. I had the courage to stand up to him once. I can do it again. *Seb knows I'm in trouble.* I pull myself up from the floor and turn to face Phil, but his palm connects with my face once again. The fiery sting scorches my already painful cheek and tears stream from my eyes. He moves to grab hold of me, but I try to duck out of his way, desperate to get to the door.

"Don't you fucking dare," he shouts, reaching to grab me again and this time succeeding. The metal knife clangs on the wooded floor as Phil drops it.

I lash out as be pulls me towards the stairs. My fists ball up and I try to punch and hit Phil, but my attempts do little to stop him. My legs thrash, kicking out and stomping. I feel some kicks make contact with his body, but to little effect. I claw and shout and scream in the struggle.

"No! No! No!" I scream, fighting his intention of getting me upstairs.

"You like it rough now, do you?"

"No, Phil! Stop! Please don't, you don't have to do this…" my heartbeat is thrashing in my ears and my head is beginning to feel light and dizzy.

"Just shut the fuck up!" Phil roars in my face. His fist slams into my face, pain erupting from the contact and dulling everything else around me. I slump into Phil's hold as my vision blurs. All my strength evaporates and I fight to keep my eyes open, but they don't get the message. Tears and swelling take their toll and my eyelids cast me into darkness.

I come round, lying face down on what feels like a bed. I try to open my eyes but only one of them is cooperating. As the light and dark shapes come into focus I recognise my old bedroom. I move my arms to help me up but I can't. They are bound behind my back.

I move the rest of my body, trying to shift position, but my legs won't budge either. I'm wide awake now; the fear has chased away my lingering haze. I'm lumped over the bed with each leg tied to the foot of the bed, anchoring me.

"Awake, I see," he barks. I start thrashing my body but it isn't enough. His voice triggers the panic now swamping my system.

Adrenaline and fear pump through my veins. I'm gasping for air. *No, no, no. Please, no.*

"You wanted to be tied up, Izzy. I said I would. I said I'd do what you wanted, but noooo, not good enough. Well, you're my fucking wife and I say how it's going to be. Do you like this, Izzy, being at my mercy? Your legs spread for me—God, you haven't done that for me in fucking years." His cruel words ring in my ears and my tears soak into the bed. I'm helpless. I'm helpless and I can't do anything to stop it.

"Please, Phil. I don't want this. Don't. Don't do this to me. I'm begging you. I'll do anything. Just no, please don't…"

"Oh, I know you'll do anything. Anything I want. Bent over our bed, offering your cunt to me like the little slut you are." He shoves my skirt further up my hips. "Never wore lace for me, Izzy, or stockings. Fuck me underwear. Well, you asked for it."

"No I'm not! Get off of me. Don't. I fucking hate you."

I'm sobbing into the bed, my body shaking with fear. He's really going to do it. He's going to rape me. He rips my knickers from my body and gropes me, squeezing and smacking my bum.

"Nooo, please, no." My voice is panicked and desperate but it doesn't stop him. His fingers drive into me viciously and I cry out at the intrusion.

"What's the matter, Izzy? Am I not doing it right? I thought you liked this?"

"No. No, no, no. Stop! Stop it. Please, stop it. You're hurting me!" My throat is raw from shouting. My lungs heave to pull in the needed air. "How could you? How could you, Phil?"

219

"You ruined everything." He plunges another finger inside me and I cry out at the pain. "I'm going to fuck your pretty cunt and spank your arse until you say you're sorry."

"Don't do this. Please, don't." I feel sick. My arms and legs are numb from where he's tied me in the wrong position for too long. He slams his hand down on my bottom and red heat blazes across my skin. He smacks again and again, not holding anything back.

"And to think if I'd just done this to you all those months ago, none of this would have happened."

Bile rises in my throat. The man I loved is physically abusing me. We loved each other once, right? *Smack, smack, smack.* My bottom is on fire and it's overwhelming. My eyes are squeezed shut and I'm preparing for another blow. I try to zone out, to think of a happy place, warm and safe, but the pain throughout my body is stopping me from finding it. I wait for the bite of his hand on my skin, but it doesn't come.

"What the...?"

"Isabel!" *Seb. He's here.* "Get your hands off her." His voice is like ice.

"Who the fuck are you?"

"Move away from her now."

"She's my wife, arsehole." I can't see what's happening, so I turn my head, and through my puffy eyes, I can make out Seb standing by the door, a murderous look trained on Phil. At Phil's claim on me, Seb storms over to him and I hear clattering and banging. There's the unmistakable thud of a punch and the sound of skin hitting bone.

"You. Will. Never. Touch. Her. Again." Each of Seb's words is emphasised with a blow. My bleary vision still sees Seb's fist connecting with Phil, punching him over and over again. Phil's body goes limp as Seb drops him to the ground. He's bent over his knees, breathing hard.

220

"Fuck! Hold on, Izzy." I feel soft hands around my ankles. "Hold on. I need to cut you out, sweetheart."

"Scissors. Bathroom." He's back in a moment and finally frees my legs, then my arms. I pull my legs together, sealing them, trying to protect myself. I finally sit up and wrap my arms around my knees. Seb has his arms around me, pulling me into his embrace. I'm still crying, I think. I don't care. I look over the bed at Phil on the floor. He's out cold and his face is banged up and bloody. "You... You knocked him out?"

"He's lucky I didn't kill him. God, Izzy." I feel a shiver run through both of us as he pulls me tighter. "Did he..." Seb pauses and tries again "Did he..." His words are soft and filled with sadness—so much so that he can't get them out.

"No. He just... touched me and hit me." Saying it makes me feel sick. The acid in my stomach is churning and clawing at my throat, pain flaring in my sore backside. I start to panic again, sobbing and struggling to breathe.

"Shh. Shh, Izzy. It's alright. I've got you and nothing bad will happen again. You're mine to protect and I'll do anything and everything to do that."

"He hurt me."

"I know, sweetheart. I'm so, so sorry." Although his words are kind, I can feel the tension keeping his body rigid.

Garbled murmurings come from where Phil is on the floor. He's obviously coming round.

"I should fucking kill you," he seethes.

"Don't kill him. Please, Seb." As much as I despise Phil, I can't let Seb do it. There would be dire consequences for us all.

"That's the only thing stopping me, Izzy." He grabs Phil by the collar and hauls him to face him. "You listen to me. You will grant Izzy the divorce. You will sell the house and Izzy gets the money. End of story."

"No," Phil's words are slurred. "Who do you think you are?"

"If you don't, Izzy will press charges for attempted rape, and you'll go to jail. Understand?" Phil doesn't say anything, so Seb shakes him.

"Okay, stop." He groans. "Fucking bitch." Seb punches him hard enough to make me flinch. Seeing him so visibly aggressive is so out of character, but I'm beyond relieved that he's here.

"My lawyer will be in touch." Leaving him on the floor, he gently scoops me up in his arms and carries me downstairs and into his waiting car. Before I know it, we're heading home.

Safe. He came for me. I'm safe.

"It's alright, sweetheart. I've got you. I'm not going to let anyone ever hurt you again." Seb tucks me up in bed and pulls me in close. His hands run over my head, cradling me like a precious child. "Shh. It's alright." His hushed voice soothes my frayed nerves. My limbs are numb and my ankles ache. I want to sleep. I want to go to sleep and forget that tonight ever happened.

"I won't ever let you go, sweetheart. Go to sleep. You're safe. We're home."

Twenty-Two

The next few days I spend locked in my bedroom or in the shower. As much as I try, I can't scrub the feel of Phil's hands off of my skin. My face reminds me of just how bad it got. My cheek has an assortment of colours decorating the bruising. Each time I catch my reflection the terror grips my stomach again.

Seb comforts me, but I don't want to talk to him about it and I can see that he struggles to know exactly what to say.

I email Mark over the weekend and tell him that I need to work from home for the next few days. I need some time for the bruising to go down before showing my face at work. Luckily I don't have any client-facing presentations coming up and I can focus on work.

On Wednesday, I'm ready to throw my computer out of the window. Being at home with my work should have been the distraction I needed from being stuck in my head. Yet I feel like I'm going around in circles. I can't concentrate, so I've opted for other distractions. I've cleaned the apartment, put all of the laundry away and drunk half my body weight in coffee. Still no luck.

I replay Phil's attack over and over. I then play over everything else that led up to the moment he grabbed me. Seb and I fighting, the idea of a house, of marriage. I want it all to stop. I want to go back to a normal life. One that isn't complicated or hurts. I want the pain to go away.

My phone distracts me from tossing the computer.

"Hello."

"Ms. Fields, it's Mr. Osbourn, do you have a moment?"

"Yes, is everything alright?"

"It's just to say that the management hearing date has come through. I have no question that the judge will grant us the decree and we can then make the application for the decree absolute."

"Okay... thank you."

"You're welcome. I'll email you over all the details and I'll be in touch before the hearing."

The line goes dead and I let out the breath I was holding. This is what I want. Getting the divorce will mean I'm rid of Phil for good.

I text Seb but the words dance in front of my eyes. Tears roll down my cheeks as I realise that I'll have to see Phil again. The relief I felt is swamped by the nausea now building in my stomach.

Come home, please. Izzy

I curl up on the sofa and wait for Seb, feeling lost despite the good news.

"Izzy, wake up, sweetheart." Seb's hushed voice pulls me awake. I blink up at him and see him smiling down at me. He instantly makes me feel better.

"Will you hold me?"

"Of course, sweetheart." Seb's arms pull me into his chest. I sigh with contentment. Seb's fingers slide through my hair, relaxing me further. He's still wearing his shirt, the top button open, giving me a tempting target to kiss. I press my lips into his throat, working my kisses and nips up his neck. He drops his head back, allowing me room to explore. His stubble scrapes my cheek as I move to take his lips.

"Will you take me to bed? We haven't... since, and I don't want to give him any more power over me."

Seb lifts his head back up and searches my eyes. Lust sparks and I feel that wanton ache in my stomach. He kisses me. Hungry lips attack mine, biting and sucking as he takes his fill. Without missing a beat, he curls his arm under my knees and lifts me clean off the chair. Seb walks us, still locked together, up to the bedroom before we fall onto the bed. His body presses me down into the mattress and I moan into his mouth.

"Let me hold you. I want to touch you and let you feel me. Slowly. We'll take it at your pace." His words are meant to be soothing, but they remind me of my attack.

"Yes. Please, Seb. I need this."

"I'm here. I'll give you what you need." He starts to undress me, meticulously slowly. His patience builds the anticipation of what's to come. The slightest touch against my skin heats my blood. I focus on Seb, holding the memories at bay. He stands and takes his fill of my naked body, spread out for him to behold. This is what I need, to get lost in him.

"You're beautiful and you're mine. Never forget that."

"I won't." It's the truth. His clothes hit the floor before he smothers my body with his, skin on skin. I wrap myself around him, my arms stretching over his back, pulling him down closer to me. He's nestled between my thighs, his cock tantalisingly close to where I want it. He rolls his hips and presses his hard shaft against my labia and clit, spiking my arousal and my heart rate. He pushes up, exposing my breasts, but only so he can tongue my ripe nipples. He's not giving me a chance to focus on any one thing. He's bombarding my body with pleasure.

After my breasts, his hand pushes my arm above my head. He does the same with the other arm before clutching them together at my wrists. I pull against his hold but it's firm. I move beneath him but gain no purchase. Panic flashes through me, drowning out everything around me. *I'm back on my bed. I can't move. Phil's hands bite into my skin...*

"Relax, Izzy. It's me. I'm not holding you down." I hear Seb, but everything I was feeling is dowsed in cold water.

"I'm sorry." I relax under him, but the desire isn't there. "I want to, I do..."

"Shh, it's alright." He puts his arms around me and I snuggle into his chest.

"I think I need to get away for a few days. I can't concentrate on work, I keep going over the attack in my head and all the stuff leading up to it. Mr. Osbourn called today and told me that the hearing date has come through as well. It's all so... It's too much. I'm feeling overwhelmed."

"Okay. Let's get away."

"No, I mean I want to get away on my own." I feel his body tense, but I need to do this for myself.

"Where will you go?"

"I'll speak to Jess. I'll still text you, I don't want you to worry, but I need... space. Just for a few days. Get my head clear."

"If that's what you need."

* * *

"Thanks for letting me stay."

"Are you kidding me? You're always welcome. I'm just sorry you feel that you need to get away."

"Just for a little while. I can't think clearly at home or around Seb. Plus I'm not going into work until this has cleared up." Jess winces, taking another look at the bruising that looks like a rainbow now with yellow, green and purple patches.

"I can't believe Phil went this far."

"I don't want to think about it. Sorry, but that's part of the problem. It just keeps playing over and over in my head."

"Okay, well, whatever you need, I'm here. We can talk, go out, watch movies. You'll have the place to yourself tomorrow as I'll be at work, but I'll come right home."

"Thank you, Jess. How about a film? Or you can finally tell me what's going on between you and Greg?"

"There isn't anything to tell. I've told you."

"But you've been seeing each other for weeks now. That's a good thing?"

"Not so much lately. You know how I am. I like my own space. Now, action film? You can't beat Daniel Craig as Bond." She steers the conversation onto lighter topics as we sit and get comfy for the night.

After a restless night I finally make it downstairs to make a cup of coffee. Jess has left me a note on the fridge telling me she'll be home for dinner. I check my phone and I've got a message from Seb.

I missed you last night. I hope you're feeling better. If you need to go out, please make sure Jess is with you. Or phone me and I'll take you where you need to go. S

I missed you, too. I didn't sleep well. Don't worry, I'll make sure I'm with someone. Thank you for giving me space. Love Izzy

Whatever you need, sweetheart. S

I check my emails and make sure there isn't anything pressing that needs to be dealt with. I fire off a quick message to Mark and tell him that I'll be working from home and that I've had a few personal issues involving my divorce.

I sip my coffee and look around Jess's kitchen. My head feels like it's going to explode. My life has gone from predictably boring—a routine that gets me through the day—to a chaos of changes. Being allowed to be myself, my submissive self, with Seb, finally understanding what that actually feels like, but having the other elements that come with Seb. His need to take care of me, his constant contact and want to control other aspects of my life outside of the bedroom, a new house and even marriage. I was being honest when I told him I felt overwhelmed.

Getting through the divorce is my priority now. Having Phil out of my life forever is the one thing I want more than anything. What he did to me, taking something that I thought of as special between me and Seb—my submission—and using it against me, hurts me more than the physical pain he put me through.

Phil ignored me in our marriage, cheated on me, used me for his own personal gain. Now he's physically assaulted me. I hate him for it, I hate him for all of it. I pull up my personal emails and find the most recent one from Mr. Osbourn. Four days' time and I'll get to move forward with the divorce and put him behind me.

After my mini pep talk, I focus on work and actually get it done. The one thing that I allow my mind to wander to is finally getting my divorce. By focusing on that, I am able to forget everything else that has been swamping me and find the headspace I need.

"Izzy, I'm home."

"I'm in the kitchen." I've made the kitchen into my mini work den today. When I peeked in the mirror, even the bruising looked better.

"Good day?" Jess asks.

"Yes, actually. Much better. You?"

"Same old. But tomorrow will be better. I'm taking you to the spa for the afternoon. My treat. You can forget all this shit and relax. It will do you a world of good."

"Really? Are you sure you don't have work?"

"My work is fine. I'm hoping that you can sort yours." She looks at me hopefully.

"I told Mark that I had some divorce stuff happening, so I think it should be alright. Thank you, Jess."

"My pleasure. Now, what are we having for dinner?"

"Pasta?" I offer, thinking it would be lovely to have a big bowl of carbs and sit in front of the TV again.

"Sounds good. You cook, I'll do the dishes."

"Deal."

* * *

Off to the spa with Jess. Feeling much better today. Love Izzy

That sounds like a great idea. Have fun. I'm glad you're feeling better. S

I miss you. Love Izzy

I miss you, sweetheart. S

As much as the space is doing my head the world of good, I've missed Seb. I've not been sleeping well, and now that I see the end of Phil in my life, I know that Seb and I have some things to work on.

Jess and I are sitting wrapped in soft fluffy bath robes by the edge of the pool. She's booked us both a massage in a while, but right now I'm happy to just sit and do nothing.

"Thank you for this, Jess. It's exactly what I need."

"You've been through a lot in the last few days. Having some time to yourself is the least you deserve."

"I know. Just being on my own has helped. I've been able to get my head in shape, understand what I need to focus on. Divorcing Phil is the top of the list. Then I can work on the rest of it."

"And what exactly is the rest of it?" Jess asks.

"Talking with Seb. Telling him I'm not comfortable with some of the elements of our relationship. I want to take my time with Seb. I feel like Seb's rushing me. He's doing it to try and give me reassurance, at least that's what I think, but it's the exact opposite."

"Have you told him that?"

"No. But I will."

"Good for you. Remember he loves you."

"I know." I hold on to that little bit of information and pray it's enough to get me through the next couple of days.

After leaving the spa, I pack up my bits from Jess and make my way home.

The space, even for a couple of days, has done me the world of good. I can think clearly. I've got some fight back in me and I'm determined not to show Phil that I'm scared of him.

I'm home. I'm just coming up in the lift. See you in a minute. Love Izzy

As I was expecting, Seb is waiting for me at the door when I get to it. He smiles at me, but I can see the tiredness around his eyes. He engulfs me in a huge hug and I let my body slump into his. He presses soft kisses into my hair and I hear him breathe deeply, like he's relaxed now that I'm back in his company.

I ease from his hold and we move into the living area. He sits down and pulls me down on top of him. I wrap my arms around his neck and just enjoy being this close to him again.

Although it's only been a few days, it feels like everything has changed. I left feeling overwhelmed and confused. Now, I know what I want—Phil out of my life—and I know it will happen.

"The case hearing is on Monday. Then it will be just a matter of time before I'm rid of Phil," I whisper as I'm wrapped in Seb's arms.

"Good."

"Will you make love to me? Just... I missed you." I kiss his jaw, the rough bristles tickling my lips.

"Yes, baby."

Twenty-Three

6 weeks later

The decree nisi has been granted by the court and Mr. Osbourn is putting the application for the decree absolute together. It's been nearly seven weeks since Phil attacked me. Seeing him in court was the hardest thing I've done, but the judge ruled that there was evidence to grant the decree. Phil didn't have a say.

After court, I knew that I could start putting what Phil did behind me and focus on the problems I was having with Seb. We talked. Properly. I told him that I wanted to take a break from the D/s side of our relationship. Part of what was so overwhelming to me was the difference between my past relationship and the amount of changes to my new life. I wanted some time to adjust, for us to find what was right for us.

I knew that I still wanted to submit to Seb. That part of me had finally been given the chance to grow, thanks to Seb, and I didn't want to give it up. However, I needed to know that Seb and I could work as a couple as well as a Dominant and submissive. I knew that part of our relationship worked. It was the rest of it that I needed time to trust in.

I was scared that calling a halt to the D/s would send Seb running, but I should have had more faith. I was also scared that if I let Seb dominate me and tie me up, I'd remember Phil's attack, although the vanilla sex has been great.

My saving grace is work. The hours I need to pour into my new position are now a welcome distraction. Mark gave me my promotion. I'm now the senior account manager at White Cube. Seb took me out to celebrate. We had one of our first ever dates. It was perfect. Great food, good wine, and, I'm hoping, fantastic sex.

As soon as we're back in the apartment Seb drags me to the sofa and sits down, manoeuvres me so that I'm straddling his hips, the soft denim pressed tightly to my thighs. He holds my hands and places them on his shoulders and then moves his hands to rest by his side. He doesn't kiss me, pull me closer or creep his hands up my thighs. He waits.

"I want you to be in control tonight. Anything you want, you have to tell me. I won't touch you without your instruction first." I hear his sexy smile through his words and it sets my sex throbbing in anticipation.

I wiggle on his lap to test if he'll stop me. A slight moan and a momentary closure of his eyes is all he gives away. My hands slide up into his hair and give a gentle tug, enjoying the rush of power that it brings. With my fingers clutched in his hair, I drop my lips to his and kiss him. He matches my pace, only taking what I give him. My tongue strokes against his, dipping in and out as our lips dance against each other. Still, he doesn't speed up or overpower. I kiss him harder, pressing my whole body against his. I want him to react, to growl and flip me over, and to feel his power over me.

My frustration mounts, as does the ache of my clit. "Touch me, Seb."

"Where? Tell me. You need to tell me exactly what you want." I moan into his mouth as I try to understand exactly what I want.

"Squeeze my bum. Feel my breasts. I'm already hot for you." My body aches for his touch, and something about saying exactly what I want makes it sexier. His hand strokes the underside of my breast before he rubs my nipple with his palm. His other arm slips around my thigh to squeeze my bum, pulling me closer into his hard erection. My clothes are still a barrier and I want to feel skin on skin. I want him naked. I want to explore the lines of his muscles and worship his chest.

"Carry me to the bedroom," I mumble between kisses. He lifts me and I wrap my legs around his waist. He sits me down on the bed, but waits for what I instruct. "Undress, Seb. I want you, I don't want…"

"Shh. Not going to happen." He sheds his shirt and jeans as I slip out of my dress. He's pulling me back on top of him before I know it. Now there is nothing between us, and his thick erection is waiting for me to sink down onto it. I lean over him to re-capture his lips, and at the same time, I wrap my hand around his cock and slide his head to my entrance before sitting back down on him. I lower myself slowly, taking him inside me. My hands press against his pecs as I rock back and forth, seeking that delicious friction against my clit. My eyes drift to his stomach, his muscles taut with tension as I speed my pace. I spread my legs wider and lean back, making sure that I take every inch of him.

I groan out at the pleasure sparking through my body. His hands have stayed away from me, but I miss them. I want to reach the places that Seb takes us when we're together—the abundance of pleasure and passion that can't be contained by either one of us.

"Touch me, Seb. Please. Touch my clit. Make me come."

"Fuck, yes." Seb's curse makes me smile in triumph. His thumb moves to my clit and he runs the pad over the swollen nub. A wave of heat rolls through me and my head goes slack. I want what we had back. As good as this is, there is something missing between us.

Seb's thumb presses harder against my flesh and spikes my pulse, his gaze insistent upon me. My hips work in time with his thumb and I'm racing towards my orgasm. My body tenses as I reach the edge. All I need is a few more stokes, a few more thrusts, and I'll come apart. "Please, Seb. Just a little bit more…" He flicks at my clit and that's all I need. My body contracts around him, making me shudder and arch my back, grinding down harder onto his cock. As I come, Seb follows, his jaw tensing and straining as his body releases.

I slump down against him and match my deep breaths to the rise and fall of his chest. "Mmm, thank you."

"You're more than welcome, Izzy."

* * *

I take advantage of the evening light and meet Jess for a drink after work. Spring is arriving, slowly. The hope of a warm summer isn't far off.

"Hey, you. I've ordered gin and tonics." Jess has an outside table at one of the bistros in town.

"Thanks." I sit and sip my favourite drink.

"Izzy, are you alright? You look… tired." Her eyes hold the concern that's in her voice. She's been like this since I stayed with her—always checking, always asking. She's avoided telling me I don't look great until today.

"It's alright. I'm not sleeping particularly well at the moment. I'll try and catch up at the weekend."

"Still bad? How are things with Seb?" She reaches for my hand and I appreciate the comfort.

"I'm just… I'm frustrated and confused. I wanted us to have a break. To live and be in a relationship without the Dominance and submission stuff. I thought that was what I wanted. But now…" I reach for my drink and take a long sip.

"You're not sure anymore?"

"I miss it. I miss the connection that it gives us. It's like we're stronger, more together when we play."

"So just tell Seb, or give it time, but don't shut Seb out. Perhaps you should speak to someone?"

"What, like a counsellor?"

"Yes, did you ever speak to anyone about what happened to you? I know that he didn't actually… you know, but he physically assaulted you." I finish my drink, thinking over her advice. I haven't talked to anyone. Maybe it would be good for me.

"I'll think about it. I'll call you later in the week." I get up and rummage in my bag for my wallet.

"No, don't worry. These are on me."

"You sure?"

"Yes, you buy next time."

"Okay, thanks, hun." I give Jess a quick hug and make my way back to the office to pick up my car.

It's past eight before I slide my key into the door to Seb's apartment.

"I'm home," I call, already knowing that he'll be in the kitchen. I walk through and find him sitting at the breakfast bar with his iPad in front of him. He turns as I come into the room and gives me his sexy smile as my welcome.

"Good day?"

"Not bad. You?"

"Better now you're home. I want us to spend some time together. First, I want you relaxed."

"Relaxed?"

"Yes. I'll run you a bath. You relax."

236

"Deal."

Tonight is the fourth night in a row that I've been home late, so spending some time with Seb sounds great.

"I'll even rub your shoulders, take some of that stress away."

"I don't deserve you."

"Yes, you do. Go and get undressed and I'll set it running." I do as I'm told and head off to the bedroom.

I feel like a shell of the woman I was only a few weeks ago. I've fallen into a routine and I don't want it to continue. The divorce is all but finalised, Seb's shown me that we are more than just a couple in a D/s relationship. I want to feel that special tie between us, where I was so caught up in him that nothing else mattered. I wrap my robe around me, trying to pull myself together with its tie, and walk over to the bathroom.

Steam and citrus mist the air and I breathe in the comforting aroma.

"Tie your hair up." Seb perches on the edge of the bath, shirt sleeves rolled to the elbow, making for a very sexy sight. I slip the robe from my shoulders and step into the bubbles. It's exactly what I need. The warmth seeps into my muscles, unknotting the tension as it travels through my body. I sink back and sigh with pleasure.

"Good?" Seb's velvet voice is at my ear, his lips a hair's breadth away from my ear.

"Wonderful, thank you."

"Sit up and let me rub your shoulders." I lean forward and wrap my arms around my knees, finding a comfortable position that will allow Seb the access he needs.

"Just relax." He starts by simply placing his hands on my shoulders, making sure I'm expecting his touch. He strokes down my shoulders before running a firmer touch from the base of my skull down between my shoulder blades. The pressure melts through my tension and sends tranquillity through my body. It's bliss. Seb continues working his magical fingers across my skin for another few minutes until I'm so relaxed I can barely hold my head up. "Ready to get out?"

"Hmm," I respond, content with drifting in this hazy state.

"Out you get. I'd like us to talk, just spend some time together."

"That would be nice." Seb holds up a bath towel for me to step into. I pull it around myself before Seb pulls me to him.

"Go and get your hair brush and join me in the front room." I smile into his chest. I love it when he plays with my hair. I obediently head into our room to retrieve my brush. He's sitting in his chair with a cushion by his feet. He knows I like this, that I feel content being close to him and sitting with him. It feels like a lifetime since I was last seated at his feet. Here, I have the space and the reassurance to speak to him.

Seb's positioned the cushion so that I can lean against his leg. I hand him the brush and lower myself to the floor. He shifts, moving his body forward so he can continue to pamper me. Seb's fingers work the tie from my hair, spilling my brunette tresses down my back. He places the brush at the crown of my head and gently tugs it through, carefully un-knotting the strands.

"How are you feeling?"

"Good. You know I love you playing with my hair."

"I know. Comfortable?"

"Yes, I could fall asleep if you're not careful." I absolutely would. My eyelids grow lazy with every brush stroke.

"Before you fall asleep, I want you to talk to me. Tell me how you are feeling about us, about what's happened over the last few weeks. You wanted to leave the D/s out of the relationship. How do you feel now?"

Sitting here like this, I feel I can open up to him.

"I was pleased that you did that for me—gave up something so important to you—or rather a part of you, for me. For me, I needed things to slow down. I needed time."

"And now?"

"I miss it. It's fun being with you, you know, in a vanilla way. We play, like the other night. But..."

"Something is missing."

"Yes." Seb echoes my own feelings. "I gave you my submission freely. I love everything that you do to me, but Phil made me feel vulnerable and afraid and I hate him. I don't want to feel like that. I only want to feel you and your touch. Your command. But there is a shadow of him in my memory and I can't shake it." Seb's rhythmic strokes keep me focused on the now, sitting at his feet.

"The sub always has the control, Izzy. You say no, or black, that's it. Your submission is a gift, but I can only hold it for as long as you allow it. You have the power. I miss you and I know you miss us as well." He stops brushing my hair and pulls me onto his lap. I open my eyes and look at him. He holds my gaze and waits.

"I love you, Seb."

"I love you, sweetheart."

"Can we take it slowly? I want to get back to what we had before. I don't want to be afraid."

"We'll take it at your pace. Remember, you're in control." His eyes roam over my face and I can see them dropping to my lips. I part them in invitation and he takes it. As his mouth plunders mine, his hands lock my wrists in place behind me. His lips grow more urgent, more forceful, and I moan into our kiss. With his free hand he holds my neck keeping me hostage to his desires.

I miss being able to lose myself in his hands, to feel what he wants me to feel—the bite of his teeth, the smack of the flogger or the sting of his palm. Safe in his arms, I relax and feel my body melt into his hold.

"Don't move," he whispers across my lips. He lifts me from his lap and sits me on the sofa. Firm hands press my legs wide, spreading myself for him. His hands continue to trail down my legs and clasp my ankles. My body flinches, automatically fighting his grasp. His hold remains firm and adrenaline spikes, setting my heart pounding in my chest.

"Seb," I cry out, fear already drowning my desire. "Not my ankles. He…" Seb releases his hold and picks me back up.

"Shh, shh. We'll work up through the parts you have a bad response. You want to try, though?"

"Yes, I'm sorry." I bury myself against his chest. "Everything before the ankles was good."

"Okay. We'll get there, sweetheart."

* * *

After my mini freak-out, the sexual strain has started to show between us. I've been working longer hours and Seb has several trips away coming up. He's avoided spending any time away over the last few weeks, but he can't keep putting them off.

He leaves for London on Monday morning, and I don't want him to leave with questions over us. I want him to know that I am his submissive as well as his lover. He's in the bathroom and I know just what I want to do for him. I take off my pyjamas and kneel at the end of the bed, facing the bathroom. I let my body relax and try to clear my mind, thinking only of what I want to show Seb.

I listen for the water to stop and hold my breath for Seb to walk back into the bedroom. My head is bowed, so I listen for his movement. After what feels like hours, I hear movement, followed by nothing. My entire body vibrates with the apprehension of what Seb will say. What he will do. I refuse my desperate need to look up to him and keep looking at the carpet.

"Isabel, you're a very pretty sight like that."

"Thank you, Sir."

"Was there something you wanted to say to me?" His voice rumbles low and deep and ignites my desire for him.

"No, Sir."

"Is there something you want to do?"

"Yes, Sir." I hold my breath.

"Tell me what you want to do. Now." My skin flushes at the thought of what I could say.

"I... I want to suck you. I want to make you come like I did the first night I came here."

"Good girl. Do it." He's telling me what to do and giving me the freedom to get lost in him. I eagerly pull the towel from his body, freeing his cock. He's already thick and hard, and I shift my legs further apart as my own need blossoms.

I lean forward and lick the underside of his head before swirling my tongue around and wrapping my lips over his shaft. My lips press down and I take him to the back of my throat. The low vibration from Seb's chest spurs me on and I grip the base of his shaft with my hand, squeezing tightly as I work my head up and down. I pump fast and hard, spearing my own throat with his cock. There is nothing pretty about this, it's raw and sexy. It's all about me showing Seb how much I still want to please him.

My lips grow hot and saliva seeps down around my hand that still has hold of his cock.

"God, Izzy... Yes. Yes..." I look up through my lashes to see Seb's expression as he hardens. Salty come pumps down my throat and I suck my lips up and off his shaft.

I sit back on my heels and feel... proud. Warmth radiates from my chest.

"Well done, Izzy." His sexy smile is the perfect praise.

* * *

Seb's alarm clock jolts me awake. He switches it off before rolling over to me. "Morning, sweetheart." He kisses me and then makes his way to the bathroom. I slip from the covers and go down to make coffee. Making coffee in the morning used to be a sign of my submission, that I'd be giving everything over to Seb. Now, it's just part of our routine. I make coffee, we get dressed for work and go our separate ways. We both return at varying times, with a few texts over the course of those hours. We eat and go back to bed. I can see it before my own eyes. The life I was so desperate to leave is starting to play out in front of me again.

The welcome aroma of coffee gives me the kick I need to take the drinks back up to our room. Seb is still wet from his shower, dressed only in a towel. I fight my mind to stay focused, especially since yesterday morning.

I place the cups down and sit back on the bed.

"Will your feelings for me change if we can't get back to what we were before?" I blurt it out before I can stop myself.

Seb stops packing and gives me a look that has me lowering my gaze on instinct. I hear him chuckle before the bed dips beside me.

"No, of course not. I want to be with you. I want to marry you, for God's sake. Don't you remember that?"

"Even after… everything?"

"Of course. That will never change. You still submit to me, there are just a few things you don't like anymore, and that's understandable. Lots of people have triggers. We will work on them and in time they will probably disappear." His words are just what I need to hear.

"I haven't forgotten that you proposed. I know I'm not quite divorced yet, but things haven't changed. I'm not sure I see marriage as something I want. I don't want you to think this will change overnight for me. You said you wanted someone with the same desires to share in your relationship and match your dominance with submission. I'm not sure I can do all of that right now."

"We're working on that. You are submissive, Izzy. It doesn't just go away. You offered me your submission yesterday. You let me take control. You wanted to take it slowly and we are. Don't worry yourself into something that isn't a problem." He pauses and tilts my head up so I'm looking at him. "Don't let him win. You listen to me. Understand?"

"Yes, Sir." I smile at him and he kisses it right off my lips.

Seb's words from earlier play over and over in my mind. *Am I letting Phil win?* With the divorce all but finalised, I should be free. I should be celebrating my life and moving on with Seb. Phil did a horrible thing to me, but it could have been worse. Am I giving too much power to one horrible incident?

I force my worries aside and pick open the Everlyn account. I've been working on several new campaign options for them and will be presenting my concepts to the direct marketing department of White Cube. If we get them on board, we can pitch the integrated campaign to the client.

For the rest of the day, I focus on work and hold on to the belief in Seb's words this morning. We are moving forward. We love each other. That is enough.

"Hey, Luke, how's business?"

"Good, I can't complain. I don't usually hear from you outside of Solace, Sebastian. What can I do for you?" He's right. Although we've known each other for several years now, our dealings are usually confined to Solace. However, I know that Luke can help, and right now, I need it.

"I could do with your advice. Izzy's bastard ex-husband attacked her. He tied her up and all but raped her. She's doing really well but he's left her with some triggers. We dropped the D/s to start with and have been reintroducing it slowly over the last week or so."

"Is he still breathing? The ex, I mean?"

"Only just. I swear, Luke, I would have smashed his skull in if Izzy didn't stop me."

"Well, I can understand that, mate, but it wouldn't have helped you."

"I know, but it didn't help me leaving him."

"Has she talked to anyone? Professionally, I mean?"

"No. And that's what I was phoning about. Can you recommend someone?"

"That's the first thing I'd get her to do. I have a female counsellor at the practice. I'll set it up if you want?"

"Let me talk to her first, but that would be great."

"Anything else I can help with?"

"Well, I might need your advice on how to work through some of her triggers, but we're not there yet."

"You know she's going to need time, support and patience."

"And I'm giving all of that to her."

"Were you in a TPE?"

"We tried it. I wanted to see if it was for us. She struggled with certain elements. Although underneath it all, she wants to please me."

"Good. And what about now?"

"She misses the D/s as much as me, but is nervous of it. We're taking it slowly, but it's good. For a moment I thought she was going to call it quits on us all together."

"Time and patience. Get her into counselling, though."

"I will. Thanks, Luke."

"No worries, mate. It's been a while since I've seen you at Solace. This explains it."

"We'll go back. I'd love for you to meet Izzy."

"Has Natasha?"

"Not yet."

"Oh, man, I'd get that rectified sooner rather than later. Natasha won't stay quiet for long."

"I'll handle her. I've spoken to her, but they will need to meet soon. Thanks again."

"Let me know about the counselling session, and how the meeting between Natasha and Izzy goes. I'd love to be there."

I end the call, settled that I have some reassurance to help Izzy.

The look on her face when she asked if I still wanted to be with her nearly stopped my heart. How could she think that? The worst of it is, I don't know what I have done to make her believe that I don't love her. I certainly have some work to do to show her that I'm serious, but forcing the proposal isn't the way to go. She doesn't trust the idea of marriage—another thing that fucker has been able to ruin.

The last few months have been heart wrenching. I felt completely lost for the two days that she went to stay at Jess's. I hated every minute even though I knew it was something she needed to do.

Izzy is mine to protect and I let that shit touch her.

Fuck, I don't want to be stuck in London. I need to be supporting Izzy. I pace around the tiny hotel room and consider calling her. We talked yesterday. She's throwing herself into her work and I know she's using it as a crutch. I fire off a text to her before grabbing a drink from the mini-bar. My next conversation is going to require a drink.

I take a seat at the too-small table and call Natasha.

"Hey, stranger. What did I say about leaving it too long?"

"I know. I'm sorry. There's been a lot going on, and I'm not the only one who could have called, you know?"

"Fine. So, to what do I owe the pleasure of this call?"

"I thought it was about time that I introduce you to Izzy. I know you want to meet her."

"Yes, I do. I can come round at the end of the week?"

"No, I was thinking maybe Sunday?"

"Sunday? What, for family lunch?"

"How about brunch?"

"I'll be there at 11:00?"

"Perfect. There's a few other things you need to know, though."

"Sebastian, why do I get the impression that I'm not going to like this?" I take a swallow of the too-small drink in front of me before gathering the information I need to tell Natasha.

"Izzy's got her decree nisi, so the divorce is nearly done."

"That's great."

"But her ex-husband attacked her. He tied her down and assaulted her." Just saying the words rips chunks out of my soul. Natasha is suddenly quiet on the other end of the line. She knows how I feel about Izzy and how this will have affected me.

"How bad?" Her voice is soft and I can hear the concern for us both.

"Bad enough. Bad enough that Izzy is struggling with letting me dominate her."

"That's understandable, Seb."

"I know that, and I'm not rushing things."

"Good. Has she spoken to a counsellor?"

"No, but I'm going to send her to one that Luke has recommended."

"Well, that's a start. I'm sorry, Seb. Is the bastard in prison?"

"No." I stand and pace around the room. Talking all of this through is becoming unbearable while I'm away from her.

"Seb? Are you still there?"

"Yes, I'm here."

"Good. Did you want to talk to me about anything else? I'm not sure what help I can be, but I'm here if you need anything."

"Thank you. I think it's time that you two meet. She doesn't know a lot about you." I try to think back to what I've actually told Izzy about Natasha and draw a blank. "So, I'll see you Sunday and we can talk some more?"

"Are you sure we can't meet sooner?" She has a pleading tone in her voice and it makes me worry what she's thinking.

"No, I'm away at the moment, so Sunday will be fine."

I disconnect the call and mentally start to prepare for Sunday.

247

It's rare that I get to finish work early and make it home before Seb, especially on a Friday. But with him having been away for most of the week, I want to have some time with him. I have stacked the fridge up with all our favourite ingredients for Seb to whip something up for us.

I've spent most of the week thinking about what Seb said before he left. He's right. I need to move past the fear. Seb has all of my trust. From the very beginning, I've trusted him with my body and my heart. Now should be no different.

The doorbell rings and draws me from my melancholy thoughts. It's nearly six and Seb should be getting home shortly. I open the door to an intimidatingly beautiful woman. Taller than my short five foot three inches, she towers over me in her gorgeous black boots. Sprayed-on jeans make her legs look a mile long, and her raven hair tumbles in bouncy curls to her shoulders. Whoever she is, I want to scratch her eyes out for just standing on my doorstep.

"You must be Isabel. Is Seb home?"

"No, he's not home. Can I help you with something?"

"Well, I came to introduce myself, although I was hoping Seb would be here too. I'm Natasha. May I come in?"

She walks through and takes a seat in the kitchen as if it is perfectly normal behaviour.

"Um, sure." I trail after her and wish I had the confidence to match hers.

She sits down and looks over me. I'm suddenly under her spotlight and I feel decidedly uncomfortable. She's acting as if she has the upper hand, and she does.

Fortunately, I hear the front door and I leave Natasha in the kitchen while I head off to Seb.

"Hey, Izzy. I wasn't expecting you home early. It's a nice surprise. What's wrong?"

"Natasha is here to see you." His face flashes with annoyance before he covers it back up.

"Seb, is that you?" Her sing-song voice trills down the hallway and I see Seb's body tense in recognition.

Seb places his hand at the base of my spine and leads me into the kitchen. Natasha is sitting at the table, displaying no urgency to get up to greet Seb.

"Natasha, this is an unexpected visit." Seb's words tell me that he's as surprised to see her as I am. It's a relief.

"I'm sorry for the intrusion, Sebastian." She tilts her head to the side before turning to face me. "Isabel, Seb's an old friend and he's told me a lot about you. It's a pleasure to meet you." She offers me her hand and I shake it politely.

"Natasha." We shake hands and it abates my initial frosty feelings towards her.

"Izzy, would you open a bottle of wine while I talk with Natasha. Natasha, shall we?" He gestures for her to leave the kitchen and I'm left wondering what this is all about. I grab three glasses and pour the Semillon that's in the fridge. I carry them through, eager to hear what they are discussing. There is an air to Natasha that reminds me of Seb, the way he carries himself. She's beautiful and full of confidence in a powerful way that I don't often see in a woman.

249

They are standing in the middle of the room, but they don't appear to be speaking to one another. More like glaring at each other. I set my glass down on the table before offering Seb and Natasha theirs.

"Thank you, Izzy." Natasha smiles again, and this time there is a softness there that I didn't see before. I take that as my opportunity to get to know her as she seems to want to know me.

"So, Natasha, how do you know Seb? Do you work with him?" She looks at Seb for a moment, and he nods as if agreeing to something, before she answers me.

"We met at University originally, but it wasn't until a few years later that we became… friends. We share a common interest. I think you've seen Solace. Well, I introduced him to it."

Her words turn my stomach to stone. *Solace. She's been with Seb?*

"Oh dear, Izzy, no. Not like that." I look at her and I see concern on her face. "We have never been more than friends. Seb likes his women submissive. And I am anything but." She takes a sip of her wine and smiles at Seb. He hasn't said anything during her explanation, nor has he set her right.

"So, you're a…"

"A Domme, Izzy. I like to be in charge, just as Seb does." That explains the feeling I got around her, then.

Seb pulls me against his side.

"Was there anything else you wanted, Natasha?" Seb is polite, but I can hear the annoyance beneath the surface.

"There was one thing. It's something Izzy can do. Would you excuse us, Seb? Just for a moment? And then I'll leave you to your evening."

"Natasha…" It's a warning between the two of them, and again I'm reduced to the odd one out in the room.

"It's fine, Seb. I'd be happy to talk to her." My smile is genuine, clocking this up to another part of him that I'm getting to know. If she's known him since University she'll certainly be able to fill in the gaps I may have.

"I'll start dinner, then. Natasha, I'm sure I'll see you soon. Perhaps you'd like to call first next time."

"Now where's the fun in that?" She gives him a wicked glare, coupled with a perfect smile. If I was that sassy with Seb, I know I'd be in for a punishment. They lock eyes and I wait for one of them to back down. The tension is thick and it sends my pulse racing, nervous of what's going to happen. Finally, Seb turns to kiss my cheek and disappears into the kitchen. *Oh boy!*

"What can I help you with, Natasha?"

"Well, I want us to be friends. Understand that I've known Seb a great deal longer than you, and despite my best efforts, he's never found the woman for him. Until now. I'm curious, in a good way. Seb has taken a rather long time to introduce us. Plus, I like messing with him when I can." Her smile lights up her face and I am more than relieved that she isn't interested in Seb. She's stunning.

"Seb told me you were his perfect partner, that you were it for him." Her confirmation fills me with joy. "He's also told me what happened, and I'm sorry you had to go through that. Remember, though, that being submissive isn't something that will disappear. It's part of you." I try to stand tall against her scrutiny, but her presence has the same effect on me as Seb's does when he wants to dominate me. My eyes slink away from hers.

She takes a step towards me, encroaching on my space. I feel her hand on my shoulder, offering reassurance, I think. "Don't let it ruin what you have with Seb. This is new to him. You need to help him as much as he is supporting you." I look back at her and see that she is genuinely concerned.

"If you need to talk to someone, you can always call me." She pulls a card out of her purse and hands it to me before turning on her booted heel and heading for the door.

I sit on the sofa and reach for my wine. I take two big gulps to settle my nerves. She's been perfectly nice, but it doesn't dispel how unsettled I feel.

"Izzy, are you alright?" Seb comes to sit beside me and wraps an arm around my shoulder. I lean back against him, happy to be cuddled.

"I'm fine. She just wants to be friends."

"What did she say? I'm sorry if she made you uncomfortable. She has that ability."

"She didn't. Well, maybe a little. She didn't say anything I didn't know already." I turn and curl my legs underneath me. "I wanted to spend some time with you tonight, just us."

"I was hoping you'd say that." He finally smiles and some of the tension begins to loosen.

"Will you help me? I do want to submit to you. Sexually. I know we're taking things slowly, but I need... more. I don't want to be afraid that you'll do something and I'll get hit with a memory."

"Of course I'll help. It's what I've been trying to do. I think you should speak to a counsellor. I have a friend who's recommended someone to me. I can set up a meeting."

"I was thinking you could help by taking me to Solace." His hand stills and he tips my chin up to look at me, confusion clear on his face.

"Solace? Why?"

"Because I think seeing scenes where women are vulnerable but are consenting will help. I need to see that the submissive does hold the power."

"I can show you that without taking you to Solace. You said you wanted to take things slowly. You don't need to rush things, Izzy."

"I'm not, but I'm sick of feeling like I lost a part of us in the attack. I want it back. But I'm not even sure what it is." I puff out a sigh. This wasn't how I thought this conversation would go.

"I'll take you, but it's on my terms, and after you've spoken to the counsellor. That doesn't mean we can't have fun tonight. I've missed you, too." His arm snakes around me, pulling me across his thighs so I'm straddling him. "I'm going to strip you before I spank your beautiful back and pretty nipples with a crop."

His voice has dropped and holds the command that he uses when he's dominating me. It sends a shiver down my spine and my body presses against his growing erection, eager to feel his touch.

"Yes, Sir," I purr.

"Your only job tonight is to do what I tell you and to enjoy it." He reaches up to kiss me. A leisurely kiss that tells me he's in no mood to rush things tonight.

"Take off your top but leave your bra on." I follow his command, locking my eyes on his. My blouse and vest top hit the floor so I'm left in my work trousers and my bra. Seb tilts me forward and buries his face against my chest. He nips and bites at my breasts. A rough contrast to his tender touch a moment ago.

His hands run down my arms and he pulls them behind my back, thrusting my boobs further into his face. He moves my wrists into one hand and clamps his fingers around them. I try to think about what he's doing with my body, pushing the cup of my bra down so he can suck my nipple into his mouth. Instead, my mind lingers on the hold of my wrists. I twist them but he keeps his hold.

His earlier instruction to do as I'm told and enjoy vanishes. I wriggle on his lap and pull my arms out of his grip. "Not my wrists. Please, not yet." I thrust my weight against Seb and kiss him, determined not to spoil everything.

"No wrists." Seb lifts me from his thighs, turns me around and dumps me back on the sofa with a start. It's so out of the blue I can't help but laugh. "Keep your hands above your head. I won't touch them, but you have to keep them in position." I raise my arms while Seb unfastens my trousers and peels them from my legs. He stands, looming over me. His broad shoulders and the dark look on his face re-ignite my craving for him.

His fingers toy with the top of my knickers before slipping beneath the top. He trails his fingers over my skin, his touch only just not tickling, as he removes my knickers.

"Spread your legs for me. I intend to have you moaning my name, but I want to look at you first." His carnal words spike my arousal. I move my legs wide, wanting nothing more than to get lost in Seb. He continues to stand over me, scrutinising my body, but I can see his appreciation, the outline of his hard cock pressed against his trousers.

Finally, he lowers his body and settles between my legs. The burning desire for him to lick me has me clenching my own fists. I shift my weight down into the sofa, inching my bum towards the edge to give him better access to my pussy.

A feather-soft touch grazes my labia and I almost buck off of the sofa. Seb's next touch is firmer, stroking me with just enough pressure to settle my body. While he explores, I lock my arms overhead, determined to keep them in place.

Seb grows bolder with his caress, his thumb seeking out my clit and rubbing the tight bundle of nerves. Before his lips even touch my swollen clit I'm moaning his name, my ardour clearly visible from my soaking pussy.

His tongue dips between my wet folds, tasting my arousal.

"Hmm. You're very sweet, Isabel. You seem to be enjoying this."

"Yes, Sir," I sigh.

"You're turned on by submitting to me."

"Yes." A shudder runs through me as I take a deep breath. Seb searches my face before his face erupts in his perfect sexy smile. It's infectious.

He wastes no more time with small talk and sets about making me moan.

* * *

The Clark Practice is a swanky building in the centre of Bath, all glass fronted with minimal furniture. I am due to meet Dr. Amanda Cross at 11:30 a.m. It seems that Seb has some sway and managed to make me an appointment for Tuesday morning. I sit, gnawing on my lip as I wait for 11:30. My stomach is in knots. Like the incoming tide, anxiety hits my chest, wave after wave, each time the door to the patient area opens. My rational mind tells me that there is nothing to be frightened of or apprehensive about, but my rational brain has never won out in these situations.

"Ms. Fields?" A petite woman in her early forties calls my name. I stand and follow her through the double doors, relieved to finally be getting this over with. She escorts me into a comfortable room. A large desk stands beneath a frosted window and two small sofas sit at right angles to one another in the corner of the room. She gestures for me to take one and she takes a seat on the other.

"My name is Dr. Amanda Cross. This is your first session with me. Have you been to a counsellor before, Isabel?"

255

"Please call me Izzy, and no. This is all a bit new to me." I twist my fingers in my lap, attempting to stay as still as I can.

"Okay, Izzy. There's nothing to be worried about. We're just going to talk and see where that takes us, alright? Everything you say here is in complete confidence, so please try not to worry."

"Sure, that's fine."

"Good. Can you tell me why you've come to talk with me? And what you'd like to get out of these sessions?" Her question forces me to really think about what I want.

I fill Dr. Cross in on some basic background and what has led me to come here. I provide a concise rundown of my marriage and how Seb and I met. It all really skirts around the real issue, but I need some time to work up to that.

"I would like to talk about something that happened to me. To help me get over it. I don't want it to affect my life anymore, and a few people have suggested that talking about it might help."

"Can you be specific, Izzy?"

"Um, sure. Well, my ex-husband assaulted me. He forced himself on me." I take a breath and look around the room, reassuring myself that I'm safe. "He didn't rape me, but he would have if Seb didn't step in."

"This is what you're looking to move past, the attack?"

"Yes, and how it makes me feel now. How I react when I'm with my... boyfriend."

"And how do you feel now?" Amanda's voice is soft and soothing. It has a lilting quality that is relaxing.

"Hurt. He was my husband and he hurt me. He made me feel vulnerable and cheap. I was powerless, and he wouldn't stop. We spent years together, yet he could treat me so appallingly. Like it was his right to do so. He put me in a situation that took something from me. Now, he's cast a shadow over my relationship with Seb. We have a Dominant/submissive relationship and because of what Phil did, certain things frighten me, or rather they make me panic."

"Has Seb ever done anything that would make you feel that way with him?"

"God, no. He would never hurt me."

"That's good. Then what happens between you that makes you fear your feelings?"

I remember what it is. The placement of his hands. Around my ankles or my wrists. The points that Phil used to tie me. It took my ability to fight away and I felt helpless. I close my eyes, fighting off the sting of tears. I take a few deep breaths and choose my words. "When we're together, when he moves to touch me in a particular way, my mind goes back to what Phil did to me and I panic."

"You have triggers that take you back to the trauma. That's very normal, Izzy."

"But I don't want to have them. I used to enjoy what Seb did to me. It's not like we can't be intimate anymore. It's just, tainted by Phil. He's taken what I love and tarnished it." Tears drop from my lashes, mourning the beautiful connection that Seb and I had. "He's taken everything away from me. He ignored my feelings, ignored *me* for so long. When I finally found what I wanted, what I needed, he still had to have his way. He wouldn't just let me leave him and move on with my life. Now, I'm going to be a disappointment." My words rush out, strung together in a panic. Amanda leans over and offers me a tissue to dry my eyes. She gives me some time to get myself together before speaking again.

"Izzy, I think you have a lot of emotions and feelings inside that you're not sure how to make sense of right now. You said you wanted to move past the way you feel—the feelings associated with your attack. I'd like to focus on those triggers first. But I think that there are some other underlying issues that

257

you might want to think about airing as well." I nod at the woman, feeling content to talk to her and have her help. "You said that Phil has taken everything from you. I want to show you that you have the power to take it back."

"Really?" The hope in my voice is so profound. I didn't realise how much I needed to hear that from someone else. "But how?"

"It's going to take some time, and I'd like you to work with me on it. But above that, you need to believe that he can't take your happiness away. What he did to you was a specific episodic trauma. I want you to think about it as such. A one off. By recognising that and working up to facing the triggers, you'll be able to control your reactions and move past them."

"That sounds very... simple."

"It's not going to be fun and games all the time, but I can see how much you want to beat this. I'd also like to try EMDR therapy."

"What's that?"

"It's short for Eye Movement Desensitization and Reprocessing. It's been very successful in treatment of PTSD, trauma and disturbing memories. It helps the brain to re-process the event so that you can move past it."

"Okay," I agree tentatively.

"I'd ask you to talk over the attack and recall the feelings you had while asking you to focus on my finger. You focus on moving your eyes. After talking over the attack, your memories are replaced by more peaceful ones and you're able to re-process them." It sounds like a simple technique, although I know reliving the memories will be painful.

"That sounds simple enough." She smiles at me and places her hand over mine in a comforting show of support.

"I'd like to schedule a few further appointments with you. Do you feel comfortable with that?"

"Yes, that's fine. Thank you."

"Okay. Remember what I said. It was a single incident that you were unable to control. You're in control now. You're with Seb. You know he won't hurt you. We'll work on the triggers and the memory with the EMDR."

I leave the Clark Practice, and I feel lighter than when I walked in, as if by talking through everything, the burden has been lifted. I can see a way through. I feel hopeful.

Amanda said that it will take time and that my triggers won't disappear overnight, but that doesn't mean I can't try to work on them as well.

I head into work with a brighter outlook. I can focus on working and not letting Phil get to me more than he already has.

When I turn my computer on, there's an email waiting for me from Mark. I head over to his office, keen to look at whatever he needs. We've started to work well as a team. The last couple of months have been great for White Cube. I knock and poke my head around his door. "You wanted to see me, Mark?"

"Come in please, Izzy. Shut the door." Mark's face looks grave. I immediately think back to the campaigns we were working on last week. None of the new content is due to start being released until the end of the month, so it can't be that. I take a seat opposite his desk and look nervously at him.

"Izzy, I'm afraid... I'm afraid some information has been brought to our attention and it has some serious implications for you." I flinch at his words, unease coursing through my body.

"What information? Mark, what's going on?" My heartbeat thuds loudly in my ear.

"Are you familiar with The Erotic Fantasy, a Tumblr blog called 'My Secret Side' or Fetlife?" Mark names some of the websites and social platforms that I used to frequent regularly, where I would set my imagination free and fantasise about everything I wanted in my life. My face flushes red, knowing that Mark has seen or has access to my private profiles. I can't look at him and lower my eyes.

"Yes, I am," I choke out, panic impairing my voice.

"They have been directly linked to you. In our area of business, our expertise, we can't allow our name or our client's names to come into disrepute. There is a clear clause in your contract that states that the online behaviour of employees must not risk the reputation or credibility of the firm or our clients. This is… Well, it does."

"These are very private, Mark. They don't have my name on them. They can't be linked back to me. I've had these for years and it's never been a problem." I can hear where he's going and I can't believe it.

"Well, someone has linked you. It's been reported to me." Mark sits back in his chair, seemingly as uncomfortable as I am having this conversation.

"Who? Who would think to do this? I don't understand, Mark."

"I'm really sorry, Izzy. If it were up to me, it would be fine. But HR has a very strict policy and I can't do anything to stop it. The risk to some of our clients is too big."

"Can you at least tell me who complained about me?"

"I believe it was Phil Fields."

"Phil? My ex-husband, Phil?"

"I'm sorry. I can't undo the complaint based on who it came from. There is a clear trail from one post on your regular Facebook account that links back to your Tumblr blog. That then leads to the others. It's enough, Izzy. I'm sorry. I'm afraid that you'll be on gardening leave until the end of the month when you'll no longer be working for us." He's going to fire me because of my private online profile.

"What? This isn't right, Mark. I'm good at my job. You've seen what I've done on the client accounts. We wouldn't have won Sportletic's new account without me."

"I know, Izzy, but my hands are tied." It's Mark's turn to blush now. It makes me wonder if he's seen some of the content of my Tumblr account.

"What if I delete them?"

"It's too late. I need you to send me the latest reports you're working on and clear out your desk." Mark turns blurry in front of my eyes as the tears fill and overflow, landing on my clenched hands.

I've only just reached the belief that Phil can't take everything from me. Yet, an hour later, he is taking my livelihood away. My job, my career. "He did this for revenge because I divorced him. I've worked so damn hard these last few months for you."

"Izzy, please, I don't want to have to let you go. But you've breached your contract." The shock of this soon yields to fury. *This can't be happening. This isn't real.* The anger turns my tears hot and makes them run faster, but I have to compose myself. I can fall apart later. I dash the tears and stand abruptly, seething that Mark would take Phil's side over mine.

I head to my desk and grab the few personal belongings I have at work and shove them in my oversized bag. My laptop at home has duplicates of most of the reports and campaigns I've worked on.

Mark is standing over me as I finish up, and he escorts me back downstairs.

"I am really sorry, Izzy. I'll write you a great reference, and like I said, you'll be paid up to the end of the month."

"It's fine. Goodbye, Mark."

I walk to my car brimming with tears. After I open the door and dump my bag in the passenger seat, I take a few deep breaths to try to steady myself. It doesn't work, so I hold my breath, squeezing my eyes shut and trying to force the tears to stop. They continue to leak from my eyes, and I gasp out. I try to blink my fuzzy vision away but it's still there. The tears keep coming. *Get home. Just get home.* My heart is hammering in my chest, my breathing uneven. I pray that I can hold it together long enough to get home. Angry that the waterworks always get in my way, I swipe them from my cheeks and start the engine. *I can do this.* I can at least do this.

I know that Seb won't be home. It's the middle of the day, and I'm grateful that I don't have to face him. What would I say?

I walk about the house in a daze, slowly drifting through the rooms, thinking about how I wish everything could be different. That *I* could be different. A myriad of emotions are fighting for dominance inside of me—hurt, betrayal, panic, shame and anger. Anger is winning, but it shows itself through ugly tears and big sobs.

What am I going to do? How am I going to support myself? What will I do for money? Before I have a chance to make it to the bedroom, I've convinced myself that I'll never be able to find another job, nor will Seb want a divorced, unemployed girlfriend who can't give him what he needs.

I pick up my phone and call Jess.

"Hey, what's up?"

I steel myself, sucking in air to try to keep my voice from cracking. "I… Jess, I need… I, I, I need help."

"Oh, hun. What is it?"

"Work…" I gasp between the sobs lodged in my throat.

"Where are you? Are you at home?"

"Home," I cry out, giving up on the battle to remain composed.

"I'll be over. Just give me a few minutes, okay?"

"Th-thank you." I collapse onto the sofa and pull the cushion up to my chest. I cling to it like a life raft as I'm swept out to sea in my own fears.

True to her word, Jess is banging down the front door a few minutes later. I let her in. She barges through and has me swaddled in her arms before I can ask. She manoeuvres us back into the front room and onto the sofa.

"What's happened, Izzy?"

"It's Phil. He's ruined everything."

"Phil? I thought this was about work?" I pull away from her so that I can talk.

"It is. I got... I got fired." Tears drop to my cheeks, blurring my view of Jess.

"How? I don't understand."

"He told Mark about my private blog and websites I used to visit."

"So?"

"So, because my work revolves around social media, there is a clause to state that I can't do anything that could jeopardise the reputation of the company. Apparently the subject matter of my blog wasn't deemed appropriate." I can feel the rage building in the pit of my stomach. The more I speak the words, the more I explain, the more I hate Phil. Every single word adds weight to my hatred, my resentment of the man I used to love.

"Are you sure that's a clause in your contract? Have you checked it?"

"No."

"I can look over it for you, see if there is something that can counter this?"

"No, I can't go back. I just needed someone to..."

"Have you spoken to Seb?"

"No. I can't. Not yet." How can I admit that this has happened? I wrap my arms around myself, shielding me from what I will have to tell him.

"He'll understand. He'll look after you. You don't need to worry, Izzy." She strokes my shoulder, trying to comfort me.

"I know that, but I don't want that. I want my own job, my own independence. I'm good at my job. Phil has abused and attacked me and now he's taken something I love. I hate him! Phil…"

"Shh, it's alright. We can deal with one problem at a time."

The anger is bubbling up again, but it's accompanied by a panic, a fear that I'm not used to feeling. It's clawing at me, tearing down all of the good that I've built up with Seb. Everything that I wanted to move toward is falling away.

I stand and begin pacing the room. I can't cope. This is all too much. Suddenly, I hear the front door shut and Seb walks into the front room.

"Hey, I wasn't expecting you to be home." He halts and looks between me and Jess. "Is everything okay? Has something happened?"

"Perhaps I should go," Jess offers, and stands between us. I see her give a concerned look to Seb before heading to the door. I can't wait any longer and lunge towards Seb, needing his comfort.

"I appreciate you being here for Izzy," he whispers.

I peep up and mouth *thank you* to Jess as she sneaks out of the apartment.

He lets me cling to him for a few moments, gathering my strength. After this morning talking things out with Dr. Cross I was feeling strong. I don't want Phil to have the power to make me feel bad.

"Do you need to go back to work?" I ask, letting go of him and putting some distance between us.

"Yes, I'm meeting a client this afternoon. Look, Izzy, just tell me what's going on." The concern in his voice cuts through the air.

"I was fired. Mark fired me. Phil told Mark about my Tumblr and other sites. He's still controlling my life and I don't want him to." I push back from his chest so he can see the mess that I am.

"Fired? What for?"

"Breaching my contract. There was a link to one of my BDSM accounts back to me. That was enough. I don't have a job now." I can see that Seb is trying to rein in his temper.

"I want you to take me to Solace tonight." I blurt it out, but stand my ground. I need to show Seb that I can get back to what we had. I need to fight for us.

"Izzy, I don't think that's a good idea. Now, please, tell me what has happened, and think very carefully before you answer." He shifts his body so he's standing directly over me, challenging me. I walk up to him and wrap my arms around his neck.

"Please take me to Solace," I whisper in his ear. "I want you to dominate me. To take back what he's taken from me." I bury my face into his neck, his body now stiff with tension after my quiet words.

Seb scoops me up and plants us on the sofa so I'm snuggled on his lap.

"Sweetheart, you need to help me out and explain. Why were you home with Jess? Did you go and speak to Dr. Cross?"

"Yes, I saw her this morning. I'm going to continue to see her."

"That's really great, but I don't think we need to go to Solace straight away."

"You don't understand. I need this. I need to do something positive, fight back against him and show him, or me, that he won't have any more power over me. It's my life that I want, and I want us."

"You have us, Izzy. Nothing has changed. And we don't need to worry about your job. I'll take care of you."

"Thank you, but I also need and want my own independence." I'm off his lap and stomping around the room. He doesn't understand. He doesn't see why I need to have something that is for me. I need to take the power that Phil took back.

"Okay, Izzy, but I'm not taking you to Solace when you're like this. We need to talk and you're upset right now."

"Upset? Really? You think I'm upset? What gave you that impression?" I scoff.

"Izzy, don't be like this."

"I want to go, Seb. If you won't take me then I'll go on my own."

"Like hell you will. You won't set foot inside without me."

"Really?" I shout, suddenly more than happy to take out my pain on the man I love.

"Yes, really. I will not play with you when you're like this."

"Fine, play with Natasha. Show me what you'll do to me."

"What? No. Never."

"Why not?"

"Because I love you, and I'm not going to touch another sub. No one but you, Izzy." Seb crosses the room and grabs my shoulders, making me face him. "No one but you, even when you're being ridiculous. Look at me. Look. At. Me." He holds my gaze and I feel every word he says.

"I won't let him win, Seb. I can't. All I wanted was to be free from him and have my life with you. First he argued over the divorce, then he attacked me and now he's taken my job. He's taking everything from me and I want it back."

"He hasn't taken me."

"But he will," I plead. "What if I always get panicked when you go to tie my hands or ankles? What if I can't see past the fear? I want to be the person you've been looking for, your ideal submissive, but I'm scared that I'm nowhere near close to that, and now this. I can't lose you too."

"No, you won't. That will never happen."

"You don't know that."

"I do. I love you. I'm your partner, your lover, your Dom. It's my job to protect you, to cherish you and watch over you. It's also my job to tell you when you're being irrational and talking crap." With his words, my anger ebbs and my heart bleeds for what's happened to us over the last few weeks.

"I need this, Seb."

"I know, sweetheart. But not like this."

"Then how? I'm sick of feeling scared. I'm sick of feeling what Phil did to me when we're together. I need to get over these memories. I need it." Desperation has taken root and I now have a single-minded focus on fixing us.

"Okay, but not tonight. What did Dr. Cross say?"

"She said that I need to look at the attack as a single event and realise that Phil can't take my happiness. She's going to try some eye movement therapy with me as well."

"That's good."

"So what's stopping us from going to Solace? You said we would after I saw a counsellor."

"That was before today happened. Take some time, Izzy. I'm not going anywhere."

"You don't understand, Seb."

"And you don't get to dictate to me. I told you we would do it my way." His voice switches and it knocks the frustration out of me. "I'll phone Natasha and we'll watch a scene."

"How will that help?"

"I'll speak to her and choreograph it. It will be everything I want from a scene with you, but you'll be safely in my arms. You can see how nothing bad will happen. I know you're hurting, sweetheart, but you need to listen to me and trust I know what's best. I won't be pressed on this." His comforting words are edged with the dominance that has the ability to melt my body.

"When?"

"Tomorrow night."

"Really?" My hopes rise at his suggestion.

"Really. Trust me, Izzy. We'll get through this."

White-hot fury burns through me at what that bastard has done to Izzy. Not content with emotionally and physically abusing her, he's taken away her livelihood and with it, her newfound confidence and happiness. She should have let me kill the fucker.

She's finally sleeping, exhausted from the stress of the day. I've never seen her so wound up, so frantic. At least when she told me she wanted some space she seemed calm about her decision. She's clawing to try to regain her footing and grasping at any solution, no matter the cost.

Taking her to Solace would be a disaster. I'm not sure that waiting until tomorrow will be much better, but I know Izzy well enough to know that she won't back down from this. I just hope that Natasha will help. Pacing the room, I call her.

"Hey, look, if you're upset about my little announcement…"

"That's not why I've called. Natasha, I need your help." No matter our differences, Natasha has always been there to support me.

She's instantly supportive. "What do you need?"

"I need to take Izzy to Solace, but I'm not playing with her. She thinks by going to the club she'll magically get back some sense of control that her ex-husband took away. She has a couple of triggers when she submits. She's seeing the counsellor that Luke put me in touch with, but that fucker has just had her fired. She's seeing overcoming these barriers as the only positive thing she can do." I sit at my desk and try to relieve the steel ropes that have replaced the muscles in my neck.

"What do you have in mind?"

"Izzy is drowning in self-doubt, lack of confidence and independence. I need to show her that she doesn't have to worry about any of that. She needs to believe in us. I need to reach the woman who arrived at my door all those months ago, ready to submit to me and put her trust in me."

"Okay. I still don't understand why you need my help, but for once we agree on the goal of the situation."

"I want you to do the scene that I would do, if I was with Izzy before the attack. I want her to see how I would take her submission and use it to solidify our trust." I imagine everything I would do to her in vivid detail—her position, the bindings, the words I'd use to reinforce my message.

"Okay, I can see where you're going. Have you got it all worked out?"

"Yes." I hesitate. "Thank you, Natasha."

"Hey, anytime. I can see how much she means to you, and I think this is a good way to try and get through to her. It will make her see that her submission is a gift, that she holds the power. Now, you need to take me through this scene step by step. If it involves a spanking, I think Sarah would be perfect for this."

Despite being put to bed like a child, I obviously needed the sleep. Twelve hours later, I feel a whole lot more confident about getting a handle on my life. Seb has brought me coffee and is working in his study. Thankfully, he isn't hovering.

My eyes are red raw and my stomach rumbles in protest at not eating for most of yesterday. I wrap myself in my robe and head to the kitchen, determined to start my day positively and not disintegrate into the emotional wreck that I am under the surface. I remember all of the events from yesterday, culminating in fighting with Seb, insisting that he take me to Solace. In my not-so-rational mind, ripping the plaster off in one go will hurt less than trying to pull it free slowly. In the stark reality of morning, I'm not so sure. Seb has agreed, though. Surely that means that I'm not completely certifiable? *No, I'm stronger than this. I've been a coward for far too long. Phil can't do this to me anymore.*

I brew a fresh pot of coffee and set about making breakfast. As I whisk the eggs, my mind skips to my first visit to Solace. A huge part of the thrill of that night was the anticipation and the build-up. My nerves were both fighting against me and adding to the slow burn of lust, ready to catch fire at Seb's request.

My anticipation is tainted, now. I know what I fear—being tied down with no way out, no physical way to shield myself from hands set to deliver pain and not pleasure. The powerless position I could be in, with no safeword and no-one to save me. I squeeze my eyes tight and breathe out the bad memories. Letting them overtake me won't help later on.

The eggs are thoroughly beaten, so I start them cooking in the pan. I'm not hiding that I'm up and about, but Seb hasn't ventured out to see me. I finish off the eggs and then take a fresh mug of coffee in to him. He's been nothing but supportive of me and I know that it's been difficult for him.

"Hi." I peek around the corner of his office door.

"Good morning. You can come in, you know?"

"I know. I didn't want to disturb you. I know you're home today because of me."

"Yes, and there is nothing wrong with that." He beckons me over, and I walk to his desk, setting the mug down next to his open laptop.

"How are you feeling this morning?"

"Hungry. I made some eggs. I don't think I ate yesterday." Seb stands and walks over to me. He takes my hand and leads me back out into the kitchen.

"Sit and eat," he orders with a pointed look at the kitchen table, and I'm happy to oblige. I fork my eggs under Seb's patient gaze, knowing that we'll be talking after I've finished. He moves to pour himself a new cup of coffee, the one in the study forgotten.

Last night, I felt like my whole world was coming down around me, that because of my decision to leave Phil, to take something for me, I was being punished. By Phil. Today, I still feel like my world is in shards of glass, smashed on the floor, but I still have Seb standing by me. He is the beacon of hope that I need to reach for. He can light my way back. I just need to have the courage to face my monsters to get there.

"I've spoken to Natasha and we will go to Solace tonight." His words are spoken with a tense edge, despite his relaxed appearance. "We do this under the same understanding, though, Izzy. You follow my rules, my command, and you submit without hesitation. Wear your anklet. Understand?"

"Yes."

"Good. Come here." He opens his arms and I run into them, suddenly feeling like a small child needing comfort. "It will be alright, Izzy. You have to believe that I won't let anything bad happen to you."

"I know." I mumble the words against his warm chest and hope that he's right.

* * *

A blanket of dark cloud has been drawn across the world as the sun sets in the sky. It's still early to be at Solace, but Seb has been very particular on this. It will be by his rules or we leave. I'm in the same backless dress as I was last time, the same skyscraper heels. I won't be swayed from my decision, and although Seb refuses to play with me here, I want to know how he would. I need my mind to let go of the fear and accept what Seb's actions would be.

I miss the satisfaction from submitting to Seb. I miss the connection and the respite from my doubts. I want to fight for that as much as I want to fight Phil for taking it away from me. *Will that be enough, though? Will I be enough?*

The same smartly dressed 'butler' opens the oak door as Seb cradles me against his side. We walk into the entryway and my heart jumps as the door closes behind us. The nerves that are firing at a hundred miles an hour aren't because of what might happen tonight. They are because of my fear that this won't work and I'll be stuck in panic mode.

Seb moves silently through the restaurant to the frosted glass doors. Natasha is sitting at a secluded booth to the side of the room with a beautiful woman next to her. Natasha looks mesmerising—her hair pulled back and braided in a French plait, containing the curls, a dark coloured corset making a feast of her breasts, which are spilling from the top. My eyes reluctantly leave her as we reach the doorway that Seb ushers me through.

"Last chance, Izzy. You don't have to do this. You have nothing to prove."

"I know." I look up at him and see the concern darkening his aqua eyes.

"Once we enter, you're my submissive. You do as I say with no hesitation. I'll check in with you more often than usual. Remember, 'yellow' if you need to take a moment and 'black' if you want to leave. We won't be actually doing a scene, but I will be touching you. Understand?"

"Yes." I melt into the authority of his voice and feel the stirrings of desire in the pit of my stomach.

Seb's lips crash into mine in a brutal but possessive kiss. It knocks me off-kilter and I react on instinct, giving in to his demanding tongue. His purposeful strokes claim me and I whimper under his intensity. I feel my nipples pebble against the fabric of the dress, my body already flushed from his kiss alone.

As quickly as he started, Seb moves away and pulls me to his side as he opens the door through to the more intimate areas of Solace. He guides us to one of the small, secluded bars and orders me a gin and tonic and himself a sparkling water. We sit in the corner of the bar in plush, wing-backed chairs. Seb's gaze is locked onto me. Every breath, every fidget of my body has his full attention.

Coupled with the worry that I might never be able to relax into submission again is my fear that Seb will grow to resent me if I can't. And to top off my growing pressure, I've forced Seb's hand in bringing me here.

I force my negativity away and try to focus on why I insisted on this. I sip my drink and let the ice-cold liquid settle my knotted stomach. From my position, I can see out into the hallway. Natasha is standing on the periphery, the woman from the restaurant in her shadow. The woman whose eyes I wanted to scratch out now looks as formidable as she does mesmerising.

I think back to Seb's words that it will be Natasha who will be doing the scene for us to watch. Heat flourishes across my cheeks at the thought of seeing Natasha being intimate with the woman beside her. My heart drums in my chest, imagining her carrying out the explicit acts that Seb has done to me. With me. The beautiful images from my Tumblr blog—women tied, bound and willingly submitting to the wills of their Doms.

"I'm glad that Natasha can hold your attention, sweetheart." Seb's deep voice forces my attention back to him. The gleam in his eyes fails to hide his mirth. I dip my eyes from his gaze and busy myself with my hands in my lap. "Don't hide from me, Isabel. I like that you're interested in what's going to happen tonight."

"Sorry. I didn't know how I'd feel about seeing Natasha… here."

"And how do you feel?" His question ignites my blush once again.

"Um, eager… I've been trying to anticipate what will happen and I'm hopeful that this will do what I want it to."

"What about watching Natasha? You've met her before. Are you comfortable with that now that you're here?"

"Yes." I look up and try to sound as confident as possible.

"Good girl." Seb sweeps a thumb across my bottom lip, sending sparks through my blood. My eyes dart back to where Natasha was standing, but she's nowhere in sight.

276

I take another long draw of my drink before Seb stands and pulls me up beside him. My hands attempt to pull down the hem of my dress, but to no avail. It is still as ridiculously short as when I first put it on.

"Stop fidgeting. You look delicious." I still and take a deep breath. Pulling myself up in stature, I let Seb guide me the rest of the way, down the staircase and along the corridor to the other set of frosted glass doors. As we approach, they open and we're welcomed into the main room. How I thought I could ever come here alone is beyond me, but my resolve is still strong. My heartbeat betrays my nerves but I refuse to show my trepidation.

Seb runs the tips of his fingers down my back before placing his hand just above my bum. All of his light, gentle touches have been building up. He's making sure that I'm used to his hands on me, that I'm happy with it. The familiar yearning that his touch elicits is growing in presence and I welcome it.

Much like the first visit, we walk slowly around the room. As it's early, there are few people playing. The only other people we come across are seated in secluded areas, perhaps waiting for the evening to develop. We approach the area where we watched the Dom and his sub on the St. Andrew's cross. This time, I see Natasha and her sub. Natasha has her back to us, but I can see the expression on her sub's face. She's high on pleasure as Natasha brushes her skin with the ends of her flogger. Seb has drawn me close against his side and he whispers to me.

"This isn't part of what I have planned. This is the warm up, if you will, for our scene. I want you to watch carefully and look for Sarah's expressions."

"Who's Sarah?"

"Natasha's sub." I watch as Natasha takes her time to pet and soothe Sarah, to keep almost constant contact with her, ensuring she is happy. Yet, at the same time as showing the highest level of concentration and care of her sub, she looks

277

totally dangerous. Her stance, the power that she exudes is like a physical force field around her.

My eyes flick between the cuffs around Sarah's wrists on the cross and her face. At no point does she try to pull away or escape. If anything, she is relaxing further into her bonds the more attention Natasha gives her.

"They will finish in a minute and move across to the spanking bench. That's when our scene will start." Seb's chocolate voice tickles the shell of my ear and sends a course of goose bumps across my skin. So far, all I've felt by watching is a deep sense of desire and even envy. I want to be able to put myself in the position that Sarah is in. I want the attention that I know Seb will show me.

The mental and physical frustration that have been wearing on me are beginning to take their toll. Yesterday saw the first fissure break, and I know that it won't take much to let the cocktail of fear, frustration, desire and hope overcome me.

Natasha unties Sarah and steadies her as she moves across to the spanking bench as Seb said. As they move, Seb shifts behind me and encircles my chest with his arm so I'm braced against his body. His other arm is gripping my hip, keeping me in place.

"We'll watch, and I'll tell you everything I'd do if it were you and me up there. I want you to respond as if we are in their position. If anything gets too much, use 'yellow'. You will do as I say without any hesitation. Understand?"

"Yes," I breathe.

"Cross your hands in front of you at the wrists and keep them down."

I do as I'm asked and keep my arms flat against me.

"Good girl." Seb's lips press softly against my temple. "Natasha is binding Sarah's hands with silk behind her back. It will be tight enough that she won't be able to free herself, but won't cause her wrists to hurt." Seb describes the scene that I

278

watch in front of me. As Sarah's hands are tied, I see Natasha check her work and then lie her sub gently across the spanking bench. Her hands are, again, in constant contact with Sarah's skin. If she is in need of reassurance, she has it. I can see Natasha walk around and kneel by Sarah.

"She'll be checking in with her. Knowing Natasha, she'll also be building the anticipation for the sub. Sarah can't see us now, so Natasha will likely be telling her about all of the eyes fixed on her exposed pussy, how they can all see how much she likes to submit. When I do this to you, Isabel, there won't be anyone else looking at your pretty pussy. It will be for my eyes only. I'll be the one to make you hot and needy. I don't want to share a single part of you with someone else."

His hand runs around from my hip to give my bum a harsh squeeze before going back to its original position. Seb's words and seeing what is unfolding in front of me is a heady mix that has all of my senses focused on what's around me. There is no room for anything else, and for that, I'm grateful.

"In this position, bent over, your arse will be on perfect display for me. I'll be able to spank you if you've been naughty, or give you the attention I know you crave from me." Again, his hand moves around to squeeze my bum, and as he does, the hem of my dress hitches up higher on my thigh.

Natasha is still in front of Sarah, talking to her, but I can see that Sarah is growing restless. She is fidgeting against the bench. The light in the room is just enough to show the glistening wetness between her legs, betraying her arousal. My temperature rockets and I fight my own need to fidget.

"What are you thinking, Isabel? I can feel all of your reactions like this, and I need you to talk to me."

"I… I can see how turned on Sarah is. I can see that she's wet."

"Yes, I have no doubt that she will be enjoying this. Are you? Are you wet already from what you've seen?"

"Yes, I like watching this. I'm not sure if I should, but it's very intimate." I try to articulate my foggy thoughts.

Seb's fingers toy with the exposed flesh of my thigh, his other arm keeping me anchored to his chest. Natasha moves around Sarah and picks up her flogger again. With rapid movements, she lands light blows up and down Sarah's back, bum and thighs. Her strikes beat out a steady and sure rhythm that relaxes my overactive heart. Now it's Seb's turn to keep constant contact with my skin. His fingers dig into my thigh, rub circles and inch higher before moving to a new spot. Watching the spanking and feeling Seb's innocent touch is making me desperate. *I want to feel his touch. I want to be under his command.*

"Natasha is going to move Sarah again into a more personal position. She's going to continue the spanking across her lap so she can be in total contact and control of her. Her hands will still be tied. Sarah will have to give Natasha permission to do this, but I doubt that she'll have any thought of objecting. Have you noticed how turned on she is? How much her body wants what Natasha is giving to her?"

With Seb's direction, my eyes linger on Sarah's parted legs and I can see that her pussy lips are wet and dewy. Natasha stops her flogging and comes to stand at the side of Sarah. Making sure we have a clear view of what she's doing, she sweeps a finger through her wet folds. Sarah groans in response, the first time I've heard her, and I can't help my own mewl of need.

Seb's hand trails up behind my backside and skims a feather touch against my pussy. That touch is nowhere near enough and I want Seb to touch me like Natasha is touching Sarah. "Sebastian, will you touch me? Please?"

"Mmm... certainly." His fingers sweep over my lips, sending shocks to my neglected clit. "You're wet Isabel. You're beautifully wet. Do you want my fingers in you? Do you want me to bury them deep into your tight pussy until you clench around them?"

Oh sweet lord. "Yes, please… Please, Sir." His finger pushes inside me and I'm enveloped by relief followed by heat. Pleasure spikes as he slowly draws his finger back and replaces it with two, making my knees quake in my standing position. My hands haven't moved from in front of me, but I feel desperate to wrap them around Seb, to get as close to him as I can. I'm split between wanting to watch the play between Natasha and Sarah and just focusing on Seb. I know that it's both actions that have led me to let go of my fear and open up and relax into Seb. *That and him getting me so damn horny I'm begging for it.*

Natasha and Sarah have moved. I can see that Natasha is sitting now, and Sarah is kneeling at her feet. She is offering her hands to Natasha for her to bind them again.

"Sarah will have her hands tied in the front this time." Seb's fingers still play with me and I can feel the building of my orgasm. He pulls his fingers out of me, leaving me empty, and I hold back the whimper lodged in my throat. His hand moves to mine, still diligently crossed in front of me. He rests his hands over mine and I fight my body's instinctive need to tense up.

"Shh, sweetheart. Don't panic. Focus on watching Sarah. She's offering her hands to Natasha. She knows that Natasha won't do anything against her wishes. She's giving this to her—a sub to her Domme—like you give me your trust and your submission. Remember that first time? Remember your nerves, your lust, your strength to win through all of your doubts?" Seb's words sink into my soul and I relax my hands. He rubs my wrists, making sure that I'm not going to tense on him again, and I can see that it's working. I'm still here at Solace, not back with Phil. I can see Sarah's hands are now bound and she's resting her chest across Natasha and I can feel Seb adding pressure to my own hands, binding them with his.

"Natasha is going to start hand spanking Sarah. They have talked about what the spanking is for. I want you to listen to what I say and repeat what I say. I will spank you as well. Do you understand?"

"Yes."

"Good girl. I'm going to hold your hands as well. I want you to give them to me. Place your crossed hands in my palm so that I can keep you still." He moves his arm off my clavicle and I place my wrists in his hand. As I do, a loud smack sounds out and echoes through the room. My eyes flash to Sarah and recognise the pleasure spread across her face. Seb glides the remainder of my dress over my behind, giving him easy access.

As I watch Natasha's hand arc down onto Sarah's offered bottom, Seb lands his own soft smack to mine. "I will trust my Dom." His deep gravelly voice resonates deep within me and I can't help but feel the first crack in my emotions.

"I will trust my Dom," I whisper back, trying to feel the words he's asking me to say.

With Natasha's next spank, Seb smacks me and delivers more words. "I will listen to my body."

I repeat the words, now understanding what Seb is making me do.

"I will communicate openly."

I repeat the line.

"I am wanted."

I breathe through the words as I echo them back.

"I am needed." Seb's voice is calm and measured, telling me everything that I need to hear.

"I am needed."

"I am loved."

My eyes can't hold back the tears any longer and they fall at my admissions back to Seb. All of my fears and worries are being laid bare for Seb to wash aside and replace with his strength and love. "I am loved."

Determined to break me open completely, Seb continues. It's harder to watch Sarah now through my bleary eyes, but I can hear her throaty moans of pleasure under Natasha's hand.

"I am my own person," I repeat, feeling the power that saying these words aloud gives me.

"I am independent."

"I am independent."

"I hold the power."

"I hold the power."

"My Dom loves me."

"My Dom loves me." Seb loves me. For who I am. With every hit, Seb opens me up to the truth that he's been trying to tell me from day one. Finally, I'm in a position to accept and to hear him. My body softens against him, using him to support my limbs under the onslaught of emotional release. He turns me around, finally releasing his grip on my hands. I quiver, standing before him. Seb recaptures my hands and brings them to his lips to kiss.

"Do you understand now? Do you see? We'll get through this, Isabel. I'll be by your side. You've done so well tonight, sweetheart. I'm so proud of you." He draws me in to an engulfing hug and I rest my head against his chest, listening to his racing heart.

I love this man with everything I have. I know that tonight has helped to lay some of my triggers to rest, but I'll have to listen to Seb, be guided by him and trust that he can help me when I can't see my way to helping myself.

"I'm sorry for how I've treated you. I seem to always be apologising."

"Shh, not now. Now is for us. Just us. You have no idea how well you've done tonight. At the risk of pushing us too far too quickly, I want to go to our room."

"That sounds perfect."

283

"I meant what I said, Isabel. We'll get through this together. Trust that."

"I do, Sebastian. Thank you for getting me back to this place."

"Always."

"Always."

Twenty-Seven

6 months later

"Thank you, Amanda."

"I'll see you next month."

I get up and leave Dr. Cross's office after my latest session. Over the last few months, we've been working through a lot of my negative views and where they stem from, and with Seb's help, I've been making real progress. I don't see Amanda as a counsellor, but a confidante with whom I can share my troubles. She helps me to see my own problems and to work through them without simply telling me what to do.

It's early evening and my next stop is Jess. I have a favour to ask her, and hope that she's free. As I pull up outside her house, I see Greg storm out, slamming the door behind him and barging past.

"Jess?" I call out as I open the door. "It's me."

"Hey, come in, come in."

"You sure? I just saw Greg and he didn't look happy."

"Well, Greg is never happy. Drink?"

"Just a tea, please. Is everything alright between you two?"

"It's the usual story. We're not exactly seeing eye to eye. What are you doing here, anyway? It's lovely to see you." She brings two steaming cups of tea over to the table and we both sit down.

"Well, I sort of need a favour. Are you free now?"

"Now? Um… yes. What do you need?"

"I need you to come with me to an appointment. It shouldn't take long. A couple of hours, tops."

"Sure. Where are we going? Are you alright?" The concern in Jess's voice is heart-warming and I struggle to keep my amusement to myself.

"Yes, I'm fine. It's a good thing. I just need you to hold my hand."

"Izzy, you know how I feel about being kept in the dark."

"You'll see." I grin at her, my smug smile beaming from behind my tea cup.

An hour later, we're both sitting in the small waiting area of a tattoo shop. The walls are dark and littered with pictures, randomly arranged in gilded frames.

"I can't believe you're doing this," Jess whispers beside me.

"I know. It's exciting." My heart is beating fiercely in my chest.

"I'm all up for holding your hand, but why, exactly, are you having a tattoo?"

I've been purposefully vague to her but it's time to come clean.

"It's my wedding gift. Or engagement gift, really."

"Engagement? You're going to marry Seb?"

"Yes." My smile splits my face and my cheeks begin to ache with the joy at admitting to the decision that I came to a few weeks ago. Jess bundles me into her for a hug and we rock back and forth on the small sofa.

"Oh, you totally deserve this, Izzy. What made you change your mind?" She pulls back from our hug.

"Nothing specific. I think I just needed time to make the decision for me. It was always Phil or Seb taking charge of my life, and I wasn't even sure I wanted to be married again. If I was going to get married, I wanted it to be my decision, not because I wanted to please Seb. This is my choice and I choose Seb."

"He's going to be beside himself. He doesn't know yet?"

"No. I hope so."

"Don't start doubting now."

"I'm not. Don't worry. He's stopped asking and I think that helped. It took the pressure off me and let me find my own answer and trust my feelings. It's taken a while to believe in them again."

"Izzy? We're ready for you now." A willowy young woman calls us over and escorts us to the back of the shop. She points to a large leather chair that reminds me of a dentist's chair, and a pulse of fear runs through me. "If you take a seat, Tanya will be over. She's just printing out your design. Then we'll get it placed before we start."

"Thank you." I sit back in the seat and Jess pulls up the small office chair beside me.

"So, what are you having done?"

"My anklet, or a drawing of my anklet."

"I didn't know you wore an anklet?" Jess looks a little puzzled, and I guess she would be.

"It's something between me and Seb. Don't worry. He'll understand."

"Hi, nice to see you again, Izzy." Tanya is next to me now with a thin sheet of paper in her hand. "You ready? I just need to get this positioned. If you can take off your shoes." I take off my shoes and rest my foot on the chair so Tanya can press the design around my foot and get the perfect position for the chain.

"I brought the actual anklet to help. Jess, it's in my bag." Jess rummages for a second and pulls out the little black box.

"Perfect. I'll add some embellishments to the basic design." A fuzzy purple ring appears on my ankle and I panic, thinking about how this could come out—a horrible black ring forever around my ankle. Stop it. It will be fine. I chide myself and take a breath. Tanya knows what she's doing. She adds a few details with a pen before sitting back.

"Right, happy?" I glance down and look closely, seeing the small details and crystals she's drawn on by hand.

"Yes, let's go for it." Jess claps her hands in excitement as Tanya busies herself with the final preparations.

I lean right back in the chair and look up at the ceiling, expecting the worst. I feel Jess's hand close around mine and I squeeze it hard.

"Right, ladies. The sound is worse than the pain. Keep still and just say if you want me to stop at any time, okay?"

"Yep," I force out.

"Right. Sound first, then you'll feel a slight scratching sensation."

A high-pitched, whiney buzzing fills my ears for a few seconds before stopping. Then, it's back. Tiny, sharp pinpricks press into my bony ankle and send flashes of pain through me. I close my eyes and breathe through it, grasping Jess's hand harder. I bear the uncomfortable pain for a few moments before I get a rest. Tanya starts again seconds later, and I go back to trying to block it out. Just as I think the pain is going to be too much, it eases somewhat as she moves round to a more fleshy part of my ankle.

"You're doing really well, Izzy," Tanya says, and I open my eyes to watch her. The metal contraption she holds looks clunky in comparison to the tiny black she's marking on my skin. I watch for a few more moments, now used to the pinprick sensation.

"It's looking great, Izzy." Jess is more engrossed than me. I close my eyes again and hope that Seb will be as pleased as I am that I'm giving this to him. "So, when is the wedding?"

"Wedding? Oh, not for a while. I've not even told him I'll marry him yet."

"Ha, don't make me laugh. He's been wanting to put a ring on you for nearly a year. Get ready for a winter wedding." Her comment doesn't upset me. It makes me giggle, but I quickly stop, wary of moving about too much.

We sit quietly with just the buzzing for a few minutes before Jess starts up the conversation again.

"When's Phil's hearing?"

"In a few weeks."

"Are you alright, you know, with being a witness?"

"Yes. Although I didn't press the charges, I still get to stand up for myself, even if it's a bit late."

Phil assaulted Sophie, the girl he was cheating on me with, after she kicked him out. The police came to question me and I ended up telling them about my attack. I am now a witness for the prosecution against him.

"I'm proud of you. You didn't have to do anything."

"I know, but how could I not? Having Seb to support me and being able to talk it through with Dr. Cross has also helped. Hopefully, it will give me some closure as well."

Our conversation trails off and I try to focus on something other than the buzzing sound of the gun. I zone out for a while, contemplating how my life has changed over the last few months. Six months ago I didn't think I'd ever get out from

289

under the overwhelming changes to my life. Now, I know that it was all worth it.

"Right, Izzy, I'm about done. I need to wash you off and get you wrapped up." Tanya stops the pin-scratching and I relax my body, unaware of how much tension I was holding on to.

She cleans and then wraps my pretty anklet in cling film, and my excitement dies at the fact that it won't be perfect and pretty to show Seb.

"Take off the film when you get home and then soak it and wash it with warm water and antibacterial soap. Let it air dry. You can show your guy then. You have to apply Bepanthen before wrapping it back up, okay? It's all on our website."

I thank Tanya as I pay my balance, and Jess drives us back to her place where I pick up my car and head for home.

Seb and I are still renting the same place, but I have started looking for something to buy. I'm in no rush, though, and neither is Seb. The last six months have meant change for Seb as well as me.

We have reached a point we're both happy with when it comes to D/s. I always submit in the bedroom, when we are at home and when we go to Solace. It's a good compromise and one that we both benefit from. Seb can still get the high from the TPE element, but without it causing me to worry or question myself to the point of confusion. We check in through the day, but the rules aren't as rigid as they were. When Seb is away, the frequency increases.

I can trust that Seb, as my Dom, will stretch my submission, but he knows where my weak spots are, and when he needs to pull back. We are happy, but it's within my power to put the cherry on the cake, and I intend to do just that.

I park and enter the house, a ball of excitement. Seb is in the kitchen and I call out as I rush upstairs to clean my new ink. I run a shallow bath and rest my foot in it for a few minutes before cleaning it with soap. I change into a black lace dress, which is short and has a revealing neck line. It is one of my Solace dresses—the ones I wear only when submitting to Seb—and I pad barefoot back to the kitchen.

My heartbeat echoes inside my ears as I walk over and sit at the kitchen table. Seb's eyes watch me as I saunter across his line of sight and they fix on me as I sit.

"Good evening, Isabel."

"Good evening, Sebastian." His sexy smile is in full effect and I can't keep my face straight.

"Do you have something you want to say? You look like you want to play, sweetheart." He turns off whatever was cooking and stalks over to where I've sat.

"Maybe, Sir." My voice drips with satisfaction. I know I'm being a tease, but right now, I don't care.

"Don't start something you can't finish, Isabel." He's behind me in a second, his hand gripping my hair, tilting my head back to look at him. The adrenaline spike sends a warm rush of desire to my clit and I can feel the clench of my pussy already.

"I think dinner can wait tonight." He plunders my lips with hot, aggressive kisses and I melt under his dominance. His hand keeps a tight hold of my hair, ensuring I can't escape, while his other freely runs down the front of my dress, discovering my lack of underwear.

"Isabel," he growls. "You need to tell me what's going on right now, or I'll take great pleasure in spanking you on the table until you do." The warning in his voice sends erotic shivers through my body. I'd like nothing more than to bend over and feel the palm of Seb's hand against my skin.

"I'd like that, Sir."

"Fuck, yes, you would, wouldn't you? Do you have your anklet on?"

"Yes, Sir. See?" I lift my leg and rest it against the edge of the table. Seb looks at it and I feel the grip on my hair loosen as he takes in what I'm showing him.

"Izzy, is that… a tattoo?" The emotion is clear in his voice, and my heart stills for my next words. I drop my foot and turn in my chair to face him.

"Yes, I wanted to give this to you. As a gift. It's a little raw, though."

"A gift? Is it my birthday?" I can see his hunger warring with his confusion at my explanation.

"An engagement gift for you."

"Engagement…" He repeats the word in a gravelly breath, catching on to my meaning.

"Yes, I want to marry you, Seb. I want to submit to you and be your wife. If you'll still have me?" His beautiful aquamarine eyes dilate and his sexy smile is back. He bends to kiss my forehead.

"Of course I'll have you. You're it for me, Izzy. I love you and you've made me the happiest man by agreeing to marry me. Thank you, sweetheart."

He bends to cradle me in his arms and lifts me.

"Hey, where are we going?"

"I want to make love to my wife in our bed. I'm suddenly only hungry for one thing. But don't worry, I'll spank your gorgeous arse over the table later."

"Here they are." Jess walks in, carrying a bouquet.

"Jess, you've got the wrong flowers. That isn't my bouquet." I freeze in the middle of her lounge, already dressed in my gown and just needing the flowers before we make our way to the ceremony.

"I know, but these are what you're having. They are from Seb."

"Seb? Why is he choosing my flowers? They aren't anything like…"

"Stop! Calm down. Read this as well. It's from him, and perhaps it will help to calm your nerves." She passes me a thick envelope, the same as the previous notes he's sent me. I perch on the edge of the sofa and gently peel it open.

Dearest Isabel,

It was once tradition for the husband to pick flowers for his wife and leave them on her doorstep. This is the closest I could come to that tradition, and I wanted to give you one final message.

So that we are clear, this is the meaning behind these flowers.

The red rose signifies our love. I love you with everything I am and that will never fade.

The lily is for majesty. You hold all of the splendour I could wish for. Our story is just that—it's ours and I am going to cherish it.

Blue hyacinths are for constancy. I am your constant. You've come so far in believing that, and I need you to hold on to that forever.

I'm not saying that everything will be smooth sailing, but we will remain constant.

The baby's breath is for everlasting love.

I'll look forward to seeing you walk towards me, ready to become my wife, holding the message I want to share with you.

I love you Isabel York.

Always yours,

Sebastian.

The End.

We'd like to thank you for reading Forever More by Rachel De Lune. Desire *more* from your romance novel? Get a FREE Novella! Sign up for Rachel's infrequent mailing list and be notified of GIVEAWAYS, Advanced reader opportunities and Pre-order notifications!
Join us at:
http://eepurl.com/bckw0r

If you enjoyed Forever More and would like to give back to the author, please consider writing a review! Reviews are a tremendous help for authors. So if you were moved and enjoyed this book enough to write even one sentence of encouragement it would be a huge boon.

Connect with Rachel De Lune:

Facebook:
http://on.fb.me/1FXxBwa

Twitter:
https://twitter.com/rachel_de_lune

Google+:
https://plus.google.com/103010030570874602054/posts

Goodreads:
https://www.goodreads.com/user/show/19186002-rachel-de-lune

Pinterest:
http://www.pinterest.com/RachelDelune/

AUTHOR WEBSITE:
http://www.racheldelune.com/